LIVING
THROUGH
TRAGEDY

Read
Already

LIVING THROUGH TRAGEDY

From the Editors
Of *True Story* And
True Confessions

Published by True Renditions, LLC

True Renditions, LLC
105 E. 34th Street, Suite 141
New York, NY 10016

ISBN: 978-1-938877-67-4

Visit us on the web at www.truerenditionsllc.com.

Contents

HE RAN OVER OUR LITTLE BOY
Can our marriage survive?

I was making photocopies for my boss when someone tapped me on the shoulder. I turned to find the office manager standing behind me.

"Chloe, could you come to my office, please?" she asked me.

Wondering what she wanted, I glanced at my watch and then back at the copier. "Mona, I have to finish these copies for Richie's eleven o'clock meeting. Could I come see you when I'm done?"

She shook her head. "No. You really need to come now. Forget about the copies. I'll have somebody else make them."

I opened my mouth to argue, to tell her that this was an important meeting, that I was Richie's assistant and it was my job—not someone else's—to make sure he had everything he needed for it. But something about Mona's expression stopped me.

She looked serious and, worse, sorry for me. I bit my lip and nodded, afraid I was about to lose my job. I hadn't done anything to deserve being fired, but business had been slow lately.

I followed Mona to her office in silence, too nervous to ask questions. My husband, Paul, and I had just bought our first house, a fixer-upper. We needed both paychecks to cover the mortgage, utilities, and grocery bills, plus buy building materials for remodeling.

Mona paused outside her office and gestured me in. When I stepped inside, I stopped and stared in confusion. My parents sat in the two chairs in front of Mona's desk. My mother was crying, and my father had his arm around her, patting her shoulder.

I knew something terrible had happened. Oh God, I thought, don't let it be Paul. My husband had taken the day off to work on our house with his dad. He'd said something about replacing a few shingles. Had he fallen off the roof? From the look on my dad's face, if it was Paul, he wasn't just hurt but . . .

My father glanced up and saw me then. "Chloe," he said.

At the sound, my mother leapt to her feet, crying, "Oh, honey," and held out her arms to me.

I didn't move. "Is it Paul? Did something happen to him?" I held my breath.

My mother's arms fell, and she sobbed again.

My father stepped forward and put his hand on my shoulder. "Chloe, you'd better sit down."

1

I still didn't move. "Just tell me. Is he . . ." I couldn't bring myself to say the word.

"It's not Paul, sweetheart." My father's shoulders sagged. "It's Leo."

Leo was my baby. My precious angel. My eighteen-month-old son. I couldn't—wouldn't—believe what I was hearing.

"What are you talking about?" I asked in a voice that sounded too shrill to be mine.

Tears filled my father's eyes. "He's . . . he's gone."

"You mean lost? He wandered off?" I asked, hoping that was what he meant.

Paul had insisted on keeping Leo home with him instead of sending him to the sitter's. I argued that he couldn't work on the house and keep track of a busy, curious toddler at the same time. But Paul said his dad would help him watch Leo. He convinced me by telling me how much Leo would enjoy "working" with Daddy and Paw-Paw. I'd smiled, picturing him with his beloved little toy hammer and saw, and relented.

And now he was lost.

My father shook his head. Tears ran down his cheeks. "There was an accident. Leo was hurt badly. He didn't make it, sweetheart."

I couldn't breathe. This was a nightmare. It couldn't be real, couldn't be true. I wasn't going to believe it.

My father hugged me and cried. I started breathing again and patted his back. My mother came and put her arms around both of us.

"Where is he?" I asked.

My father took off his glasses and wiped them with his handkerchief. "At the hospital. Paul and his parents are there. We'll take you."

Mona stepped into the room. "I'm so sorry, Chloe." She had tears in her eyes, too. I was the only one in the room who wasn't crying. "I'll get your purse from your desk for you. Just wait here a minute."

The ten-minute drive to the hospital took forever. I opened the passenger door before my father even had the car fully stopped in the parking lot. Without waiting for him or my mother, I ran into the building's lobby.

"I'm Chloe Eastman," I said to the woman behind the information desk. "Leo's mother. Where's my baby?"

"One moment, please." The woman typed and watched her computer screen. She picked up the telephone and spoke quietly into it and then hung up. "If you'll have a seat, Mrs. Eastman, someone will take you to him in just a few minutes."

I wasn't waiting a few minutes. "You don't understand. He's been in some kind of accident. He's hurt." I leaned forward, gripping the edge of her desk. "I'm his mother. He needs me."

She looked at me sadly. "I'm terribly sorry, Mrs. Eastman. The doctor will be up as soon as he can. Is anyone here with you? Maybe your husband?"

"He's with our son." I could hear my voice rising too loud for a hospital, but I didn't care. "And that's where I need to be!"

A hand touched my back. "We're her parents. We'll take care of her," my father said from behind me. "Come on, sweetheart."

"No, Dad. I have to see Leo now!"

Just then a man in green scrubs approached the desk. "Mrs. Eastman?"

The woman behind the desk nodded.

"I'm Dr. Martins. Come with me. I'll take you to your son."

We walked down a hallway and entered an elevator.

The doctor pushed a button. "I'm very sorry about your little boy. I understand your father-in-law administered CPR, and the medics tried to resuscitate him when they arrived. But the car went over his torso, and the internal damage was just too severe. There was nothing anyone could do."

A car had hit my baby! Part of my brain heard what Dr. Martins said, but another part refused to understand. "This is some kind of terrible mistake. I'm his mother. I know if I can just hold him, he'll be okay."

My mother started sobbing again.

My father said, "Oh, God. Sweetheart, you have to—"

"It's all right," Dr. Martins interrupted. "This happens. It's a defense mechanism, perfectly normal. She's coping with the situation the way she has to."

The elevator door opened, and Dr. Martins led us down another hallway. He knocked before opening a door. "Mr. Eastman, your wife is here."

Paul was sitting in a chair, his parents on either side of him, Leo in his arms. My little boy was wrapped in a white blanket, like I'd swaddled him when he was an infant.

As I walked toward them, my mother-in-law left her chair for me.

"Oh, Chloe," Paul said and started crying.

I sat, never taking my gaze off my baby. With his eyes closed, long lashes against his round baby cheeks, he looked like he was sleeping.

I smoothed his soft hair. "Give him to me, Paul. Let me hold him."

Paul slid Leo into my arms.

Kissing his forehead, I rocked him back and forth. "Everything's okay now, Leo. Mommy's here," I crooned and stroked his cheek.

My mother gave a strangled-sounding cry. Paul put his arm around me, and both he and my father-in-law sobbed.

Colleen, my mother-in-law, put a hand on my shoulder. "I think we'd better leave you alone for a little while." She ushered my father-in-law and my parents out of the room and closed the door behind them.

I lifted one of Leo's arms free of the blanket. It hung limp in my hand, but that didn't concern me. That's the way all small children feel when they sleep deeply.

I held his little hand to my cheek and whispered, "Wake up, sweetie. Wake up for Mommy."

But he just slept on, so quiet.

I shook his hand and spoke the same words, only louder this time. "Please, Leo, please wake up."

Paul laid his head on my shoulder and continued to cry in broken sobs.

Finally, I stopped shaking Leo's hand and lowered it gently to the blanket. My vision blurred as hot tears filled my eyes and ran down my cheeks. I had to face the truth. My baby was gone.

I don't know how long we sat there, just the three of us. I held Leo and cried, and Paul held both of us in his arms and cried, too.

At last, I turned to look at my husband. "I don't understand. How could this have happened?"

Paul lifted his head, looking far older than his twenty-six years. "Chloe, I don't know." He drew a deep, shuddering breath. "I thought he was in the yard with Dad. I never saw him, never knew he was there, until I started backing up the car and . . ." He buried his face against my shoulder again. "That terrible thump."

I froze, staring at the top of Paul's head while I tried to comprehend what he'd just said. I whispered his name, and Paul raised his head.

"What are you telling me?" I asked. "You did this? You ran over him with the car?"

Paul closed his eyes, as if he couldn't bear to face me, and nodded.

Clutching Leo in my arms, I jumped to my feet and turned to face my husband. "I don't believe it!" I shrieked. "I told you! I told you I'd take him to the sitter's. But, no, you had to keep him at home with you."

I glanced down at Leo, at his sweet, still, little face. My jaw clenched and I looked back at Paul. "And now he's dead. What kind of father kills his own son?"

Paul just sat there staring at me with tears streaming down his face. He never argued, never protested. How could he? Everything I said was true.

By then I was screaming, swearing at him, crying over and over, "You killed my baby!"

The door flew open and our parents rushed in, followed by a nurse and Dr. Martins.

4

"Why don't you all go out in the hall for just a minute," the doctor said. "We'll give her something to calm her down."

"I don't want to calm down!" I turned to look at Paul. "He killed my baby!"

The nurse was herding everyone toward the door, but my father-in-law, Brent, stood his ground.

"Wait," he said, looking at me. "You can't blame Paul, Chloe. It's not his fault. It's mine. He had to make a trip to the hardware store for more roofing nails. I was supposed to be watching Leo."

Brent raked a hand through his gray hair. "The dog started barking. I turned around and saw her running across the street after a squirrel. I started to go after her. Halfway across the yard, I remembered Leo and turned back. But by then he was in the driveway, and the car was already moving. I yelled for Paul to stop, but it was too late."

I stared at my father-in-law, seeing the sequence of events in my mind. He'd tried to save my dog, only to let my son be run over instead.

"That's supposed to make me feel better?" I asked. "My husband killed my baby and his father helped him! How could you have been so careless?"

My father-in-law looked at his feet.

The nurse pointed to the door. "Please go now, sir."

When we were alone, Dr. Martins turned to me. "I'm going to give you an injection, Chloe. A tranquilizer, so you can sleep. You'll need rest to cope with this."

I nodded.

"Will you let me take your son from you now?"

I crushed Leo against my chest and half-turned away from the doctor. "No, please don't. I can't. . . ." I started to cry again.

"That's fine," the doctor said. "You can hold him as long as you want." He pointed to a stretcher in the corner of the room. "Would you like to lie down with him over there?"

I nodded. The nurse pushed up my sleeve, swabbed my arm, and gave me the shot. After she and the doctor helped me onto the stretcher, they left the room.

Curled on my side with my arms around Leo, I pressed my lips against his silky hair and breathed in the scent of him.

"Good night, sweet baby," I whispered. "Mommy loves you."

When I woke, I didn't remember where I was or what had happened. Then memory flooded back, like a bad dream. Except it wasn't.

I reached for Leo, but he was gone. Someone had covered me with a blanket. Across the room, Paul slept in a chair. His mother sat next to him, staring out the window.

I sat up. "Where are my mom and dad?"

5

My mother-in-law turned. "In the cafeteria with Brent, getting coffee."

Paul opened his eyes. We stared at each other. I wondered if I looked as bad as he did.

"I want to go home," I said.

He nodded and stood. "Okay, let's go."

I shook my head. "Not with you. Not to our house." I couldn't even stand to look at him. "I'm going home with my parents."

Paul winced as if I'd slapped him. I curled my hands into fists, feeling my nails digging into my palms. I would hit him if he argued. But he just sighed and nodded again.

My mother-in-law bit her lip. "I'll go down to the cafeteria and get them."

I wasn't about to wait there with Paul. We had nothing to say to each other, as far as I was concerned. "Never mind. I'll go myself."

My parents and I made funeral arrangements. I chose a casket, flowers, and a burial plot in the cemetery near our church.

Afterward, we went to my parents' house. I gave my mother a list of the clothing and personal items I needed from my own house and then went upstairs to my old room. It was still exactly the way I'd left it when I married Paul and moved out four years earlier.

On the nightstand stood a framed photograph of Paul and me at the prom. I stared at it. We looked so young, so innocent, so happy—so unsuspecting of what was to come. Wishing I were dead, I swung my arm and sent the photo flying across the room. It hit the wall with a crash and fell facedown on the floor. I flopped across my single bed and cried for my baby.

Two days later, I saw my husband for the first time since leaving the hospital. The funeral director had us arrive at the funeral home a half-hour before visiting hours, so that we could spend private time with Leo before everyone else came to pay their respects.

My parents and I took our time with him first, while Paul waited on the other side of the room with his family.

Lying in his tiny coffin, Leo still looked like he was sleeping, but it wasn't the same as at the hospital. The makeup that had been applied to his face made him look artificial, like a doll—beautiful, but not my little boy. His cheek felt hard and cold to my touch. I tucked his favorite stuffed animal, a bedraggled blue bunny, under the blanket next to Leo, smoothed his hair, and walked away.

I watched from across the room as Paul, his parents, his brothers and sisters, and their families approached the coffin. Paul and his dad stood with their arms around each other, sobbing over Leo. They looked so pitiful, so completely destroyed, that I felt sorry for them. And I didn't want to feel sorry for them. I excused myself to go to the ladies' room.

When visiting hours started, we formed a receiving line. I stood first, next to my parents, with Paul's family after them. Paul stood last in line, next to the coffin.

While I greeted people, smiling and thanking them for coming, listening and nodding over their expressions of sympathy, I glanced at my husband. He couldn't keep his hands off Leo, continually straightening the blanket, touching his hair, his face, his little fingers, and crying all the while.

If I'd had a whole heart left, I supposed it would have broken, watching Paul. But my heart was already shattered. I didn't have a piece big enough to spare for him.

After visitation, we went to church for the funeral, and to the cemetery for the graveside service. Our minister talked about how difficult it was to understand why God would allow such a tragedy to occur, but that the ways of the Lord are mysterious and beyond human comprehension. He said we should pray for the strength to endure this test of faith.

But I wasn't so understanding as to keep singing the Lord's praises in the face of this trial. God had sat back and watched my husband run over my baby, and I just didn't have a whole lot to say to Him.

Throughout the services, I sat with my parents and never spoke to Paul. When it was all over and we were walking back to our cars at the cemetery, he followed me.

He touched my sleeve. "Chloe, will you . . . are you coming home now?"

Just the thought of going back to that house, of seeing Leo's empty room, his bed, all his clothes and toys, and having to look at Paul, who'd killed him. . . . I jerked my arm out of his grasp and turned away. "No. I can't."

A week passed and then another. I returned to work, but I continued to live with my parents. I didn't see Paul or talk to him.

About a month after Leo's death, my mother-in-law showed up unexpectedly one Saturday. My mother invited her into the kitchen and made tea. The two of them made small talk, but they were both obviously uneasy. I didn't contribute much to the conversation. We all knew she hadn't come just for chit-chat.

"Colleen, how's Brent doing?" my mother asked.

"He has his good days and his bad days." My mother-in-law sipped her tea and looked at me. "It's Paul I'm really worried about. I don't know if you knew, Chloe, but he went back home—to your house, I mean—last week." She shook her head and frowned. "I know he's not sleeping or eating right."

Could she possibly believe I slept or ate well? We stared at each other for a long moment.

"Chloe, are you ever planning to go home?" she asked, coming to the point finally.

"I don't know. I haven't decided yet. When I do, I'll discuss it with Paul." I didn't add "not with you," but I could tell she knew that was what I meant by the way her face turned pink.

My mother gave a disapproving frown. "Chloe . . ."

"What you're doing to Paul isn't right," my mother-in-law said. "His own grief is destroying him. How is he supposed to survive with the burden of your blame on top of it?" When I didn't answer, she continued, "It was an accident, after all. And Jesus tells us we have to forgive one another, Chloe."

Gritting my teeth, I slammed my cup down on the saucer, sloshing tea all over the tablecloth. "That's easy for you to say, Colleen. You're Paul's mother. But in case you forgot, I'm Leo's mother. I'd like to see how forgiving you'd be if someone killed your son!"

I thrust my chair back from the table and left the kitchen. As I stomped upstairs to my room, I heard my mother apologizing.

When my father came home, he knocked on the door to my room.

"I heard about Colleen's visit today," he said, sitting on the edge of my bed, where I was lying on my back.

"Mom thinks I'm wrong, doesn't she? She thinks I should go back to Paul like a good little wife."

My father patted my knee. "Your mother's pretty traditional."

He didn't have to tell me that. I'd lived with her long enough to know.

"But when push comes to shove, she'll stand behind you, whatever you decide. We both will."

I rolled to my side and propped myself on my elbow. "Do you think I should go back to Paul?"

He shook his head. "I don't know, sweetheart. That's a decision only you can make. Nobody else has to live your life, so nobody else has the right to decide—or to judge you for what you decide."

I sighed. "I just don't know, Dad."

"Let me ask you a question. Do you still love him?"

I thought about it. I'd been in love with Paul since I was sixteen years old and we were assigned as lab partners in high school biology. I'd never thought he was great-looking before, but the way he made me laugh every day as we dissected a frog changed the way I looked at him. One day I realized he'd gone from just-above-average-looking to beautiful in my eyes. That's when I knew I loved him.

Ten years, marriage, and the birth of our son had only deepened that love. Until a month ago, he'd still made me laugh every day. I certainly hadn't felt like laughing since then. But someday I might, and the thought of Paul not being there when I did saddened me.

8

Under the pain of losing Leo, I supposed I continued to love Paul. But I wasn't sure that was enough.

"I guess I do, Dad. But loving and forgiving aren't the same thing, are they?"

My father looked at me sadly. "No, sweetheart, they're not. And if you can't forgive him, I don't think you should go back. Colleen's right about one thing. Paul's going to have to live with guilt for the rest of his life, God help him. That's bad enough. But if he has to see blame in your eyes every day, too, even if you never say a word about it, that's more than any man should have to deal with."

I nodded. "But I don't know if I can forgive him."

"I don't know if you can, either, Chloe. The loss of a child has to be just about the worst thing that could ever happen to anyone. I don't know how you go about forgiving someone for that, accident or not. But if you can't, I think Paul's better off without you."

That night, I dreamed I was back at Leo's funeral. The church was empty when I entered. I walked down the aisle toward the coffin, dreading the sight of my baby lying still and silent in death. But when I came closer, I realized the coffin was too big to be Leo's. Irresistibly drawn despite a sense of dread, I stepped nearer and peered inside.

Paul lay in the coffin.

He wore a black tuxedo, like the one he'd worn on our wedding day, with a white rosebud and baby's breath pinned to his lapel. His gold wedding band glinted on his left hand.

But the main thing that struck me was his face. It was unlined, relaxed, young-looking—as if in death he'd found the peace that had been destroyed the day our son died.

Staring down at Paul, I felt desolate. First I'd lost my baby and now my husband as well.

"Paul," I moaned. "Paul, don't leave me."

But he didn't answer. He was gone, just like Leo.

I cried out in sorrow and regret, and the sound of my own voice woke me. Lying in my bed, I was crying and shaking and calling Paul's name. The clock read two in the morning.

I knew I should've been relieved that it was just a dream, but I couldn't shake the sense of loss and despair I'd felt in the dream.

I wanted my husband.

The need to see him, to touch him, to know for certain he was still alive was stronger than my anger. I slid out of bed and dressed.

Downstairs, I wrote a note to my parents, telling them I was going home. As I signed my name, the thought occurred to me that Paul might not want me back. I hadn't stuck by him when he needed me. I'd added to his pain by channeling my own pain into anger at him.

9

And since the day we'd buried Leo, Paul had never called me, never tried to see me, and never asked me to come home. In fact, now that I thought of it, he hadn't actually asked me to come home at the cemetery. He'd only asked me if I was coming home, not said he wanted me to.

The thought that Paul might've decided he was better off without me made me bite my lip so hard I drew blood. But even if that were true, I still had to see for myself that he was okay and tell him how sorry I was.

As I drove home through dark streets, I thought about Leo's death and admitted finally that Paul really wasn't at fault. He'd had no reason to think for a minute that his father hadn't had our son safely in hand.

It was harder to stop blaming my father-in-law. He should've been holding onto Leo, not running after the dog. But when I was honest with myself, I had to admit that it could have happened to anyone, even me.

One day a couple of months earlier, Leo and I had walked out of the grocery store together. One of the plastic grocery bags I carried gave way, and I let go of Leo's hand just in time to prevent a glass jar of spaghetti sauce from crashing on the concrete. The next thing I knew, I heard squealing, skidding tires. Released for an instant, Leo had dashed out into the parking lot. He wasn't hurt—the car never touched him—but that was due to the driver's quick reflexes and good brakes, not to my vigilance.

I'd been so ashamed of my failure to protect my son from danger that I hadn't told Paul about the incident. Maybe if I had, he'd have thought to warn his father that day to hang onto Leo until the car was out of the driveway.

I also knew that if I'd insisted that Leo go to the sitter that day instead of staying home with Paul and his dad, Paul would have given in and Leo would still be alive.

We'd all made mistakes. It was easy to try to assign blame, but pointless. Blame wouldn't bring Leo back. He was gone. But Paul wasn't.

When I turned in the driveway, the house was dark. I peeked in the garage window and saw Paul's car before heading up the sidewalk.

Although I had my key ready, the side door wasn't locked. As I flipped on the kitchen light, I heard footsteps on the stairs and thought for a moment Paul had heard me come in. But the click of toenails on hardwood from the hall prepared me for my dog, not my husband. Sparks, a beagle-spaniel cross, trotted into the kitchen, wagging her whole body. Bending, I scratched her ears and rubbed her belly.

When I straightened, Sparks headed for her food bowl, and I looked around the room. I'd expected to find dirty dishes in the sink— Paul hated doing dishes—but I didn't see even a glass. Everything was neat and clean.

I walked down the hall and found the living room equally tidy. Standing in the room that had always been cluttered with newspapers, magazines, and Leo's toys, I felt like I was in a house no one lived in. The orderliness and silence gave me a chill.

What if my dream was a premonition? I'd never had dreams that had come true, but that didn't mean they weren't possible. What if Paul couldn't live with his grief and guilt and had done something terrible? People committed suicide for less obvious reasons.

Heart pounding, I headed up the stairs. Please, God, let Paul be okay, I prayed. I entered our bedroom in the dark and held my breath as I switched on a lamp. The bed was empty, neatly made—another chore Paul detested.

Fearing the worst, I even checked the bathroom but found nothing.

Then I looked down the hall at Leo's room. Following the glow of his nightlight, I made my way into his room.

Paul lay curled on his side, asleep, on Leo's little race-car toddler bed. One of his arms cradled a stuffed bear against his cheek. I stood still, watching him, listening to his breathing, thinking how much I loved him, just as I'd often done with Leo.

I remembered what my mother-in-law had said about Paul not sleeping and decided not to disturb him. Morning would be soon enough to tell him how I felt. To find out if he still loved me.

Just as I was debating between sleeping in our bed or spending the night in the rocking chair in the corner of Leo's room, Sparks came in. She wagged her tail and jumped onto Leo's bed, landing right on Paul's legs.

He jerked and raised his head, then saw me and froze.

"Paul, it's me," I said, fearing he'd think I was a burglar.

"Chloe?" His head dropped to the bed again. "What are you doing here?"

His voice sounded flat, as if he didn't care what I was doing but only asked because it was expected.

I swallowed hard. "I need to talk to you. Do you mind if I turn on the light?"

He sighed and sat up. "Go ahead."

His face looked haggard and haunted in the lamplight. My heart ached at the sight.

"Paul, I came here to tell you how sorry I am. I was wrong to blame you. It wasn't your fault."

"My mother put you up to this," he said, sounding angry. "She told

11

me she was going to go see you, and I told her not to. But she did it anyway, didn't she?"

"Well, yes, but——"

"I told her not to interfere, that it would be better if she just left things alone."

My heart sank. "Better for who?"

Paul rose to his feet, running his fingers through his hair. "For you, for me, for everyone." He shook his head. "I'm fine, Chloe. You don't have to feel guilty, no matter what my mother says. I accept your apology. Now go get on with your life." He turned his back to me.

My eyes filled with tears. "You don't look fine," I said. "And I don't have a life to get on with!"

"Of course you don't," he said, swinging around to face me again. "Not yet. But you will. You'll make a new one."

I knew for certain I didn't want any kind of new life that didn't include Paul. But it seemed he wasn't offering me a choice.

"Do you want a divorce?" I asked.

He shrugged. "I think it'd be best."

Blinded by tears, I stumbled to the door, trying to keep from sobbing until I was out of the house. But I stopped in the doorway and looked back at him. No matter how much the answer might hurt, I had to ask the question.

"Don't you love me anymore?"

He just stared at me for a long time.

Finally, I took his silence for an answer, and I couldn't hold back a sob.

Paul crossed the room and stood in front of me. "I almost said no, but I can't lie to you. Not about that." He lifted a hand but stopped just short of touching my face and let it fall to his side. "Chloe, I'll love you until I die. But I don't expect you to live with the man who killed your child."

I understood then. "If you love me, then don't expect me to live without you," I said, slipping my arms around him.

For a moment he stood still, stiff and resisting. But then he put his arms around me, and we cried together—for our son, for each other, and for ourselves.

It still took a lot of convincing that night before Paul agreed to pick up the pieces of our lives and continue with our marriage. His guilt for what he'd done was so terrible that he believed he didn't deserve to be happy. In the end, it was only out of concern for my happiness that he was even willing to try.

But after six months of grief counseling, which we attended together, Paul started to forgive himself and allow himself to be happy again.

We aren't the same people we were before we lost Leo. But we wouldn't want to be. He was our child, and he left his mark on our lives. Not a day goes by that I don't think of my son, sometimes with tears, but often with a smile and even laughter over the memory of something he said or did.

Shortly after the one-year anniversary of Leo's death, Paul and I agreed to start trying for another baby. The decision was both scary and exciting, but we felt we were ready. That was four months ago, and today I learned that I'm pregnant. Paul should be home from work in a few minutes. I can't wait to tell him.

THE END

RAPED—AND IN A COMA
Who hurt my sister!

As I stroked my sister's hand, I said, "Oh, Kira, how I wish that you could talk to me. I miss you so much." I watched her eyelids, hoping desperately that they would flutter.

I'd been praying that she would awaken and call me by nickname, Roadrunner. She had given me the name when I was twelve. She'd said that I was all legs and had run like a giraffe. I'd hated the name, but right then, I'd have given anything to hear her say, "Hi, Roadrunner."

At twenty-three, I had grown into my long legs and had outgrown my tomboyishness, but Kira had not been able to witness the changes. She'd missed my first date, my senior prom, and my high school graduation.

My sister had been in a coma for eight years.

I remembered every detail of that fateful night as clearly as if the horrible accident had happened only hours before. . . .

Hey, Roadrunner, give me a hand," Kira had said. After lifting her beautiful hair, she'd stood waiting for me to zip up her pink dress.

That night, Kira had looked so beautiful, so elegant. I'd envied her slim attractiveness, her long, shapely legs, and how confidently she'd walked in her high heels. I'd also envied all her boyfriends, especially Nicholas, who'd been taking Kira to dinner and then out dancing at a new, popular club.

"Why so glum?" she had asked.

After plopping on the bed, feeling as lumpy as the worn mattress, I had answered my sister truthfully.

"You're headed out for a night on the town and I'm doomed to cold pizza and boring television."

"Oh, Roadrunner, don't you worry. Your time will come. You're just a late bloomer, that's all," she'd assured me. She had ruffled my hair and told me to get to bed at a decent hour.

"I get it. You don't want anyone to witness your coming home after curfew," I teased her.

Kira had smiled and left our room. I'd heard the sound of her heels echoing on the wooden hall floor. After the doorbell had rung and Mom had called out, "Be home at midnight," the house had suddenly felt empty and cold. I could hear the television blaring and imagined Mom, sipping her coffee and staring into space.

The room that Kira and I'd shared had offered blessed sanctuary from my mother's depressed moods. Her suffering had started after my father's death from cancer the year before. If she wasn't morose, then she was bitter. Either way, life at our home was very unpleasant.

I'd thought that Kira was lucky. At eighteen, she'd left for work as a receptionist every day and dated almost every night. At fifteen, I hadn't had the same freedoms.

The next morning, the warmth of the sun had heated the bedroom like a sauna. The clock told me that it was already nine o'clock.

Why didn't Kira wake me? I thought. I'm going to be late for school.

My anger turned to worry when I saw that Kira's bed hadn't been slept in.

Later, the painful news of Kira's car accident came in the form of a state trooper at our front door. Mom and I sat by Kira's hospital bed while she struggled to breathe. Tubes and machines had been hooked up to her and it seemed as though she was a robot in some awful, futuristic movie.

Days, months, and years passed. The tubes and machines had been removed, but still, Kira clung to life. Sometimes, I wondered if Nicholas had been lucky—he had died instantly at the scene.

As Kira lay in a nursing home bed and as I sat beside her, I couldn't stop my selfish tears. I had lost so much—the love of both my sister and my mother. My mom had died suddenly a few years earlier.

"Joyce, are you all right?" The nurse's voice was soft and caring.

When Maura touched my shoulder, all my resolve weakened and I broke into heavy sobs. The kind nurse let me cry and hugged me tightly.

"I'm sorry, Maura," I managed to say, when I'd finally stopped sobbing.

"Sorry? Sorry for what? For being human?" she asked.

"Some days are harder than others. I hate seeing Kira like this," I confessed.

"It's a tragedy, Joyce. She is lucky, though," Maura told me.

"Lucky? How can you say that? She's trapped in a body that doesn't move, with a mind that's lost to us." I was shocked by Maura's statement.

"She's lucky to have someone who still loves her and who still takes the time to visit. So many people here have been abandoned." A shadow of sorrow veiled her face. I realized then how hard it must have been for her to work at the nursing home, day after day, watching the forgotten patients fade away.

"What did you bring Kira today? A new CD? A book that you'll read to her?" she asked brightly.

"You're certainly curious," I said, laughing. The shopping bag at my feet held a new robe. The fabric was soft and it was trimmed with white lace.

15

"That's lovely, Joyce. Let me bathe Kira, then we'll dress her."

As Maura and I bathed my sister, I saw that her once-shapely legs were like sticks. Her lustrous hair had dulled, and her expressionless face was waxen. I noticed, too, that she had gained some weight. Her stomach appeared swollen.

"Do you think that the weight gain is a good sign?" I asked hopefully.

"Maybe, but it could be just water or fluid retention. We've changed her diet a bit. I think I'll call the attending physician and have it checked out," Maura said. "I should have some information by your next visit."

During the following week, I thought frequently of Kira, but trusted that Maura would call me if there were any problem at the nursing home. The children in my second-grade class kept me busy and at night, I welcomed the sitcoms that I watched. The laughter helped to relieve my daily pressures.

I welcomed Saturday morning, despite the overcast skies. I straightened my small apartment, did my weekly grocery shopping, and then drove to the nursing home. I noticed that the sun was breaking through the clouds as I pulled into the parking lot.

When I entered the front hallway of Pleasant Vistas, I saw Maura at the front desk.

"Hello," I said cheerfully. "How's Kira been this week?"

Maura, who usually smiled broadly at me, looked concerned and motioned me toward the staff coffee room. My stomach tightened and my thoughts flitted from bad to worse.

Is Kira ill? Is she dead? Why hasn't anyone called me? I wondered frantically.

"What is it, Maura? What's happened?" I clutched my purse as I spoke and suddenly, I wondered if I really wanted Maura to answer my questions.

"Joyce, I'm not sure how to tell you this. It's unbelievable, really." Maura stared at the floor.

My heart lifted. "Did she wake up? Did Kira wake up?"

Maura shook her head, then looked directly into my eyes. What I saw in her expression frightened me.

"No, Joyce. Kira's pregnant," she said.

"Pregnant? That's not funny, Maura. How could you be so cruel?" I couldn't believe that she'd had the nerve to tell me such a thing.

I could feel my face flushing with anger. My poor sister, lying mute and helpless, had been the brunt of some horrible joke.

"I'm so sorry, Joyce, but it's true. The doctor confirmed it today. In fact, she's almost six months along."

"How could this have happened? What—" My voice trailed away

as I realized that the only way that Kira could have become pregnant was unthinkable: Someone had raped her.

"What kind of place is this? Who could have done this? What are you doing about it?" My throat constricted and my voice became shrill and hysterical.

Maura reached across the table and grabbed my hand.

"Joyce, I don't know. I just don't know how it happened. I feel so awful. It's horrible." Her eyes were filled with tears

I stood up, ripping my hand from Maura's. As I started to run away, I heard her calling after me that the police had been contacted. She was trying to assure me that the rapist would be found.

Too little, too late. This shouldn't be happening at all, I thought. It was a nightmare too unbearable to believe. I just couldn't understand how it could possibly be true.

When I got to her room, Kira was lying still on her bed, innocent and vulnerable. Some miserable man had raped her. She hadn't been able to scream; she hadn't fought back; she couldn't identify him. My poor sister was helpless, and she carried a helpless baby inside of her.

As she slept, I watched her shallow breaths and the swelling of her belly beneath the cotton blanket. I had no idea what I was going to do.

I sensed someone else's presence in the room then, and was surprised to see a man standing in the shadows. I started and my heart pounded.

"I didn't mean to frighten you," he said. "I'm Detective Polymer. I've been assigned to your sister's case."

"Aren't you the lucky one?" I commented, acid dripping from my every word. "Is there any question that she did not give her consent? Or, perhaps she looks especially seductive with a feeding tube trailing from her nose?"

I knew that I was being irrational and that my anger was aimed at anyone in my range. I was furious with Maura, with the detective, and with every staff member in the nursing home.

"You have every right to be angry, Miss Amato. This is a horrible situation," he said softly.

"Situation? This isn't some situation. This is my sister. Her name is Kira. Kira never harmed anyone in her whole life."

For the rest of that day and night, I could think of nothing else except for the animal that had done such a thing to Kira. My mind was filled with so many questions: Should she carry a monster's baby? How would her health be affected? What could I do? Would the police take her case seriously? By morning, I was ready to find some answers.

Kira's doctor discouraged the idea of an abortion at such a late stage. He was certain that Kira could carry the baby to term and that

17

the chances for a healthy child were good. But, he was uncertain if Kira's condition would deteriorate during, or after, childbirth.

"We'll make certain that she is properly nourished for the baby's sake. There should be no problem finding adoptive parents," he said. "I know that this will be difficult for you, Joyce, but we can get through it."

"Why should we even be going through this?" I asked. There was no hiding the disgust that I felt.

Later that afternoon as I sat beside Kira, I wondered what I should do. What would she have wanted me to do? The question weighed heavily in my mind. I'd never felt so alone.

"Joyce," Maura said as she entered the room, "Detective Polymer would like to talk with you again. Should I send him in?"

"No, Maura. I'd rather talk with him in the coffee room. I'll be there in a few minutes," I told her.

As I searched Kira's expressionless face for a clue of what to do, I couldn't keep the tears from falling. The grief I'd faced over the past years welled up inside of me and I felt as if I might burst and crumple into a million pieces.

Later, as I spoke with Detective Polymer, I was struck by his obvious concern and by the anger that I heard in his voice as he outlined the investigation that he'd planned to find the rapist.

"We've gathered a list of all male personnel who've worked here in the last year. A number of them still work here, and the others will have to be located."

"So what? Do you think that any of them will really confess?" I couldn't keep the derision from my voice. "Kira certainly cannot identify anyone."

"We'll narrow the investigation and request DNA samples from all of the men who have worked here during the time period of the rape. We can search for paternal probability from the testing. We won't need any witnesses. The perp's samples will condemn him," he told me.

Detective Polymer sounded so sure of himself, so certain that he would find the rapist. I prayed that he was right. I wanted justice for Kira, and I was the only one in the world who cared whether or not it was found.

"Detective, how soon will you know anything?" I asked.

"The questioning of the men who are still employed here has already begun," he explained. "Meanwhile, if you can think of anyone who has shown a special interest in your sister or of any other information that would help in the investigation, please don't hesitate to call me."

When he handed me his card, I noticed the deep scar on his wrist.

It was jagged, white, and ran beneath his jacket sleeve. For the first time that day, I thought of someone else other than Kira and myself. I was curious, but I said nothing. After all, he was a stranger to me.

At work the next day, the children's shrill screams and bickering set me on edge. I felt my irritation rising as the day wore on. Instead of calming the situation, though, I snapped at Alex, a child who'd been misbehaving. My anger only increased his mischievous behavior and shortened my temper. I feared that I was losing control.

Instead of the normal hugs that I usually received at the end of the day, the children were distant and wary. I wondered how much my self-absorption had contributed to their misbehavior.

Could I handle my job—and the weight of Kira's situation?

I knew that needed a level head. I needed to talk with someone who understood the challenges of working with children day after day. Specifically, I needed to speak to Florence. She was a woman who had managed to continue working, despite the death of her husband. I'd always admired her strength.

When I neared the classroom next to mine, I could hear Florence stacking up the chairs inside.

"Florence, do you have a few minutes?" I asked.

"Yes, but only, if we can go somewhere with adult-sized chairs and a glass of white wine," she told me. She promised to meet me at a nearby pub when she'd finished cleaning her classroom.

As we sat in an Irish pub and sipped our wine, I told her about what had happened to my sister.

"How could someone be such a beast?" she asked in horror. Unfortunately, neither of us had any answers.

"Florence, I'm so tense that the children are driving me up the wall. I snapped at Alex today, and, of course, that only set him off even more."

"Hey, don't be so hard on yourself. Alex can be an imp, and I've been tempted to take him over my knee on a few occasions myself." Florence laughed. Her laugh was deep and hearty. Florence put all of herself into life—even her laugh.

"But, you didn't put him over your knee, Florence," I told her. "You wouldn't do something like that to a student."

"Cut it out. Stop blaming yourself. What are you really feeling guilty about?" Florence asked, in her no-nonsense manner.

As her eyes bore into me, I could feel the tension mounting as all of the confusion and sorrow swelled inside of me. Suddenly, a tirade of words poured from me.

"I didn't protect Kira from what happened. She has no one but me and I didn't help her. I visited her week after week and couldn't see what was right in front of me. I should have known something was wrong. I failed her." Finally, my guilt was exposed.

"Well, do you want some psychological babble, or some practical advice?" Florence asked as she motioned to the waitress for another glass of wine. "I could give you both, you know."

As I sat there in the shadows, I didn't think that either would be helpful, and I told her so.

"Well, you could feel sorry for yourself or you could figure out what you're going to do for Kira now," she said.

"That's easier said than done, Florence. It's all so overwhelming. I feel so helpless."

"Joyce, I've known you for a long time, and I've never known you to be helpless. Misguided maybe, but never helpless. Now, do you want my help or not?"

Our conversation lasted through dinner, right up until the eleven o'clock news. Florence had switched to club soda and I was riding high on caffeine by the time we'd left the pub. When Florence drove out of the parking lot , I waved good-bye. My sense of helplessness had been replaced with resolve.

I'd decided that I would help Detective Polymer with the investigation in any way that I could. In fact, I had already begun to write down a list of the staff who'd been involved with Kira.

The next day, I called the police department during my morning break.

"Detective, I'm taking you at your word. I have a list of people and a few ideas to pursue. When can we talk?" I asked.

"I'll be in court this afternoon. With any luck, I'll be out by four. Will that work for you?" he asked.

"Not really," I told him. "I have a parent conference until five."

"I'm off duty by five, and then I—" he said.

"Do you want my help or not?" I interrupted. I was determined to keep my feelings of helplessness at bay.

"Hold on, Miss Amato. I was going to suggest that I meet with you then."

As I blushed, I was glad that he couldn't see my face through the phone wires.

Later, when Detective Polymer entered my classroom, he towered over the tiny chairs and desks. The image of him trying to sit on one of them conjured up an amusing picture. I was almost tempted to offer him one of the small stools.

He solved the problem by plopping down comfortably onto the floor.

"Do you mind if I take off my jacket?" he asked. He began to pull it from his broad shoulders before I could answer. As he rolled up his sleeves, I noticed the scar stretching beneath his sleeve.

20

As I eased to the floor across from him, I felt his eyes on me. I noticed that they were probably the most beautiful eyes that I'd ever seen on a man.

"Well, what do you have for me?" he asked.

"Here's a list of all the men who have worked specifically with Kira, including the minister and four doctors."

His eyebrows rose.

"I thought that all men were suspects, not just the low-paid ones," I countered with a hint of defensiveness. "Besides, you told me the other day that you were investigating everyone. This is a complete list."

"You're right, of course. I was just reacting to your thoroughness, that's all. Of course, you know that there'll be an uproar when we ask for blood samples from the doctors. The nursing home administrator already raised a ruckus yesterday when we asked him for a sample."

We shared a smile as I imagined Mr. Stern even being asked. He definitely was not the type of man who would take kindly to any kind of accusation.

"I didn't even think of Mr. Stern. Thank you for being so conscientious," I told him.

Detective Polymer brushed off the compliment by telling me that he'd been only doing his job.

"We've found three of the men who've left the area since the probable incident time. They've been very cooperative. The last one moved out of state, though, and we're still trying to track him down."

"Any suspects, Detective Polymer?" I inquired.

"They're all suspects. Now, it's a matter of elimination," he explained.

The following weekend, at Kira's bedside, I willed her to wake up, to tell me what to do, to tell me who had done such a terrible thing to her. Despite my wishes, though, she continued to sleep. There was no way that I could reach her.

Over the next few weeks, Maura kept me abreast of what had been happening at the nursing home. She laughed at Mr. Stern's and the doctors' indignation at having been considered as suspects. She felt sorry for one of the nurses' aides who had been terrified of losing his job. Everyone knew that he had been one of Kira's primary caregivers. A shroud covered the nursing home as everyone watched one another with suspicion.

Through it all, Kira's pregnancy became more and more obvious. I could no longer pretend that it wasn't real. A child was going to be born—Kira's child. It would by a child of rape, but the baby would also be my niece or nephew.

"What are you going to do about the baby?" Florence asked

one afternoon as we decorated the bulletin boards outside of our classrooms.

"The doctor suggested adoption. He said that there would be no problem in finding a home for an infant," I informed her.

"Is that what you want? Is that what Kira would want?" she asked softly.

"How am I supposed to know what Kira would want?" Sarcasm had crept into my voice.

"You, yourself, have said how much Kira would have loved working here at the school. You're the one who said that she'd wanted to have a carload of kids."

"I don't think that Kira expected to have her carload of kids by way of a rapist," I snapped.

"True enough," Florence responded calmly to my angry outburst. "But still, it is her baby."

"What am I supposed to do? Raise it?" The thought had never really even entered my mind before.

"Actually, raising the baby should be something that you seriously consider," Florence answered.

Having been properly reprimanded, my thoughts whirled. What would Kira have wanted? Would she have wanted to give the baby away? Or, would she have wanted for me to raise it? Could I raise my sister's child? Did I want to? The thought of a child bearing any resemblance to the rapist made me cringe. I decided that it was just impossible. I couldn't raise that baby, and I wouldn't.

"This topic is closed," I said as I glared at Florence. That time, Florence had gone too far. She had asked too much of me.

As the days passed, the pregnancy swelled Kira's thin frame. When I looked at her, I could see nothing else. She was misshapen and grotesque. It was as if she was merely an incubator for the child, not the baby's mother.

During one visit, Maura stopped in to talk with me as I sat by my sister's bed.

"Have you noticed the color on Kira's cheeks? If I didn't know better, I'd think that she was happy about being pregnant," she said, smiling.

Maura had been right. Kira looked more like her old self than she had in months.

"What have you heard from Detective Polymer?" Maura asked. "I haven't seen him around in some time."

"It's a dead end. Everyone has been cleared, except for that one nurses' aide. They haven't located him yet."

"I could be wrong, but I don't think that Harry Norton could have done such a thing. He always showed nothing but respect for the patients. He was the only one who could calm Mr. Roake and, trust me, that was a challenge."

"If it's not him, then we've got nothing," I said. "Who else is there?"

Maura shrugged. "You've got me. I've thought about it endlessly and I can't think of anyone else who has even been near your sister's room."

"Maybe a visitor? Another patient?" I suggested.

"Anything's possible, I guess, but none of the visitors has access to other patients' rooms. And, I can't think of any patient who would be physically capable of actually raping anyone."

In truth, I couldn't either, but someone had raped my sister and I'd vowed that that someone would be found. I was determined to hound the police, the nursing home—everyone, to find the man who had done such a horrible thing to Kira.

Every day for a month, I called Detective Polymer. I became his worst nightmare. I wouldn't let him forget about Kira, not even for a day. On weekends, I left messages on his voice mail.

One day, he had clearly had enough. When I called, he told me that he had to speak to me about something.

"Miss Amato, all the time that I spend on the phone with you could be better used by doing my job," he told me.

"Kira is your job, Detective," I reminded him.

"Yes, she is my job, but so are a lot of other cases. There are other victims, too, Miss Amato, and all of them deserve my attention, as well."

"You're right. I'm sorry. But, you will call me as soon as you have new information, or when you find Harry Norton, won't you?"

For the next two weeks, I fought the urge to pick up the phone. I was losing my patience. Finally, one evening, Detective Polymer knocked on my apartment door.

When he came in, he slowly surveyed the room. I figured that it was probably a habit that he'd developed from investigating crime scenes.

"I like it," he told me. "It's cozy."

"It's early poverty mixed with my mother's few good pieces," I joked.

After I'd invited him to sit on my sofa and offered him a cup of coffee, he looked at me seriously.

"We found Harry Norton working in Memphis. He's been cleared."

The last suspect had been cleared. My heart was heavy with disappointment. A sense of new hopelessness added to my despair.

"What happens now?" I asked.

"Something will break. Some puzzle piece will pop up. It's not over, Miss Amato. Not yet," he promised.

There was a firmness of conviction in his tone. For once, I didn't feel quite so alone.

"There's a pot of spaghetti on the stove, Detective. Would you care to join me?"

"Sure, why not? That sounds better than the frozen dinner waiting at my place. Can I give you a hand?" he offered.

He followed me into the kitchen and I handed him the lettuce to shred for a salad. We chatted comfortably about a current movie that we had both seen.

While we ate, he talked about his younger sister, who was the light of his life. He bragged about her high school grades and her swimming achievements.

"It must be devastating to lose the ability to communicate with your sister like you have," he said.

Then, I told about the night of Kira's accident. I described how the drunk driver had crossed the highway median and slammed into Nicholas's car head-on. I told him that Nicholas and the drunk driver had been killed instantly. Only Kira had survived. I wondered out loud if it would have been better if she had died.

"Life doesn't always make sense. Sometimes, the ones left behind suffer so much." His eyes were filled with naked pain.

Uncertain of how to respond, I just watched him in silence.

As he touched the scar on his hand, he began to talk. His words unleashed an outpouring of regret.

"My partner and I answered a domestic call. A husband had been threatening his wife and baby with a gun. Bobby and I thought that we had talked the man down. His gun was at his side and he had agreed that I could talk with his wife outside. I suggested that she bring the baby with her, and he started shouting obscenities at us.

"When Bobby tried to calm him, the husband raised his gun and shot Bobby point-blank in the chest. I leapt for the man, knocked the gun from his hand, and threw him to the floor. I shouted at his wife to take the baby to the neighbor's and called for an ambulance. What I didn't foresee was the knife that the man had hidden behind him. The blade sliced right through me."

"Your partner?" I asked hesitantly.

"Bobby died on the operating table." His eyes glistened with tears.

After Detective Polymer left, the scent of his cologne lingered in the room. Despite his reassurance, I doubted that any justice would be found for Kira. Defeat smelled stronger than the masculine cologne.

Soon, it was two weeks before Kira's due date. I smoothed a rose-scented lotion on her swollen hands. The fragrance reminded me of the times when Kira and I had stopped to smell the roses on the way to school, roses in the garden that our mother had once planted so lovingly.

"I brought another CD today, Kira. I thought that you'd like to hear the latest Bruce Springsteen CD. You've always liked his voice."

It was a struggle for me to listen, though. I have never liked popular rock music. But, the psychology student who'd examined my sister had encouraged auditory stimuli, as he'd called it.

My heart beat erratically when I thought of that student. I tried to remember when he had been there in the nursing home, doing his research on coma patients. He had been a fixture around the nursing home for weeks. There wouldn't have been a record of him, though, as he hadn't been an employee. I struggled in vain to remember his name.

I ran down the hall frantically, almost falling over Mr. Roake's wheelchair. He shouted at me as I raced to the coffee room.

"Maura, what was that psychology student's name?" I asked breathlessly.

"Oh, I haven't thought of him in ages! Is it possible that he could be the rapist? He was so shy, though. He was afraid of his own shadow," she said.

"So? Wouldn't he be a perfect candidate? He was afraid of women who could say no, maybe, but not of coma patients. Please help me to remember, Maura. What was his name?"

"Emil. Wasn't his name Emil Valente?" She was lost in thought, trying to remember whatever she could.

"That's it! Valente! His name was Emil Valente! Maura, you're a marvel," I told her, before hugging Maura so tightly that she complained of not be able to breathe

Immediately, I called Detective Polymer and left him an urgent message. It seemed an eternity until he called me back. Actually, only forty-five minutes had passed.

"This had better be important," he said. "I'm up to bat soon and I'm a great hitter."

"You go save your team. I'm coming to you. Where is the park?" I asked.

As I drove to the city park, I remembered all the conversations that I'd had with Emil. The times that he had observed Kira. He had been charting her responses to silence and music, before and after verbal stimuli, and at changes in the hours from dusk to dawn. He was convinced there was a change in her facial muscles when she heard certain vocalists, in response to human speech, and during the early mornings when the sun was rising.

The staff had found him amusing, but had given little credence to his research. Still, it had been a change of routine for them and had given them something new to talk about. I had hoped that his experiments and extra attention might draw Kira out.

Detective Polymer waved at me when I sat on the bleachers.

"Hey, Burt, keep your eyes on the ball, not on your girlfriend," one of the players yelled.

So, his first name is Burt. We've talked together so many times, and I didn't even know his first name. Burt. It has a nice ring to it, I thought.

The game was in its final inning and Burt came up to bat in the bottom of that inning. He struck out.

"Great hitter, huh?" I asked when the game had ended and he was wiping the sweat from his face.

"Do you always kick a man when he's down?" Burt asked.

I blushed.

"Hey, I was only kidding. What's so important that you drove all the way over here?" he asked.

Immediately, I told him everything about Emil Valente. I told him every last detail that I could remember about the man, including a full description of his appearance.

"Slow down, Joyce, or you'll explode," he said gently.

Joyce? He'd never called me Joyce before. I had to admit that I liked the soft way that he said my name.

"So, what do you think? Can you find him? He said that he was from the state university. Will they give you his records? What if he's not in school anymore?" I just couldn't stop talking.

"I'll go to the university first thing tomorrow. Okay? Don't worry, we'll find him and check him out."

Detective Burt Polymer was true to his word. He called me the next morning.

"Emil Valente is still a student. I have his home address, but his landlady says that he left for a week's vacation to visit his folks in Florida. We'll be here to greet him when he gets back," he assured me.

The days dragged by.

When the phone rang Friday evening, I hoped that it was Burt. Instead, I heard Maura's voice on the line.

"Joyce, Kira's in labor. We transferred her to Memorial General for the delivery. I'll meet you there."

The baby! Kira was having her baby. It was really happening. I couldn't believe it. My sister, never married, who'd been in a coma for so many years, was having a baby!

My feet were like lead as I crossed the parking lot to the hospital. I didn't want to go in. Once I walked through that door, then the nightmare would become real. If I stayed outside the building, though, would I really be able to pretend that nothing had happened? Could I ignore everything? Could I pretend that there was no baby?

I wished that I could go backward in time to the years when Kira had teased me and call me Roadrunner. I wished that she could be that beautiful young girl, in a beautiful dress and high heels. I wished that I could be innocent again . . . .

The doors opened automatically as I neared the entrance. I realized that I couldn't turn back. Life was there in that hospital. Life was Kira upstairs on the sixth floor, giving birth to her baby.

"Can I help you?" an older woman asked.

"I really wish that you could," I said, without thinking.

She looked perplexed as I passed her and headed to the bank of elevators. She was no more perplexed than I.

The nurse at the central station suggested I sit in a waiting room. The chairs were cold and uncomfortable, and the coffee was strong and bitter. I was so tense that I could barely sit still. Finally, Maura appeared.

"How is she?" I asked.

"Fine. Everything's going well. They've taken her to surgery," she informed me.

"Surgery?" I repeated. What had gone wrong?

"Your sister is having a cesarean."

My eyes must have looked as confused as I felt, because Maura kept on talking.

"You do know what a cesarean is, don't you?" Maura asked.

"I know what a cesarean is, Maura," I assured her.

"You look awful. It's probably going to be another hour or so before Kira is back from surgery and recovery. Go downstairs, have something to eat, buy an interesting magazine, and I'll meet you back here," she instructed me.

"What if something happens? What if Kira doesn't make it?" I was so afraid.

"I'll be with her. I promise that if anything changes, I'll come and find you."

The sandwich was tasteless and the chips were stale, but I ate everything, anyway. Doing something, anything, kept my mind occupied. I watched a nurse, red-eyed from the long hours, sipping coffee from a paper cup. Two doctors conferred at a table across the room. An elderly woman sat staring out into space sadly.

I wandered to the closed gift shop. Through the windows, I saw a collection of stuffed animals and a rack of magazines. A helium machine stood in the far corner, waiting to blow up balloons that would brighten a patient's day.

Even though Kira was in a coma, I planned to pick up a bouquet of flowers for her room. She deserved the delicate fragrance of roses. She had loved the red, white, and yellow blossoms of Mom's rosebushes.

In the waiting room, I thumbed through a variety of magazines. I couldn't concentrate enough to read so I looked at the picture. Time passed slowly. Then, suddenly, I heard the words that I'd been praying for.

"Joyce, Kira's in her room," Maura told me as she entered the room.

I followed her down the hallway to a corner room. There was a rocking chair, and stencils of baby lambs and ducks on the wall over the bed.

Kira lay amidst a host of new tubes. Scenes from that horrible night years before flashed through my consciousness. I grasped Kira's hand tightly. Its warmth often fooled me into thinking that she was about to wake up, about to talk to me.

A mewing wail sounded from the corner behind me. I hadn't seen the crib when I entered.

"It's a baby girl," Maura told me. "She's beautiful!"

Before I could respond, Maura had picked up the bundle and held the baby out to me. The tiny baby was wrapped in a pink cotton blanket. Her face was puckered up as she prepared to wail again.

Involuntarily, I reached for her. She was so light. As I drew her close to me, her face relaxed and I sighed. A swelling filled my heart and I felt a radiance of love. I was holding Kira's baby!

Maura left the room and I sat in the rocker. An hour passed and the sun shone between the cracks in the blinds. Still, I rocked and marveled at the miracle that I was holding in my arms.

"Oh, Kira. She's a beautiful girl. I wish you could see her, hold her. She looks just like you."

Kira lay listlessly. Her raspy breathing and the creak of the rocking chair were the only sounds in the room as I cuddled the sleeping baby.

When the nurse came to take the baby to the nursery so that the pediatrician could examine her, my arms felt so empty. I was startled when the doctor came into the room.

"You'll be relieved to know, Joyce, that we've found a lovely young couple for the baby. They're eager to take her home. The paperwork is being processed."

"When will they pick her up?" I asked as numbness spread over me.

"They'll be here tomorrow. You'll need to sign the papers later this afternoon, since you're Kira's guardian. Will you still be here? I can have the contract delivered to the nurses' station," he told me.

"That'll be fine. Thank you." The doctor smiled and left the room.

As I sat in Kira's room, nurses walked in and out. I nodded off to sleep and woke abruptly, certain that I'd heard the sound of my nickname, Roadrunner, echoing in the room. I was alone with Kira, and she lay as placid as ever. I realized that my exhaustion must have stimulated my imagination. And, I figured that my wishfulness had caused me to hear things that I wanted to here.

"Am I disturbing you?" a male voice asked.

Detective Polymer stood near the doorway.

"No, not at all. Come in, I was just daydreaming," I confessed with a smile.

"How's Kira? The baby?" he inquired.

"Both are well, thank goodness," I told him happily.

"I have news. Emil Valente confessed to raping your sister." Although his tone was serious, his eyes were filled with emotion.

I leapt up and before I knew what had happened, I had thrown my arms around him. I felt a mixture of relief and joy. But, my joy was mixed with sadness. Suddenly, I didn't want to lose that precious baby.

In the circle of Burt's arms, I wept. I wept for Kira, the baby—and myself.

"Let it out, Joyce. It's okay. I'm here," he said as he stroked my hair.

As the sobs subsided, a name kept repeating in my head. Elizabeth. It was Kira's middle name and I knew, then, that it would be the baby's name. My baby's—and Kira's. Because as I held that precious new life in my arms, I knew that there was no way that I could ever let her go. I would raise her, and love her, and tell her all about her mother. And, one day, if there should ever be a miracle and my sister was to wake up, her beautiful daughter would be there to meet her mother.

THE END

ATTACKED AND BEATEN
BY MY BEST FRIEND'S HUSBAND

I had worked late at the bookstore, catching up on the accounts, and it was after dark when I finally turned the key in my upstairs apartment. I set my dog down on the floor and locked the door behind me. As I switched on the lights, my dog, a tiny teacup poodle, began to act strangely.

Sparkles sniffed the air, shook her silver head, bared her tiny teeth, and growled.

I dropped my jacket and purse on a chair by the door and turned to my dog. "What is it, girl? What's wrong?"

As I watched, her hair seemed to stand up on her back, and her growl increased almost to a roar. I stood and stared at her, surprised that such a small dog could make such a big noise. "Is someone there?" I asked her.

A movement from the shadows of the hall caught my peripheral vision, and I jerked my eyes that direction.

Mark Robbins stepped from the shadows, unshaven, and reeking of alcohol. "You stupid shrew. Your little rat is growling at me." He glanced down at Sparkles and sneered.

"How did you get in here, Mark?"

"I used a ladder to climb up and break in the bedroom window."

"What are you doing here?"

He took a few steps toward me, and Sparkles positioned herself between us. "You know why I'm here, Samantha. Tell me where I can find Vicki."

Cold fear stabbed at my stomach causing it to lurch into my throat, but I forced myself to meet his eyes. There was no reason to lie. "She's at a battered women's shelter. Now get out of my house." I took a step backward and reached for the phone on the end table, but Mark got there first and jerked the cord from the wall.

"Oh, no you don't," he hissed. "You're going to tell me where my wife is."

I screamed at him with more courage than I felt. "I don't know where your wife is. The police keep the location of the shelters a secret so that wackos like you can't find it. Now get out of my house!"

I lunged toward the door. My hand reached the deadbolt key, but Mark grabbed me from behind and spun me around. "You're the reason she left me!"

"She left you because you broke her nose and knocked out her front teeth. If you want to find her, you'll have to ask the police where she is."

He stepped closer to me until I could feel his foul breath on my face. "It's all your fault! If you hadn't interfered, she'd be at home with me, where I could take care of her and tell her how sorry I am. I could have convinced her that what happened was an accident."

"An accident?" I couldn't believe his words. "You punched her in the face several times, and this wasn't the first time you've done it. You've broken her arm, her ribs, and her collarbone. Are you going to keep it up until you kill her?" He was standing just two feet in front of me. I didn't know what to do, but I was so furious that even my fear couldn't stem my anger. "You're crazy, Mark. You need to be locked up."

"I'll tell you what I need. I need to be rid of you. Without you around, everything will be all right between Vicki and me."

Before he could say or do anything else, I let out an earsplitting scream.

"Scream all you want, Samantha. Your downstairs neighbors aren't home."

He raised his arm to slap me, but Sparkles launched herself from the floor and buried her teeth in his hand. He flung her to the carpet and kicked her small body with his boot. She cried out and lay still.

"That's my dog," I screamed. "What have you done to my dog?" My eyes were on Sparkles. I didn't see the fist that caught me off guard as he punched me squarely in the face. I reeled backward fighting for balance, but he punched me again. This time I saw flashes of light as I fell. My head struck the corner of the end table. As I lay there stunned, Mark kicked me in the ribs again and again. I put up my hands to ward off the blows, and my mind reeled. Was he going to kill me? He was still kicking when I passed out.

Vicki and I met in high school. It was sophomore year, and I was struggling through gymnastics in physical education class. The rest of the girls in class were having a good time vaulting over the pommel horse. The teacher explained that all we had to do was run up to the horse, put both hands on it and leapfrog over. I've always been a klutz. So I hung back and waited to go last, hoping that something would happen and I wouldn't have to do it at all. No such luck. When my turn finally came, I ran up to the horse, caught my leg on the edge, and landed on my head. All the girls laughed. Even the teacher had to put her hand over her mouth to keep from smirking.

Vicki stepped up beside me and brushed her hair out of her eyes. "It's okay, Samantha. I used to do it that way. You can't stop at the horse. You have to keep running and hop over. Watch."

31

She vaulted the horse, and with her help, I got over it, too. The entire class applauded.

I told her, "Thanks. I couldn't have done it without you."

"Yes you could," she assured me. "You just needed someone to show you how. Now, I was wondering if you could do something for me. I just moved here, and I don't know anybody. Would you show me around?"

"You bet," I told her.

We ate lunch together that day, and she went home with me that night and stayed for dinner. My dad had passed away the year before, but Mom took to Vicki and seemed to like her as much as I did. She didn't really have any family. Vicki didn't know who her father was, and her mother had left her in the care of a sister, who had agreed to keep the child for a couple of hours, while her mother ran errands. Vicki's mother never came back. The sister, Mary, adopted her niece and raised her as her own. Since Mary always hoped her sister would return for her child, she insisted Vicki call her "Aunt" instead of "Mom."

Mary was a waitress, and because her job didn't pay very well, she had to work most of the time to provide her niece and herself with the essentials of life. Vicki worked at a car wash on the weekends, and when she wasn't working or going to school, she was at my house. Having her around was like having a sister. We spent a lot of time studying, dreaming, and talking about boys the way girls do. Our grades went up because she helped me with math and science, while I helped her with English and French. Mary was proud of the way Vicki did in school, and she was very happy when her niece got a scholarship to the university. Vicki would be the first member of Mary's family to go to college.

We enrolled in the university together, Vicki in the business school and I in the English Department. We shared a dorm room.

I was a junior in college when I met Dave Pierce, who was in my Shakespeare class. "My parents wanted me to be a computer engineer," he confessed, "but I couldn't stay away from Shakespeare."

Vicki came along on our first date. Dave had come by our dorm room looking for me, and he had invited both of us to join him at the Student Union for pizza.

"Do you think he likes me?" I asked Vicki later.

She rolled her eyes. "You should see the way he looks at you when he thinks you're not watching. He's crazy about you."

He was, too, for as long as it lasted. In our last year of college, Dave asked me to marry him. The weekend after we graduated, we threw ourselves a potluck wedding in the university chapel. Mom and Vicki helped me make my wedding gown, all our friends brought food, and we made precious memories of each other, our families, and our friends.

Afterward, Vicki went to work for an accounting firm, while Dave and I scraped together enough money to rent a shop on Main Street. We both loved to read, and over the years, we had each accumulated a large book collection. By combining our books and setting up shelves of bricks and boards, our little hole in the wall shop became a used bookstore. We didn't have enough money to rent an apartment. So we lived in the back of the shop.

Vicki came by often and helped us set up our business and our accounts. She did well at her firm, getting regular raises and promotions, and she seemed to go on lots of dates, but she had no special man in her life.

Things went along really well for a couple of years. Dave and I increased our business, began to sell new books, and even rented an apartment. We had wanted a baby, but month after month went by with no luck. One day, Dave came into the shop with something under his arm, something small and cuddly.

"I know how much you want a child of our own," he told me, "but in the meantime, I thought we could love this little girl." He put a tiny, silver ball of fluff in my hands. "When she grows up, she'll play with the baby we'll have someday."

"This is the smallest puppy I ever saw," I told him.

"She's a toy poodle," my husband explained. "When they're this small, they're called teacup poodles. I don't know if she'll be able to sit in a teacup when she's grown, but she's the cutest thing I ever saw."

"Her eyes are sparkling so much!" I exclaimed, and that's how Sparkles got her name.

A year later, Dave was diagnosed with testicular cancer. By the time the doctors found it, it was way too late. Mom, Vicki, and even Mary helped me care for my husband during his last days.

About the time Dave passed away, Vicki met Mark. He came to work for her firm, and she was infatuated with him. Actually, he charmed her like a snake does a bird. He told her everything she wanted to hear, how he wanted a home and a family and how he loved children. Of course, that wasn't true. The only thing Mark ever loved was himself. Unfortunately, I was walking around in a daze. So I was no help. I didn't know how my life could go on without Dave, and I was too busy feeling sorry for myself to pay attention to what was happening to my friend.

Mary told Mom that she didn't trust Mark. She thought he was only interested in getting money from Vicki. Since my friend was so pretty and sweet, it was hard to believe that Mark didn't love her. Mom knew I had my own problems, and she didn't mention Mary's fears to me. We did find out later that Vicki had lent money to Mark, but we dismissed the incident as unimportant.

Then they eloped. I felt kind of left out, because I had always thought that my best friend would have a big wedding and I would be her matron of honor, as she had been my maid of honor.

"It just seemed like the thing to do at the time," Vicki told me. "You weren't up to helping me plan a wedding, and frankly neither was I. If I want a big wedding, I can always have it later."

Not long after they were married, Mark quit his job. Vicki said he was looking for something better, but from what I saw, he wasn't looking at all. He spent his days drinking beer in front of the television. When his wife suggested he put out some resumes, he hit her. The first time was only a slap. But the slaps turned to punches before long. Mark fell into the pattern of beating his wife, then apologizing and promising it would never happen again. Against all advice and suggestions, Vicki put up with it for a year.

Then three days before Mark attacked me, Mary had come by the bookstore and asked me to go by and check on her niece. When Mary had called her, Vicki had said she was sick, but when her aunt went by her apartment, Vicki wouldn't answer the door.

I found her lying on the sofa. Her entire face was black and blue and her nose was crooked. Her mouth was bleeding, and her front teeth were missing. I called an ambulance and the police. They took her to the hospital and then to the battered women's shelter.

Vicki called me later from the shelter. "Thank you, Samantha, for getting me out of there," she said. "I don't what I would have done if you hadn't helped me."

"You would have gotten away from him sooner or later," I insisted. "You just needed someone to show you how."

When I woke up in the hospital, I could barely open my eyes, and I couldn't open my mouth at all. My whole body throbbed and it hurt to breathe. A hand grasped my hand, and I looked up into Mom's worried face.

"My dog?" I managed to whisper through my teeth.

"Sparkles is at the vet. She's hurt, but she'll be all right."

"Vicki?"

"Still at the shelter. She's safe. It's lucky I came by right after Mark left. The police are looking for him, but they haven't found him yet." She sat down on the bed beside me. "Samantha, you've been badly beaten, but the doctors say you'll be okay. Your jaw is wired shut, you have broken ribs as well as internal injuries, and there were broken bones in your face. I put a note on the door of your bookstore that it will be closed today. As of tomorrow, Jessica, your clerk, has agreed to work full-time rather than part-time, and I will take over her part-time duties."

I nodded. The bookstore wasn't what I was worried about at that moment. "Mirror."

"Don't try to talk now, dear."

Maybe she hadn't understood me. I couldn't open my mouth. So I could barely understand the word I forced out between my lips. "Mirror."

She shook her head. "I don't have one with me, but you look pretty bad. Don't upset yourself. The doctors promised you'd be okay."

From the expression on her face I knew how bad I must have looked. Since I had never known my mother not to have a mirror in her purse, I was sure that she thought seeing my reflection would shock me.

I waited until Mom finally left before pestering a nurse into bringing me a mirror. The nurse tried to talk me out of looking at myself, but I kept insisting, and she finally agreed. She brought me a hand mirror and offered to hold it for me, but I took it from her and caught a glimpse of her cringing as I looked into the glass.

The bride of Frankenstein had looked better than me. The parts of my face that weren't stitched and bandaged were swollen and navy blue. I didn't even recognize myself. I glanced at the nurse. She shook her head and pity flowed from her eyes. I turned my attention back to my reflection. There was no way I could describe the shock I felt when I realized the extent of my injuries.

"How are you today, Samantha?"

I looked up. The nurse had gone, and a doctor in a white coat stood at the end of the bed staring at the metal clipboard that held my chart. He was a young man, probably in his midthirties, clean-shaven, and handsome. His square jaw and strong hands reminded me more of a cowboy than a doctor.

"I'm awful," I managed to say.

He walked over, sat down in the chair beside my bed, and took the mirror from my hands. "Don't be upset by what you see there. Your injuries are extensive, but you'll recover fully."

I was sure he was just saying that to make me feel better. "My face will never be the same." With my jaw wired shut, my words came out garbled.

The doctor understood what I had said. "Your face will be back to its beautiful self sooner than you think, and your husband will love you more than ever."

I shook my head. "My husband is dead."

His eyes caught mine. "I'm very sorry to hear that. I'm Dr. Hutchens, and I'll be back to check on you later. In the meantime, don't worry. I promise that your face, as well as the rest of you, will be all right."

35

After he left, the nurse returned. "Dr. Hutchens is the best plastic surgeon in the state," she confided. "If he says you'll be all right, you can believe him."

Maybe it would have been easier if I hadn't seen my face in the mirror. I closed my eyes and tried to forget my frightening image. I must have dozed off, because some time later, a woman's voice awoke me.

"Excuse me." A woman stood beside my bed. "I'm Detective Smith. Are you Samantha Pierce?"

I nodded.

"I need to take your statement and ask you questions about what happened to you. I'm sorry to bother you with this now, but Mark Robbins is still at large, and any information you can give me will help us catch him."

I pointed at my face. "My jaw is wired. It's hard to talk."

"I know, and this won't be easy, but if you'll bear with me, we'll take our time and make sure everything is accurate. We really need your help, Mrs. Pierce. Can I call you Samantha?"

I nodded. The detective both recorded our conversation on tape and took notes. I told her everything that happened from the time I had arrived home from work to the moment I passed out on the living room floor.

Mom came back while I was giving my statement, and she explained how she had come by my apartment and found me. She had called the police and the paramedics from her cell phone, and Mom had dropped Sparkles off at the vet on her way to the hospital.

Smith looked from me to my mom. "We photographed Samantha's injuries while she was in the emergency room. We also took a statement from your vet, because animal cruelty is a felony in this state. When we finally catch this guy, the district attorney will throw the book at him."

"Detective, I'm worried that my daughter is still in danger from this creep," Mom said. "What if he comes after her here?"

"It isn't likely, but hospital security has been alerted and given a photograph of him. They will be watching this area."

Later that afternoon, Aunt Mary visited me. She took one look at me and burst into tears. "Oh, Samantha. I'm so sorry," she muttered over and over.

"It isn't your fault, Mary. Mark is out of control."

"I came to thank you for what you did for Vicki, getting her away from him, but I can't believe what he did to you. You must be so angry."

"Yes, I am," I admitted, "but not at you or Vicki. I'm angry at Mark. He's the one who did this to me." No matter what I said, I couldn't seem to reassure her that I didn't blame her or her niece. When she finally left, she was still crying as hard as she had been when she arrived.

A couple of days later, I had another visitor, one I hadn't expected. I was lying in bed staring out the window when I heard a familiar voice say, "Samantha?" Her nose had been set, her bruises were healing, and a dentist had replaced her missing teeth. There were tears in her eyes.

"Vicki, I'm so glad to see you. You look a lot better."

The tears spilled down her cheeks, and her words echoed Mary's. "Oh, Samantha, I'm so sorry. I never thought Mark would come after you."

"I'm just glad you're safe."

She sat down on the bed. "How could he think he could get even with me by hurting you?"

"Don't worry about it, Vicki. The police will take care of Mark."

"I wish I could believe that," she said bitterly, "but they can't even find him."

"What about you? Is it safe for you to be here? He might be watching the hospital."

Detective Smith walked into the room. "He'll be in big trouble if he is. Your friend is with me."

A sigh of relief hissed between my teeth. "That makes me feel better."

"Samantha, will you be seeing your mother today?" Smith asked. "I have a couple more questions about her break in."

I didn't know what she was talking about. "What break in?"

"Mark broke into your mom's house," Vicki told me. "Don't worry. She's safe. The police thought he might do something like that. So your mom is staying at a downtown hotel registered under an assumed name, and the police have started watching your bookstore."

Dr. Hutchens entered the room then, but although I nodded to him, I turned my attention to the policewoman. "What happened at Mom's?"

"When Mark discovered your mother wasn't there, he trashed her house," Smith explained. "We lifted his prints from the fireplace poker he used to vent his rage on the furniture."

This time the tears were in my eyes. Mom loved her home and took pride in the antiques she and my father had collected.

Vicki hugged me and prepared to leave with the detective.

"We'll catch him," Smith assured me. "It's only a matter of time."

"They say time heals all wounds," I muttered as she and Vicki left the room.

Dr. Hutchens stepped up beside me. "I don't know about all

wounds, but it sure is healing yours. Have you looked at your face lately?"

I shook my head, and he went to get me a mirror. The navy blue patches had changed to a sickly yellow.

"You sound much better, too." He touched my face and looked inside my cheeks. "The swelling on your face has gone down making you much easier to understand.

"When can you take the wires off my jaw so that I can open my mouth again?"

He smiled. "Soon. I bet you're tired of eating through a straw."

I nodded. "I want ice cream, pasta, fried chicken . . ."

Laughter seemed to emanate from deep inside the doctor, and his eyes glowed as if someone had turned on a light inside his face. Later that day, he came back with a tall paper cup.

"I noticed that the first thing on the list of things you wanted to eat was ice cream. This is ice cream." He handed me the cup.

It was a chocolate milk shake. "Thank you. Thank you so much." I probably should have said more, but I was too busy sucking on the straw.

Day by day, I recovered. My headache disappeared, the dark circles left my eyes, and I could breathe easier. When I asked Mom why she hadn't told me about Mark breaking into her house, she said that she hadn't wanted to worry me. She thought I had enough on my mind.

The day that Sparkles got to leave the vet's office, Mom smuggled her into the hospital in a tote bag. I was so happy to see her that I nearly cried. She wiggled, yipped, and licked my face all over.

Dr. Hutchens arrived in time to witness our happy reunion, and he didn't seem upset about my dog being in the hospital. "From what the police said, this little poodle is quite a hero," he told us. "She gave them evidence against Mark Robbins. They took samples of his skin from her teeth." He looked from my dog to me. "You are both very brave."

Vicki came to see me again a few days later. This time she was by herself. Her face had nearly healed, she was wearing makeup, and her hair had been cut and styled. "So how's the patient today?" She set a paper bag down on the bed in front of me. "I thought you might be getting pretty bored in here. I brought you some things to do."

"Thanks. You look a lot better. I like your hair that way. I opened the bag and found several popular novels, some magazines, crosswords, and a crochet hook with yarn. "What did you want me to do with this?" I held up the crochet hook.

She shrugged. "I don't know. There is a book of crochet patterns there. If you get really ambitious and want to make an afghan, I'll bring you more yarn."

She tried to hide the sparkle in her eyes, but I knew that she remembered my attempt at making an afghan for my home economics class in high school. I had forgotten to count my stitches, and the afghan came out crooked. I had pulled the stitches out and started over, but I had made the same mistake again. Finally, I had given up.

"Okay, I'll make the afghan for you, but you have to put it out where everyone can see it." We both laughed, and I realized that this was the first time we had laughed since Mark had attacked us.

"You must be a lot better, Samantha. The last time I saw you, I could barely make out your words, but today I can understand you. How are your ribs?"

"Well, I can breathe now, and this morning I sneezed without bursting into tears. That's a good sign. But what about you? I don't see your police dog around. Did they catch Mark?"

The laughter disappeared from her voice. "No, they haven't. Detective Smith came with me. She stopped at the hospital security office. I don't know what's going to happen."

"They'll catch him," I said with more assurance than I felt. "What I want to know is, when they do, will he get out on bail?"

She shook her head. "I asked the inspector that, and she told me that the district attorney would convince the judge that Mark is a danger to us, and they will hold him in jail until his trial."

Now, if they could only catch him. For a moment I wondered whether Mark had left the area, but I realized that as long as he wanted to find his wife, he probably wouldn't go anywhere else. He was just hiding out.

Every time I asked Dr. Hutchens when he would take the wire off my jaw, he said, "Soon." Finally, the day came when he did it. I couldn't believe what a joy it was to be able to open my mouth again.

"Wow, now I can eat real food," I told him, "but the nurse will probably bring me a tray of green gelatin."

He smiled. "Maybe. We'll see about that. I'll be back to see you around dinner time."

He did more than stop by. That afternoon, Dr. Hutchens brought me a tray of food. Instead of gelatin, he brought fettuccine Alfredo, diced tomatoes, and a piece of soft garlic bread.

I was delighted. "This doesn't look like hospital food. It sure beats the broth I've been eating."

"It isn't hospital food," he admitted. "I brought it from home."

"You made this? It's delicious. Do you do this for all your patients?"

I had been joking, but he answered seriously. "I've never done it before."

As I glanced at his face, I caught an expression in his eyes that told me there was more going on than dinner. Suddenly, I was conscious of my rumpled hospital gown, my hair that needed cutting, and my complete lack of makeup. Don't be foolish, my mind insisted. Dr. Hutchens fixed my face. He's seen me at my worst. I shouldn't be self-conscious now, but the feeling won't leave. Suddenly, for the first time since my husband's death, I was excited by the presence of another man.

My self-consciousness got even worse when the doctor removed the last of the stitches and bandages from my face. This time I sat in front of a large mirror, and I marveled at what I saw. If anything, he had put my face back together better than I was before. Although I hadn't been ugly, I had been rather plain. Now I was pretty.

"You're not just a doctor," I told him. "You're my fairy godfather."

"Nonsense," he said. "You're giving me too much credit. You were always a beautiful woman. I was just doing my job."

I couldn't take my eyes off my reflection. "I hope I get to keep this face. The police still haven't found the man who attacked me. I'm being released from the hospital tomorrow, and I'm afraid he'll get me again. I'll be staying with my mother. So he won't catch me at home, but he might wait for me outside my bookstore."

Dr. Hutchens nodded. "I thought of that, Samantha, and I talked to the police about it. They assured me that they would watch your bookstore. But this brings up something I wanted to suggest to you. When I'm not working, I teach martial arts at the youth center. It isn't far from your bookstore. Maybe you could come over and join my class."

"Karate?" I don't know whether it was the way the doctor looked at me or my fear of Mark that made me answer, "I'll be there."

The next day, I was both excited and nervous at the prospect of being released from the hospital. The possibility of running into Mark nagged at the back of my mind, but it couldn't spoil my pleasure at being able to return to my mother, my dog, my business, and my life. I know Mom would be happy to quit overseeing my store, and Sparkles would be happy to have me back. Of course none of us could go home yet, and the police would still be watching my store and looking for Mark, but at least I would be out of the hospital.

The more I thought about it, the more I realized that Dr. Hutchens was right. I should study karate, not just for self-defense but for fitness as well. Maybe I could convince Mom and Vicki to study with me.

Vicki was still living in the shelter, but Detective Smith had arranged for her firm to release the accounts that Vicki was working on, and she could work at the shelter. I didn't know how long it would be before my friend could go back to her life, but it didn't seem like she would have much of a life to go back to. Maybe it was better this way. Vicki would be free of Mark, and she could begin to make a new life. She would have Mary, my mom, and me to help her.

Mom brought me some clothes to change into, and when I put them on, she complained that I had lost some weight while I was in the hospital.

I laughed. "It was all that eating through the straw."

She left me in my room while she went down to the office to sign some papers for my release. "Wait here," she said. "I'll be right back. Dr. Hutchens will be here in a few minutes. He wanted to say good-bye to you."

I walked over to the window of the room, stared out at the hospital parking lot for the last time, and wondered whether I would have to leave the building in a wheel chair. I had heard that hospitals made their patients do that, even when they were completely able to walk.

Hearing a sound behind me, I turned. I expected to see Dr. Hutchens, but instead, a man entered the room wearing scrubs and a mask over his face.

Thinking he must be in the wrong place, I said, "You've got the wrong room. I'm about to be released."

The man pushed the mask down under his chin, and I saw the leering face of Mark Robbins. "I'm in the right place. Did you miss me, Samantha? I heard they're letting you out today, and I thought I would come by and spoil your plans."

"Hospital security is right outside, Mark, and the police are everywhere. If I were you, I'd get out of here."

He walked toward me. "There's nobody outside, no one to hear you scream. Sound familiar?"

"Like I tried to tell you before, I don't know where the women's shelter is."

"This isn't about the women's shelter," he hissed. "It isn't even about Vicki. It's about you and me. I came here to finish what I started. You ruined my marriage. I'm going to ruin you."

He lunged at me. I jumped backward and screamed. Mark was between the door and me. I glanced frantically at the table beside my bed. There was an assortment of toiletries. I grabbed the box of tissues and flung it at him. It was followed by a small bottle of lotion, a bar of soap, a toothbrush, a tube of toothpaste, and a wet washcloth. He managed to dodge all but the washcloth. It hit him in the face, but he pawed it away, as if it were nothing. I hurled the pitcher of water at him. The pitcher overshot him, but the water splashed down the front of the scrub suit he was wearing.

I screamed again, as he stepped forward, closing on me. I kicked at his groin and missed but managed to land a glancing blow to his knee. He bellowed, lurched forward, and grabbed my throat. I hit and kicked at him, but my blows didn't seem to reach him.

41

I clawed at his hands with my fingernails, but he held on and squeezed. My eyes felt like they were bulging out of my face, pain shot through my lungs, and I thought my heart would burst.

Suddenly, he let go, and the breath whistled into my lungs like a gale-force wind. As my senses returned, I saw Mark lying on the floor in front of me as Dr. Hutchens held him down. A nurse hovered in the doorway.

"Call the police," the doctor shouted, and the nurse scrambled to obey the order. "Are you all right?" He was looking at me.

I nodded and massaged my bruised throat.

Mark struggled, but my doctor placed his knee in the middle of Mark's back and twisted his arm. "Move again, and you'll need an orthopedic surgeon."

Hospital security arrived almost immediately, and the police weren't far behind. Detective Smith herself read Mark his rights and snapped the handcuffs on him.

Dr. Hutchens examined my neck. "You'll be black and blue for a couple of days, but there's no damage."

"You saved my life," I whispered.

"In that case, would you call me Kirk?" His eyes were glowing again.

As the inspector had said, the district attorney charged Mark Robbins with everything from attempted murder to aggravated assault, animal cruelty, and breaking and entering. The jury found him guilty on all counts and the judge gave him thirty years with no parole and no time off for good behavior. I had to laugh when the judge said that. I had never seen Mark demonstrate any good behavior.

Vicki began her new life by opening her own accounting firm with one of the accountants at her former company. She has divorced her husband and put her disastrous marriage behind her. There is a new man in her life these days, a good man. Mom took a cruise down to the Caribbean after Mark's trial was over. Sparkles returned to her happy, boisterous self. And as for me, Kirk and I are planning a June wedding.

THE END

BLACKOUT
One Night Of Drinking
Changed Everything

Getting away for a weekend in the city was a rare treat for me, a small-town newspaper-advertising manager. I seldom got out of town, so I really looked forward to the annual advertising conference in Denver. The girls in my department were as excited as I was. The company paid for our hotel and the banquet on Saturday night, and between learning sessions we had time to shop and enjoy a few drinks in the hotel lounge.

For the three of us who were single, that might mean meeting some new men and dancing to the live band. There was no place to dance in Valley Park, unless you hit the bars on the weekend and that wasn't my cup of tea. I didn't drink much; I didn't like the taste of alcohol. And besides, with my job I needed to maintain a professional image. I guess I had accomplished that image, because I would be receiving the Advertising Manager of the Year Award at the banquet this year. My folks back home in Illinois would be so proud.

My department included Sandy and Carrie, who were single, and Paula who was married with two beautiful children.

"This isn't just my award," I reminded them. "I couldn't have done it without all of you. Let's go down to the lounge and celebrate a little before dinner."

I was actually planning on a soda and not an alcoholic beverage. As I said, I didn't like the taste of alcohol and I hadn't had more than one or two drinks since I graduated from college fourteen ears ago. In my senior year of high school and in college I went to a couple of parties. I guess I had a little too much to drink, because I remember a couple of times waking up at home or in the dorm and having no idea how I got there. Funny I should say remember, because the truth is I didn't remember a thing. But there were never any problems. In fact, my friends thought it was funny and would tease me about my lost weekend. But for me, it was a little scary, not knowing what I had said or done. A couple of times, people stopped talking to me and I had no idea what I had done to offend them, but that was a long time ago, and this was a really special occasion. And besides, I was pretty young then. I shouldn't have been drinking anyway. Now I'm a mature adult.

Anyway, I decided to treat myself to a drink—a real drink. Sandy ordered a round of something called a Banshee. They were absolutely delicious, kind of like drinking a banana milkshake. There was no alcohol taste at all, which I would later find out was not such a good thing.

We were giggling up a storm after our third round of Banshees. Paula was telling a story about her ten-year-old son who decided to raise fishing worms to earn money for a Nintendo game. He soaked the worm bedding and spun it dry in the washing machine. The whole family itched and scratched for a week before the kid confessed to what he had done. It was hilarious! With Paula's kids, you never knew what to expect.

I envied Paula. At thirty-six, I was getting past my prime. Here I was still single and not a man in my life. My biological clock was ticking and I loved kids. I thought about moving to a bigger town, but I had such job security at The Valley Park Gazette that I was afraid to give it up. I guess you could say I was comfortable and maybe just a little afraid too. I made the big move fourteen years ago to Colorado from Illinois with a group of friends just after graduating from college. We started out in Denver, but within a few months we had scattered to different parts of the state and soon I had a whole new group of friends at my job in Valley Park.

Occasionally, we'd get a new hire who was single and we'd date a few times, or I'd meet someone new at one of the banks or the hospital while making my ad contacts, but they always moved or got involved with someone else. I was beginning to feel, as my grandma used to say, like I'd been left on the shelf.

We were laughing up a storm, enjoying our Banshees, when three guys came over and introduced themselves. They were all nice looking, forty-ish, in town for an auto body shop convention. I remember sliding over to make room for the one who introduced himself as Alex. After that, everything is a blank.

It was dark when I woke up with this horrible feeling of being in the wrong place. Then, I realized I was naked and not alone in the bed. There was someone on each side of me. Surely, I wouldn't have gone to bed naked with my girlfriends!

As my eyes adjusted to the darkness, I realized with horror that I was sleeping between two men! One was the man I knew as Alex, and I had absolutely no idea who the other one was. An illuminated clock on the dresser told me it was three in the morning.

Oh my goodness! What have I done? Where am I? I couldn't stop running those questions through my head.

As I searched for my clothes, I stumbled over another naked guy sleeping on the floor. My hands were shaking. Stumbling around in the dark, I managed to find my belongings and get out of the room. I remembered that I was in a hotel in Denver and I remembered having

44

drinks with the girls, but after that—nothing!

Feeling around in my purse, I found the keycard for my room and let myself in as quietly as I could. The hotel had provided a cot so I could be in the same room as my friends, but now I wish I had a room of my own. I was so ashamed! What would they think of me? Did they see me going off to a room with three men? Or did I sneak out to meet Alex? I had no idea.

I stepped into the shower and let the hot water wash over me, as if it could wash away the shame. I knew I had sex with someone. But who? Or heaven forbid, was it with all three? The tears were streaming down my face and I hoped the shower would cover the sound of my sobs.

I was getting out when Sandy opened the door.

"Jenni, are you okay?" she asked. "We missed you at the banquet."

Oh my—I didn't even go to the banquet!

"I'm okay," I said. "Just had a little too much to drink maybe."

"We thought it was strange when you went off with those three guys by yourself," Sandy said, "but you were acting perfectly normal, so we weren't worried. You must have had a lot to drink in their room."

"I don't know," I said. "I don't remember anything other than us girls drinking Banshees and those three guys coming over to the table. Why did you let me go?"

"Come on, Jenni," Sandy said. "You said you were going to party with them and if we weren't coming then we shouldn't bother you. Actually, what you told me was to kiss off."

"You know I wouldn't say something like that," I insisted. "When have you ever seen me behave or talk that way? You know how much that award meant to me. Oh my goodness—the award!"

"I accepted it," Sandy said, "but I'm sure Ralph won't be happy when he finds out you didn't even show up to accept your award."

Ralph was the publisher of The Valley Park Gazette.

"Do you think someone will tell him?" I asked.

"Of course someone will tell him," she said. "These newspaper people are like one big family. He probably knows already."

"Why didn't you stop me when I left with those men?" I asked again.

"I TOLD you," Sandy said. "You told us to leave you alone."

"Well you ought to know I didn't mean it," I said.

"I've never seen you act that way before," Sandy said, "but you seemed perfectly normal to me. You certainly didn't seem drunk and you're a big girl, Jenni. We figured you could take care of yourself. It's after three in the morning now. I'm tired and we have a long drive back tomorrow."

I crawled onto the cot, but I didn't sleep a wink. I kept trying to remember what happened between the time I was at the table with the girls, enjoying those delicious drinks, and when I woke up naked in bed between two strange men, but nothing was coming through.

When Carrie opened the drapes and let the morning sunlight fill the room, I was still trying to figure out the night.

"Good morning, party girl," she said sarcastically. "When did you get in?"

"Late," I said. "And you could have at least come to get me so I didn't miss the banquet."

"Hey, don't go blaming us," Paula said. "You left with those guys and said not to bother you, but to tell the truth, we were pretty embarrassed. Sandy made up an excuse about you not feeling well when she accepted your award."

I couldn't blame them for being distant, but as rotten as I felt I really needed their support.

Things were never the same with the girls. We still worked together, but it felt like a wall had gone up between us. Finally, one afternoon I decided to approach Sandy about it. She was always the one I'd been closest to, so I just asked her, point blank, if there was anything I could do to change things.

"I feel bad, because we've all been friends for so long," I said. "Surely because I had a little too much to drink you can't stay mad at me forever."

Sandy looked really uncomfortable. Finally she said, "It wasn't just that you had too much to drink, Jenni. We were totally embarrassed. I mean, you appeared to be stone sober and you went off with those guys to their room like. . .like. . .some kind of a prostitute. You were making suggestive remarks and we were all embarrassed because we didn't want them to think the rest of us were like that."

"I'm really sorry if I embarrassed you, but you could have stopped me," I said.

"We tried," Sandy said. "You told us to kiss off and mind our own business!"

"I would NEVER talk like that," I gasped. "You're making that up."

"Well, I've never heard you talk like that before, either, " Sandy said, "but we saw a whole new side of you that night. I have to get back to work now, if you don't mind."

Instead of taking a coffee break that day, I went for a walk, alone. Tears were streaming down my face. It was a cold, drizzly October afternoon and if anyone saw me they would think it was the rain on my face. I choked back the sobs, knowing life would never be the same at The Valley Park Gazette. I decided to talk to Ralph, the publisher, the next day, to see if I could transfer to another newspaper in the company.

I felt a little better about things after making my decision, but unfortunately, I had to call in sick the next day. I woke up with the stomach flu, which was going around the office.

As it turned out, I missed a couple of days. I woke up in the morning, nauseated and dizzy, but by noon I'd feel pretty good. So on the third day, I went in a little late, but I did make it.

Ralph motioned to the chair across from his desk. "What can I do for you? I understand you've been sick."

"I have," I said. "I guess it's that flu that's been going around, but that's not why I'm here."

He learned back in his chair, cradling the back of his head in his hands.

"I'm here to. . .resign," I said. "Things just aren't going well and I feel it's best if I leave."

It was hard to tell what he was thinking. He didn't say a word.

"There is one thing you could do for me, though," I said, "and I would appreciate it very much. I'd like to transfer to one of the other newspapers in the company. Do you know if there are any openings in advertising? I don't need to be the manager. I just need a job. Things just aren't working out here."

I was having a hard time keeping from crying. That was the last thing I wanted to do. Crying was unprofessional, but right now I felt anything but professional.

"I've noticed a change in you," Ralph finally said. "It started a couple of months ago, when you didn't show up to receive your award at the conference. Sandy said you weren't feeling well then."

I wondered what else she told him.

"I wasn't," I said, "and I appreciated her doing that."

"I'll be happy to give you a recommendation," Ralph said. "There's nothing open in the company that I know of, but I'll print out a listing of advertising jobs in the industry that you might apply for. Would that help?"

"That would," I said.

He turned back to his computer, hit a couple of keys, and soon a paper was inching its way out of the printer."

"I'll leave in two weeks," I said. "That should give you some time to replace me."

"You can consider today your last day," Ralph said. "We'll give you two weeks severance pay. I can tell your heart is not in this job anymore, and replacing you won't be a problem. Sandy can step up to the plate."

"I'll get my things," I choked.

I found a box in the pressroom and cleaned out my desk. Nobody said a word. Finally, I was down to the last thing—my grandmother's African violet that I had hauled all the way to Colorado from Illinois.

Sandy's desk was behind me and I handed it to her. "It's kind of like passing the gavel," I joked. "Congratulations."

There were tears in her eyes as she came around her desk and gave me a hug.

"I'm sorry, Jenni," she said. "We all are."

I walked out the door with my cardboard box and never looked back. I didn't want to cry. I was so ashamed. I felt like everyone there knew the awful thing I had done at the conference in Denver. I'd embarrassed them all. I was the company joke.

I did luck out with one thing. About halfway down the list of jobs Ralph had given me, I found The Pleasant Valley Courier, a small weekly newspaper in rural Idaho. It wasn't that far away and the publisher hired me, sight unseen, after talking to Ralph on the phone. The ad manager had left in a hurry and the publisher was desperate for a replacement. He gave me enough time to sell my things at a garage sale, pack the car, and head to Idaho.

I still wasn't feeling well, especially in the mornings, but it was getting better and I told myself once I got situated things would work out. And did know one thing—I would never have another drink. From now on, I'd say I was allergic to alcohol, and I guess you could say I was, because it definitely did not agree with me. I never did remember anything about that night.

The long drive up to Idaho gave me time to think. I didn't need a therapist to figure out I had a problem. Getting a new start was all I needed to get back on my feet. Everybody makes mistakes, I told myself. In my new town, no one would know anything about me.

I arrived in Pleasant Valley shortly after noon and settled into the room at the Sunset Motel that would be my temporary home. I didn't have any food, but there were some packets of instant coffee. I fixed a cup as I blew-dry my hair, but it tasted terrible! It must have been old. It didn't look like the Sunset Motel did a lot of business.

The Pleasant Valley Courier was in an ancient building that badly needed a coat of paint, but the smiling faces that greeted me when I walked in the door made up for the dreary exterior. Everyone was so friendly.

My boss, Mr. McGee, was an older man, around retirement age, but he seemed to have no thought of retiring and spoke of the newspaper as though he'd be there for another forty years. We discussed the company insurance and other technicalities.

My office was just an ancient desk in the corner of a big room that held a couple of reporters, the bookkeeper, and my "staff," which was one rather large, but friendly, woman named Joan who welcomed me with open arms. She was tired of carrying the load herself and had no desire to be the manager.

Mr. McGee said I could start right away, getting acquainted with the computer system and getting my desk in order. By five o'clock I had already put in my first day.

On my second day, I was sitting down having coffee in the break room with Joan when a tall, nice looking man, obviously one of the press crew, came in. He was covered in ink from head to toe.

"Mind if I join you?" he asked, wiping the ink from his hands on his coveralls. "We've got a break between runs and I wanted to meet the new kid on the block." He smiled and his beautiful eyes twinkled above his ink stained cheeks. "I'd shake hands," he said, "except you'd never get this stuff off."

Joan introduced Rich, the manager of the pressroom. He'd been with The Pleasant Valley Courier for ten years and had plenty of opportunities for advancement, but he loved small town living.

"The only problem is, there isn't much for a single person to do except hit the bars," he said. "That was okay in my twenties, but not anymore. I'm getting too old for that stuff."

"Not exactly my cup of tea either," I said, sipping my coffee.

We made small talk for a while and I did my best to avoid talking about my last job. I noticed the coffee tasted really bad again.

"It's just a little strong," I said, when Joan noticed.

Rich excused himself and went back to work and Joan had barely left the room when a wave of nausea hit and I ran for the bathroom to toss my cookies. When I finally came out, I must have looked pretty bad because Joan asked if I was okay.

"Yes, thank you," I said. "I guess maybe I've got a touch of the flu."

When I got to my desk I was shaking all over. Why had it not occurred to me before? I'm way overdue for my period! But I can't be pregnant! Not now, at thirty-six, when I just started a new job. Surely God wouldn't let that happen!

I hadn't used birth control in ages because there was no reason for it. Much as I wanted someone to share my life with, my job had pretty much been my life since I got out of college. It wasn't that I never dated or never had the chance. It was just that the right guy never showed up.

I didn't dare leave work early on my second day, but that night, as soon as I got off work, I headed for Walmart and bought an early pregnancy test.

Please, God, let this be negative, I prayed. This can't happen. Not now. Not when I'm just getting a new start. Not with someone I don't even know.

But the test was positive!

I collapsed on the floor of the bathroom in my motel room; clutching my knees to my chest and rocking back and forth like a frightened child. I was pregnant and I had no idea who the father was. I always wanted a baby, but I'd given up on that ever happening when I didn't even have a serious boyfriend. Surely, this had to be a nightmare and I'd wake up soon.

But it was real.

Ever since I was a little girl, I dreamed of having a husband and family. I loved kids. I was thirty-six years old and time was running out. This could be my last chance, I told myself.

I made a bowl of oatmeal and managed to keep it down as I flipped through the newspaper, checking the ads, and familiarizing myself with what would be my clientele in Pleasant Valley.

I was checking the classifieds when an ad caught my eye. Dr. Chuck Wainwright had a hypnotherapy practice in Pleasant Valley! He was advertising help with smoking cessation, weight loss, phobias, etc. It was the etc. that I was interested in. I heard memories could be recovered under hypnosis. If that was true, perhaps I could recover the memory of that night and learn who the father of my child was. Not that I'd attempt to contact him. I was too ashamed, and whoever he was, he wouldn't want anything to do with a girl who would sleep with three guys on a one-night stand.

I made an appointment with Dr. Wainwright for Saturday. He wasn't usually in on Saturdays, but since weekends were my only days off he agreed to see me for the initial consultation. He said he would do the actual session the following week. My heart was pounding so loud I was sure he could hear it across the room.

I poured out my story, stopping occasionally to blow my nose and wipe my eyes. I was so ashamed but Dr. Wainwright had to know the truth if he was going to help me.

Finally, I finished and leaned back in my chair, sipping on the little bottle of water he'd given me.

"I'm sorry, Jenni, but I can't help you," he said.

"But you can recover repressed memories through hypnosis," I said. "I know you can. I've seen it on TV."

"Ordinary, repressed memories," he said. "This is different."

"How is this different?"

"What you're describing is an alcohol blackout," Dr. Wainwright said. "During an alcohol blackout, no memory is ever formed, so there is no memory to retrieve. It simply does not exist."

I couldn't believe what I was hearing.

"I have a couple of books I can let you borrow," Dr. Wainwright said. "It would take too long to explain it all, but other doctors have done extensive studies on this subject and books have been written about what actually happens during an alcohol blackout. What happened to you isn't unusual. People have been convicted of committing murder during an alcohol blackout and they'll never know if they actually did it because no memory is ever formed.

"But I'm not an alcoholic," I said. "I hardly ever drink. That night I only had a few fancy drinks. I wasn't falling down drunk."

"You don't have to be an alcoholic, Jenni. That's exactly what it says in the books I told you about," Dr. Wainwright said. "I'd like you to read these books, and when you're through, we can talk about other ways hypnotherapy can help you. I can help relieve your anxiety and I can help you access your higher self to get the answers you need about what to do. But I cannot recover a memory when none exists."

I couldn't believe what I was hearing. I thanked him, took the books and hurried home to read them. I can't tell you how hard it was for me to focus on my new job and deal with the horror that was happening to me, but somehow I managed.

The books terrified me. What happened to me was far more common than one would imagine. I learned a person in an alcohol blackout can appear to be perfectly sober and in her right mind. That was exactly how my friends described me when I asked why they hadn't tried to stop me from going with Alex and his friends. I learned that a person in an alcohol blackout will say and do things totally out of character. For the first time, I began to believe what my friends had told me; that I had told them to kiss off and leave me alone. I would never have used that language in my right mind.

Reading those books was a sobering experience—pardon the pun.

I had so much on my plate I didn't know where to turn. I was pregnant. I had a new job and I had to do my best if I wanted to keep it. I was totally alone. There was no one in my family I could talk to and I had no friends. So, I made an appointment for another session with Dr. Wainwright. He had been a huge help with the information on blackouts and above all, he didn't condemn me. He really seemed to care. So maybe he could help me decide what to do about my pregnancy.

"I'm sorry I couldn't help you recover the memory, Jenni," he said, "but let's see what we can do about finding an answer to your problem and releasing some of that anxiety."

He said the answers were there. My higher self knew what to do. I just needed to access my higher self, through hypnosis, and the answer would come through. Naturally, I was a little skeptical since I had never been hypnotized.

I was even more doubtful afterwards because I was totally aware of what was going on all around me the whole time I was supposedly hypnotized. And when I was supposed to visit my higher self, nothing happened and I didn't "see" anyone. But I did feel totally relaxed afterward and that alone was worth what I paid him.

"I don't think I was hypnotized," I said, "but I certainly feel better."

"Rest assured, you were," Dr. Wainwright smiled. "You may not have received your answers immediately but they will come. Hypnosis is very subtle. Just pay attention to your dreams and any information that comes your way in the days and weeks ahead."

He acted like he knew a secret I didn't know.

I scheduled another appointment for three weeks and went home.

After that, I felt surprisingly calm. I still didn't know what to do about my pregnancy but it just didn't seem so pressing. Then one day, I was in the break room having a cup of tea—the coffee still tasted like crap—and I noticed a magazine on the table. It was opened to an article about a woman who chose artificial insemination because she wanted a baby and didn't want to be married.

That's it! I'll tell people I chose to be artificially inseminated since I was getting close to the end of my childbearing years. It makes perfect sense. I have good insurance and a job. There's no reason I can't raise a baby by myself.

I felt like a ton of bricks had been lifted off my back. Dr. Wainwright was right! The answer did come, just like he said it would.

I couldn't wait for my next session. I called him and I could almost feel him smiling over the phone.

"I told you hypnosis is subtle," he said. "Your higher self gave you the answer. It just didn't happen the way you expected, when you were in trance, but it tuned your subconscious into becoming aware of the things around you. I'm happy for you, Jenni. I think that's a perfect answer."

I continued to see Dr. Wainwright about once a month after that, and we began working on using hypnotherapy for the birth of my baby.

As my pregnancy became noticeable I was very matter-of-fact about it, telling my new friends and my boss, Mr. McGee, that I'd been artificially inseminated because I wanted a child and time was running out. I had to do something now. I said I was thrilled about the pregnancy and the more I talked, the more I convinced myself I was.

Mr. McGee seemed a little upset at first since I'd just started my job and he suspected I knew I was pregnant when I started, but I explained I had every intention of working as long as possible and finding daycare after a couple of weeks so I could come back to work. That eased his mind. He had gone without a manager for the two weeks before I showed up, so he knew he could get through it.

The nausea let up and I actually began to feel good. My new friends at The Pleasant Valley Courier told me I was "glowing" and when I looked in the mirror I noticed I actually did have a kind of a glow about me. I was so thankful that I'd found Dr. Wainwright. I laughed, thinking he wasn't Mr. Right in the way I'd always imagined, but he certainly helped me get in the right frame of mind.

The only one who seemed disappointed with my pregnancy was Rich, the pressman.

"I was hoping we could do some things together since we're both single," he said.

"Maybe after the baby comes," I said. "I can understand you not wanting a pregnant date. That might look a little strange."

"I heard about what you did," he said, rather shyly. "Artificial insemination. That's very brave of you, wanting to do this on your own. I think you're going to make a great mom."

"Thank you," I said.

"As for being seen with a pregnant date," he said, "that's not a problem at all. How about dinner Saturday evening? It would be fun to go to that new little barbecue place that opened up a couple of weeks ago. Remember you did their ad?"

"I did and it sounded great, but I didn't want to go by myself," I said. "The only problem with Saturday is, I finally found a little furnished apartment and I'm moving out of my motel room. I'm going to be pretty wiped out after that."

"How about if you had some help?" he asked. "Then you wouldn't be so tired."

"You mean it?"

"Of course," he smiled, and his eyes lit up again. He reached over and patted my knee. "I'll be by Saturday morning and we'll have you moved in no time."

I was shocked when he actually showed up, and even more surprised when I learned my apartment was in the same building he lived in.

"What a coincidence," he said. "I couldn't have planned that better myself."

After I got moved in, I showered and put on a new top that wasn't exactly a maternity top, but it was loose in front and covered up my expanding middle. For the first time in months, I was excited about something. I had to keep reminding myself that I was pregnant and Rich was just being nice but even so, I would be forever grateful to him.

Dinner was wonderful. I declined the wine, but we shared a toast across the table with his wine and my glass of caffeine-free soda. I hated for the evening to end, but finally it was time to go home. My kitchen wasn't set up yet so Rich invited me to his apartment where he made decaf coffee and we watched a little TV before I headed back downstairs to my new place.

As the months past and I grew bigger, Rich and I grew closer but it wasn't until my seventh month that he kissed me. The touch of his lips on mine sent shivers through me. Did I dare tell him my horrible secret? Actually it was beginning to feel unreal to me now; I'd been living the lie about being artificially inseminated for so long.

"I can't imagine why someone didn't snap you up long ago and why you had to do this," he said, touching my belly tenderly. But it wasn't a judgmental statement. I sensed he really was in awe of why I wasn't already married. And then he added, "I'm just grateful you didn't marry someone else, Jenni. I'm glad you're here for me. I've never felt this way before. I knew it the first day I met you in the break room. There was just a spark there that I've never felt before."

"I can say the same for you," I said. "I can't imagine why someone didn't latch on to you a long time ago."

"I just never found the right woman," he said.

We shared a kiss then and I felt a tear trickling down my cheek, realizing this was all going to end if I told him the truth.

"What's wrong, Jenni?" he asked, wiping the tear away.

"Nothing," I lied. "I'm just happy. So very happy."

I was in my eighth month when the girls at work gave me a baby shower in the break room on a Friday after work. It was a surprise, with the pink and blue balloons, a beautiful cake, tiny little sandwiches from the deli, and a pile of presents. Rich and the guys from the pressroom even showed up and presented me with an ink-stained envelope containing one hundred dollars—enough to buy the used crib and mattress he knew I needed.

He stood there beaming as I opened the gifts, one at a time. I didn't know if it would be a boy or girl. I'd opted not to have the ultra sound since I wasn't having any complications. I was kind of old fashioned I guess, but I liked the idea of it being a surprise.

The shirts and nightgowns seemed so tiny. I hadn't been around babies much and it was hard to imagine anything being that small. By the time I opened the last gift, tears of happiness were streaming down my cheeks. "Thank you all so much," I said. "I love you all."

"I'll help you load those in the car," Rich said.

He helped me bring the gifts in the house too, and I thanked him again for all he'd done. When we had set the last package in place, he invited me out to dinner. I was much too tired to cook so I was happy to take him up on it.

After dinner, I invited him in for coffee. Decaf, of course, since I was thinking about the baby.

"There's something I've been wanting to talk to you about, Jenni," he said, when we were finally settled on the couch.

My first thought was, he wants to end our friendship, and of course I couldn't blame him. Who wants a woman the size of a small elephant?

"Jenni, when I grew up, it was kind of expected that mothers would be married, and, well, I don't know how to put it any other way. I love you Jenni. Will you marry me?"

My heart sank. I wanted to hear those words all my life, but I knew I had to make a decision now. To tell or not to tell. And I loved Rich too much to live a lie.

"I would love to marry you, Rich," I said, "but there's something you need to know first. You don't know the whole truth about me."

By the time I finished, I was shaking and sobbing so hard I was afraid I'd go into labor.

"I'm not making any excuses," I said. "I truly don't remember anything about that night. But I couldn't give up my baby either. So I made up that story about being artificially inseminated. I should have told you sooner, but I cared so much about you. I didn't want to lose you."

Rich just sat there and for the first time that sparkle was gone from his eyes.

"Well, this is a shocker," he said. "I'll have to think about this, Jenni. I. . .I'm sorry but it's a lot to take in."

"I know," I said. "If you don't want anything more to do with me, I understand. I only ask that you please don't tell my secret. Things are going so good for me here in Pleasant Valley. I'm happy and I want things to be as normal as possible for the baby and me. Can I trust you with my secret?"

"No worries," he said.

He got up to leave and kissed me on the top of my head. I sensed the romance was gone. I was just some poor, pathetic thing that he felt sorry for now.

I didn't see Rich for a couple of weeks after that. There was no reason for him to come into the ad department and no reason for me to go into the pressroom and he stopped coming for breaks when he knew I'd be there. But I knew I'd done the right thing, even though my heart was breaking. I had to tell him the truth.

I was at work when my water broke. I was sitting at my computer when I felt this grinding sensation and then it felt like I wet my pants.

"Oh my goodness, I'm going into labor," I said.

Joan came running over. "Don't worry," she said. "I'll clean it up and we'll get you to the hospital. I'm so excited! I'm going to be an aunt!"

We laughed and hugged each other and then she ran for some paper towels and mopped up the mess and she drove me to the hospital. Joan had to go back to work, so I was left alone, but I was so grateful for her help and she promised to come back later.

My labor was going very smoothly, using the self-hypnosis

55

techniques Dr. Wainwright taught me. I was so focused I didn't even notice someone had come into the room.

"Rich, what are you doing here?" I asked. "You're supposed to be at work."

"I heard what happened and I had to be with you," he said. "I just had to be here. I love you, Jenni. I love you and if you'll have me, we're going to be a family."

"But the baby," I said. "You know. . ."

"It bothered me at first," he said, "but I have to share something with you. I was adopted. My mother gave me up at birth. I never knew who she was and it doesn't really matter because the parents who raised me are the ones I'll always consider my real parents. But I'll always be grateful to her for giving me the gift of life. You chose to keep him or her and that says a lot. How the baby was conceived doesn't matter. It's what happens from now on. Will you still marry me, Jenni?"

I nodded my head as a strong contraction engulfed my body, and I really felt it that time because I wasn't focused on relaxing. A nurse came in and asked Rich to step back while she examined me again.

"Looks like you're ready," she said. "Is this the baby's father? And do you want him with you for the birth?"

My eyes met Rich's, he took my hand, and we both nodded yes.

Moments later I was holding our beautiful new eight-pound baby daughter.

Rich brought me home the next morning and two weeks later I was back on the job. By then, the crib and all my things had been moved to his apartment.

Life has been good to me. I was so afraid I'd lose Rich after revealing my secret but I had to tell him the truth and sometimes, I guess, God just decides we've had enough punishment for making foolish mistakes.

THE END

We partied without a care in the world.
We didn't know what the future held. . . .

MURDER IN
THE UPSTAIRS BEDROOM

I said the night of Brendan's party: "Your parents are going to kill you!"

I knew that I'd always remember Brendan's response. He'd looked at me with a sly smile and that weird light in his eyes. "No, they won't," he said, with eerie conviction.

That little tidbit of conversation, as innocent as it had sounded, would haunt me for the rest of my life. Should I have suspected something?

I had been sixteen at the time. Brendan and I had been dating for several months. Yet, no matter how much I'd gone over those surreal months, and told myself that I couldn't have known, I could never totally resolve myself of the guilt.

My horrified mind always came back to one, clear fact: I should have suspected something. How could a girl date a guy for several months, see him practically every day—and not realize that he was capable of murder?

I had nearly gone all the way with Brendan, on more than one occasion. He'd been tender and loving each time, battering my defenses and weakening my resolve to remain a virgin. He'd never gotten angry when I'd stopped him, just short of actually making love, like my ex-boyfriend had.

In those months, not once had Brendan exhibited the kind of violence that he was capable of. True, he'd hated his parents, but what teenager didn't?

It had taken me a year to gather up enough courage to tell my story. When I'd thought of how close I might have come to becoming his third victim, I'd turned cold inside. I'd had a lot of nightmares, and I'd still cried a lot when I'd thought about it.

Brendan wasn't exactly what some people would have called "a bad boy." We'd lived in a small town, where eighty percent of the teenagers smoked marijuana, and drank whatever they could get their hands on. We'd figured that the police in our town were either oblivious, or on someone's payroll, because they'd seldom searched anyone's car, or entered their homes in search of drugs. Perhaps, if they'd had been more diligent in their duties, such a horrible thing wouldn't have happened.

Or, maybe I was just looking for someone else to blame.

But, in truth, Brendan wasn't any worse—or better—than any of the other guys that I'd dated. Oh, there was a small group of geeks that didn't get high—who spent most of their leisure time on their computers, or playing video games, instead of partying. But, in my opinion, they were boring, and none of them had interested me.

The first time that I'd really noticed Brendan was when school had started again after summer vacation. I was just going into the eleventh grade, and Brendan was a senior. During the summer months, he'd not only filled out and grown taller, but it seemed as though the acne that I'd remembered had completely cleared up.

Brendan Walker had become a hottie, and I wasn't the only girl who had noticed.

Emily, my best friend, had nudged me. "Check it out, Jessica," she whispered. "Isn't that Brendan Walker—the kid with the bad skin?"

I had followed her line of vision. "Not anymore," I murmured. Just then, I'd realized that Brendan was looking back at me. He had really sweet eyes, eyes that had made me melt all over. My heart had jumped, and I'd gotten a warm, fuzzy feeling inside.

Brendan was looking at me as though he knew exactly what sex was all about, and couldn't wait to show me. Despite my determination to remain a virgin until the right guy had come along, I was very receptive to just about everything that came before that final plunge. I'd heard enough talk about foreplay to know that I was pretty normal in that area.

"I want to have sex with him," Emily blurted out. She'd clamped a hand over her wayward mouth, looking horrified.

I'd burst out laughing. "You are so lying, Emily! You won't even let Peter get to second base!"

Emily blushed. "Maybe not Peter, but I'd let Brendan do whatever he wanted to do with me." She'd suddenly seemed to realize that Brendan was staring at me—not her. "Oh, I think he's got a bead on you."

She'd sounded so disappointed that I'd known better than to laugh. "Hey, you've got a boyfriend. Don't be such a pig."

She gave me a light push. "Well, go talk to him before someone else realizes that the ugly duckling has turned into a swan."

"Be quiet," I whispered. "He's coming this way!" The closer he came, the more nervous I'd become. Suddenly, I'd wished that Emily would take a hike. What if she'd said something embarrassing?

My knees had nearly buckled with relief when Emily had told me, in a disgruntled tone, that she would catch me later. Then, she'd walked away. I'd slipped my hands in the back pockets of my jeans to keep from fidgeting as Brendan had reached me.

"Hi," he said, sounding a little shy.

But, there was nothing bashful about the direct way that he'd stared at me.

"Hi," I answered him, unable to look away from his beautiful eyes. "I'm Jessica."

"I know." He'd smiled. "We had a class together last year."

I'd racked my brain, and to my relief, I'd finally remembered. "Yeah. Civics, wasn't it?"

He'd nodded, looking pleased. "I had to take the class over."

I'd grimaced to show him that I was completely sympathetic. "That's a pain, isn't it?"

"Yeah," he agreed.

When the conversation had lulled, I'd nearly panicked. But Brendan had saved the day by asking me out for the following Friday night.

"Your parents do let you date, don't they?" he asked with a teasing smile.

I'd rolled my eyes. "Barely. They drive me insane."

Something strange had flickered in his eyes at my words. Just as quickly, though, it had disappeared. "Yeah. Mine, too. So, Friday night, then? I'll pick you up around eight. Ricky Sloane's having a back-to-school party at his place."

A forbidden thrill had shot through me at his words. Ricky Sloane had graduated the year before, and he and two other guys had rented a house together. I knew that my mother would kill me if she'd learned that I was even thinking about going to one of his infamous parties.

Fortunately, for my mother, I thought, she'll never know.

I'd tried to look cool and casual, and I'd shrugged. "Sounds good to me."

By my third date with Brendan, I'd hated his parents almost as much as he did. He'd talked about them constantly, which had prompted me to tell him all the despicable things that my parents had done. Pretty soon, I'd run out of horror stories, but Brendan hadn't. His list had seemed endless.

When we'd been dating for about two weeks, Brendan had picked me up on a Saturday night. I'd known, from the moment when I'd seen his expression, that he'd had a fight with one, or both, of his parents. But, even then, he hadn't looked angry—just disgusted.

"Mom went through my room again today," he muttered.

I was plastered against the seat as he'd floored his old car. Brendan was a careless driver, so I'd always tried to remember to buckle my seat belt. He'd teased me about it the first time, but by that point, he hadn't even seemed to notice.

"Bummer," I mumbled as I'd fastened the belt. Truthfully, I was getting a little bored with his complaints about his parents.

He'd swerved around a slower moving vehicle just as I'd latched my seat belt.

"She found my weed, and a bottle of vodka that I'd been hiding in my underwear drawer. She claimed that she was just putting my clothes away."

It had been on the tip of my tongue to say, "Maybe she was," but I'd stopped myself in time. I really liked Brendan, and I didn't want to risk his getting angry with me. "Maybe you should hide that stuff somewhere else," I suggested.

He'd given me a strange look. "She shouldn't be going through my drawers," he snapped. "That's just not right."

My mom and dad would have reminded him that he lived under their roof, and therefore, he must follow their rules. I was certain that Brendan's parents would have said the same thing—and, that they probably had, on more than one occasion.

"No, it isn't," I agreed. "But I think that all parents are the same."

Brendan had shaken his head rather vigorously at my words. "No, mine aren't the same. They're worse. A lot worse. She flushed my weed down the toilet, and poured out my vodka. She also told me that if I didn't stop bringing that stuff into the house, they were going to call the cops on me. Me! Their own son!"

Well, I might have liked Brendan a lot, and I might have been only sixteen, but even I'd realized that Brendan was being unreasonable. If my parents had even suspected that I'd smoked marijuana, or that I'd been drinking, they would have shipped me to live with my Aunt Grace, who was very religious, and lived in the middle of nowhere.

Brendan and I'd had our first fight that night, because I'd told him what I was thinking.

"I agree that they shouldn't invade your privacy, Brendan," I said. "But do you really think that it's okay for you to have weed and booze in the house? You're only seventeen."

He'd braked sharply and pulled the car over to the side of the road. Then, he'd sat there, staring at me, as if I had just informed him I was getting a sex change. The longer that he'd stared at me, the bigger the lump in my throat had gotten.

"If they hadn't come in my room," he said softly, "then they wouldn't have known that I had it. That's the whole point of privacy."

I could tell by his expression that it would have been useless to argue. So, I'd swallowed the lump and tried to change the subject.

"Hey, did I tell you that Mom burned my black blouse when she was ironing it? Can you believe that? I paid thirty dollars for it out of my baby-sitting money!"

Instead of responding to my outrage, Brendan had put his hands on the steering wheel and stared straight ahead. "She told me that I was a loser. She said that I was going to end up in prison, and that she wasn't coming to see me when that happened."

"I'm sure she didn't mean it," I'd murmured. I'd felt tears prick my eyes. My parents were tough on me, but they'd always been encouraging. I couldn't imagine them telling me that I was a loser.

"She meant it," he said flatly.

"She was probably just upset about finding that stuff—"

"She meant it," Brendan repeated, louder that time. He'd looked at me, and his eyes were filled with anger. "And I wouldn't be surprised if she really did call the cops over a little weed."

"Marijuana is illegal, Brendan," I pointed out gently.

"But alcohol isn't." Brendan barked out a humorless laugh. "How many people are killed by drunk drivers each year? And how many are killed by people who are high on pot?"

I'd shaken my head. I truly hadn't known the statistics. It hadn't made sense to me, either, but I'd known that my opinion wouldn't have changed anything. All I knew was that I didn't want Brendan getting in trouble with his parents.

"Why don't you just hide the weed outside somewhere, and not even bring it into the house?"

Brendan sneered. "You're missing the point," he told me. "She has no right to come into my room. Does your mother snoop around in your room?"

"Not that I know of." I'd taken a deep breath and smiled, hoping that I hadn't come off sounding all righteous. "But then, I haven't given her a reason to. She doesn't know that I smoke pot, and she doesn't know that I drink."

Brendan snorted. "Lucky you."

My patience had snapped. "Well, I don't rub her nose in it."

We'd argued off and on for the rest of the night. On the way home, things had gotten even worse. We'd gotten pulled over by a state trooper, who'd proceeded to search Brendan's car.

He'd found a pint of vodka and a dime bag of weed under the spare tire in the trunk and two rolled joints in Brendan's pocket. He'd also found about a dozen prescription pills among Brendan's pocket change. I hadn't known before then that Brendan had been taking pills, along with drinking and smoking weed.

I'd stood by the car while the trooper had grilled Brendan. I was shaking all over, thinking about my parents and what they would have said if I'd had to call them from jail. At the party, I'd had a couple of beers, and smoked a little weed, but that had been over an hour before. I was fairly certain that I didn't look wasted. Brendan, on the other hand, had bloodshot eyes and was noticeably unsteady on his feet. Why hadn't I insisted upon driving?

Finally, the trooper had finished with Brendan and come back to me. He'd stared at me so hard that I couldn't help but fidget. I'd jumped when he'd finally spoken.

"Your boyfriend says that you're clean. Is that true, Miss Henninger?"

I hadn't hesitated over the lie. "Yes, sir, Officer. I should have insisted on driving—I know."

"Yes, you should have." The trooper sounded very angry. "I'm going to give your friend, here, a couple of serious citations, and then I want you to drive the rest of the way home. Do you understand?"

"Yes, sir," I mumbled meekly. I was so relieved, I felt faint. I felt badly for Brendan, but I was selfish enough to be thankful that the trooper had believed Brendan's story.

The trooper had stepped closer. I'd stiffened all over, growing edgier by the moment. I guess I'd watched too many horror movies.

"Miss, you might want to think about finding yourself a new boyfriend," the trooper said in a low, fatherly voice. "I've got a daughter about your age, and there's no way that I would let her run around with a loser like him." He jerked his thumb in the direction of his car, where Brendan was standing. "Take my word for it—he's bad news."

If only I had heeded the trooper's advice that night. Maybe I wouldn't have had nightmares on a nightly basis in the years to come. . . .

But, of course, I hadn't listened to him. What sixteen-year-old girl would have? Not many, I'd have bet. I'd always believed that the quickest way to get a teenager to do something was to tell them not to do it. Only a year after what had happened, though, I'd felt like I was a hundred years old—not seventeen.

When Brendan's parents had learned what had happened, they'd taken his car from him, and they'd done a thorough search of his room again. They'd threatened to throw him out if he didn't straighten up and act in a responsible way.

Brendan, as always, had acted outraged by their anger. "Hypocrites! You know that they smoked pot when they were teenagers—and drank, too!" he said. "My dad drinks like a fish now, and Mom's always popping pills."

So that's where he gets his pills, I thought. Still, I'd realized that there was a difference—she, after all, had a prescription, even if it did seem hypocritical to Brendan. In that area, I'd had to agree that he was immature in his thinking. My parents had never hesitated to remind me that when I was an adult, I could do whatever I pleased.

Brendan's impending court date and car restriction hadn't stopped him. If anything, he'd become even wilder. On the weekends, he used a friend's car to pick me up, and we'd party as if nothing had happened. I'd had to admit that I was secretly worried about Brendan. Still, I'd believed that I was falling in love with him, so I'd stuck by his side. I'd also known that I was envied by my friends, and I'd loved every minute of it.

The first time I'd met Brendan's parents was a humiliation that I would never forget. It was on a Saturday. Brendan had asked me to come over, so I'd begged Mom for the car. She'd finally agreed, after I'd assured her that Brendan's parents would be home. At the time, I hadn't been lying. It wasn't until I'd gotten there that I'd found out that Brendan's parents had gone out, and wouldn't be back until late.

At first, I was nervous about being in Brendan's house with his parents gone, but I'd soon forgotten about that. Brendan had taken me to his room. He'd put on some music, turned off his light, and pulled me onto the bed with him. It was the first time that we'd gotten close to going all the way.

If his mother hadn't walked in, I'm not sure that I would have stopped him. I was so caught up in the moment. Brendan was very good at turning me on, and that time was no exception.

Mrs. Walker knocked once before entering. Even still, she'd caught me with my pants down to my ankles and my bra pushed up beneath my chin. I didn't think I'd ever been so mortified.

Time had seemed to freeze. I'd stared in shock and horror at Brendan's mother. I couldn't believe that that was the way I was meeting her for the first time. She'd stared at me, and Brendan had glared at her with an expression that I couldn't fathom. His hand had never moved from where it had cupped my breast.

"Get out of my room, Mother," he said coldly.

She'd sucked in a sharp gasp. If I hadn't been so mortified, I might have felt sorry for her. Her face had turned a deep, alarming red. She'd opened her mouth, then snapped it closed again. She'd slammed the door hard enough to shake a couple of books from a shelf.

"Brendan, I need to speak with you, please," she said from the other side of the door.

"Not now, Mother," he told her.

"Yes—now," she insisted.

I'd heard a muffled sob through the doorway, and I'd struggled to get into my clothes. My entire body was on fire with embarrassment. All I'd wanted to do was to slink out through Brendan's bedroom window. How could I face her? How could I ever face her again? What should I say? Should I apologize? Would it change her opinion of me? What was she thinking?

All of those questions and more had raced through my mind as Brendan had adjusted his clothes and marched to the door. He'd opened it and stepped through, slamming it shut behind him.

Shamelessly, I'd tiptoed to the door and put my ear against it. I'd just had to hear what Mrs. Walker had to say about me. I'd known that I wasn't the first girl to be caught in bed with her boyfriend, but that knowledge hadn't made me feel any better.

"What do you think you are doing?" Mrs. Walker whispered in a shrill, furious voice.

"What did it look like we were doing?" Brendan answered snidely.

Mrs. Walker gasped. "In our house, Brendan? Have you no respect for me or your father at all?"

"No, I don't," he told her.

That time, I'd gasped. If I had said something like that to my mom, she would have slapped me.

"You don't have any respect for me, or for my privacy," Brendan continued. "So why should I have respect for you or Dad?"

"Because you live under our roof—" she went on.

I'd tuned out the rest of the argument. I'd heard it all before, and to tell the truth, I was rather relieved to discover that Mrs. Walker was like any other normal parent. After everything that Brendan had told me, I supposed I was expecting a she-devil with horns, and a forked tail.

Feeling a very desperate urge to flee, I'd made sure that my clothes were on properly. Then, I'd braced myself as I'd pulled open the door and rushed between them. I'd mumbled an embarrassed apology and kept on going. From the corner of my eye, I'd noticed Mr. Walker sitting in the living room, but I hadn't even glanced his way. I was too mortified.

My embarrassment had given way to humiliation and shame when I'd gotten home. Mom was waiting for me at the front door, her face grim with disappointment.

"Mrs. Walker called me," she stated furiously.

I'd tried to make it to my room, feeling her breath on my neck all the way. All I wanted to do was to fall on my bed and cry my eyes out. But Mom wasn't about to drop it—not until she'd had her say.

"How could you, Jessica? You lied to me! You told me that his parents were going to be there! And to conduct yourself like a—"

Stunned, I'd whirled around to face my furious mother. "Like a what, Mom?" I couldn't believe what I was hearing. Suddenly, my mother was cutting me down, just the way that Brendan's parents had always criticized him. Was it catching? After one phone conversation with Mrs. Walker, was I going to be thought of as a loser by my own mother? Or worse, a slut?

Mom had sobbed, putting a hand over her mouth. Her eyes had glittered with tears. I'd supposed that some of Brendan's attitude had worn off on me, too, because I'd found myself talking to my mother in way that I never had before.

"I didn't have sex with him, Mom. I was doing what any normal sixteen-year-old girl would be doing with her boyfriend. We were making out. Are you going to tell me that you and Dad didn't make out before you got married?"

"Jessica Ann!" she admonished me.

"Oh, don't sound so shocked, Mom! I didn't do anything wrong." In my heart, I truly believed that. I'd refuse to think about what might have happened if Mrs. Walker hadn't returned unexpectedly. Would I have been having that same conversation with my mother? I'd never know. . . .

"I don't want you to see him anymore!" Mom ordered.

I'd felt curiously calm in the face of her hysteria. "I will see him, Mom. You're not going to stop me. I'm sixteen. It's time that you stopped treating me like a baby."

My mother shook her head. "So, you think you're an adult, just because you're sixteen? You think that you're invincible—that you can't get pregnant, or contract AIDS?"

"I would never be that stupid," I told her, tossing my head. "You know, I used to think that nobody's parents could be as bad as Brendan's. I've changed my mind."

Mom had slapped me then, and I'd realized later that I'd deserved it.

"Don't ever asked to borrow my car again," she said, with a coldness I'd never heard in her voice before. "I can't trust you anymore."

"Fine." I'd managed to hide my hurt as I'd dug the keys from my back pocket and tossed them toward her. "Your car stinks, anyway."

"Your dad will be hearing about this," she warned.

"Whatever," I muttered.

My mother and I didn't speak again for a full week. Brendan and I saw each other at school, but we didn't get to be alone again until the following weekend. He wasn't allowed to use his car, I couldn't drive my mom's, and Brendan's friend, Ricky, was out of town, so he couldn't borrow his car.

One night, I'd sneaked Brendan into my bedroom after my parents had gone to sleep. We'd fooled around for a long time. But, I'd been thinking more clearly then, and I hadn't let him go all the way. Brendan had stayed until sunrise, though, speculating on his court date. He was wondering what the judge would decide, and complaining about his parents.

He'd never once mentioned anything about killing them, though. To be perfectly honest, even if he had, I probably wouldn't have taken him seriously.

Brendan's date with the judge didn't go well. It turned out that his parents had called the judge and talked to him personally about

Brendan. Encouraged by Brendan's parents, the judge had decided to be harsh with Brendan, in the hopes of slowing him down.

Brendan was walking me home from school as he'd told me about it. It was about the only way that we could see each other during those days. We'd both felt as if the whole world was against us.

I'd given his hand a comforting squeeze. "How do you know they talked to the judge?" I asked.

"Because I heard the judge telling the prosecuting attorney about it," Brendan explained in a harsh, ugly voice. "I think they were hoping that the judge would send me to jail and throw away the key. That way, they wouldn't have to put up with me."

I'd started to argue, but had decided against it. Brendan believed that his parents were out to get him, and that they hated him. I didn't think that I could change his mind. Later, I'd wished that I had tried.

In the end, Brendan didn't do jail time, but he was sent to a rehabilitation clinic for thirty days. I'd missed him a lot, and I couldn't wait for him to come home. Yes, he had his flaws, but didn't we all?

Brendan had been home a week before he'd called me. It was on a Friday, and I had just gotten home from school. I hadn't even been aware that he was home, and I was hurt and angry that he'd waited so long to call me.

He must have sensed my hurt. "I'm sorry for not calling, Jessica," he apologized. "I just had to get my head straight after being in that prison."

I'd figured that there was no reason to ask him if he'd been redeemed while he was in rehab. Obviously, it wasn't the miracle cure that people talked about. At least, not with Brendan. Still, I had to be honest—I was glad Brendan hadn't turned into a geek while he was gone.

Never one to stay angry for long, I'd melted at the sound of his voice. "That's okay. I just missed you a lot," I murmured.

He chuckled. "You mean, you haven't found someone else? Someone who doesn't have demons for parents?"

"No, I haven't," I assured him. "And your parents aren't that bad, Brendan."

My statement was met with silence. It was as though I could almost feel his anger. Since I'd already had one foot in the grave, I'd decided to jump on in.

"I mean, if they didn't care about you, they wouldn't have gone to so much trouble, trying to get you into rehab."

My comment had been met with more silence.

I'd shifted from one foot to the other. Then, I'd begun to bite my nails. I had really missed Brendan, and there was no way that I wanted to lose him at that point. "Brendan? Forget I said that, okay?" I said anxiously.

"Okay. Are we getting together tonight?" he asked.

"Why wouldn't we be?" His lengthy silence had made me paranoid and nervous. "You do want to see me, don't you?"

"Yeah, sure. I'm having a party. You can help me get set up," he muttered.

I'd held the phone away from my ear, thinking that I must have been losing my hearing. "That's funny. I thought you said that you were having a party at your house. You meant at Ricky's house, right?"

"No. I meant here, at my house. The demons will be out of town all weekend," he told me.

"Really? Where are they going?" I could hardly believe that Brendan would be brave enough to throw a party, knowing that they could return at any time—just like they had the last time.

"To some conference that's supposed to last all weekend. They're staying in a motel."

I wasn't reassured, and I'd made a mental note to stay away from the bedrooms. I certainly didn't want a repeat of that awful scene, when his mother had walked in on us.

"Aren't you afraid that they might come back unexpectedly?" I asked hesitantly.

"They won't," he said firmly.

There had been no hesitation in his voice, and later, I knew why. Should I have suspected something then? I'd wondered later. I supposed I'd always wonder, and question, and take a million trips down guilt lane.

Brendan had picked me up at six o'clock so that I could help him to get ready for the party. We were going to make dip, and heat up mozzarella sticks and pizza rolls for the crowds of kids that were expected to come.

"They gave you back the car," I observed as I slid into the seat and automatically reached for my seat belt.

Brendan grinned. "Yeah."

Later, I'd felt sick whenever I'd remembered that smile. . . .

I'd noticed the smell the moment I'd walked through the front door. Despite myself, I'd pinched my nose closed.

"Brendan, what's that smell? It's awful!" I exclaimed.

"The sewer is backed up in my parents' bathroom. It happened right after the demons left." He shrugged. "There's nothing that I can do about it. We'll spray the house with something—okay?" He'd squatted in front of the kitchen sink and looked beneath it. Then, he'd handed me a can of disinfectant, a can of carpet cleaner, and a couple of scented candles. "Here, use this stuff. I'll start the dip."

Jumping into my fantasy role as housewife, I'd gone through the living room and the hallways with an armload of deodorizers. Making sure that Brendan was otherwise occupied, I'd sprayed carpet cleaner on his bedroom carpet, then closed the door. I'd tried the next door, too, but had found it locked. Was it his parents' room? I'd suspected that it was, and I'd figured they'd had to lock it to keep Brendan out of his mother's pills, and his father's booze.

The smell was stronger in the hallway, so I'd sprayed an entire can of disinfectant there, then worked my way back to the living room. When I was finished, I'd sniffed. The smell was still there, but not as strong. It would have to do.

"I'm finished," I announced, returning to the kitchen to help Brendan. I'd opened the refrigerator door, my eyes widening at the contents. It was completely full of beer. In the freezer, I'd found a dozen packages of pizza rolls and mozzarella sticks, and nothing else. I'd thought that it was strange, but I hadn't dwelled on it for very long. Brendan had come up behind me and put his arms around me, kissing me long and hard. I could feel his arousal, and a flash of heat had raced through my bloodstream.

Luckily, someone had knocked on the door just then. Our first party guests had arrived, and they had brought a keg of beer. Someone had turned on the stereo, and put up the volume so loud that I couldn't hear myself think. But I was sixteen, and I liked my music loud. Later, I couldn't even listen to music at all without reliving that nightmarish evening.

Booze and weed flowed from hand to hand—mouth to mouth. Soon, the house was crammed full of teenagers who were determined to party. Every so often, I would pause long enough to think about what would have happened if the Walkers had returned early. At the thought, I would shiver and push the idea out of my mind. It was too unthinkable to consider.

By midnight, I'd had a pretty good buzz going. I'd had three or four beers, and more hits of marijuana than I could remember. I was pleasantly floating, uncaring about anything. Brendan was in his element, regaling his classmates with exaggerated stories of his stint in rehab. Propping myself against an open doorway, I'd watched him, a sappy smile on my face.

That's how Emily had found me.

"You are so far gone!" she yelled in my ear.

I'd turned a serene smile her way and shouted back. "Yeah. Great party, huh?"

"Awesome," she agreed, looping her arm through her boyfriend's. "I just can't believe the nerve he's got, though, from what you've told me about his parents. They'd just die if they knew, wouldn't they?"

Little did I know then that her words would come back and haunt me. . . .

"Sometimes you've just got to take a risk." I shrugged.

Emily had nodded, then leaned close to me so that the others wouldn't hear. "Hey, Peter and I need some privacy, if you know what I mean. Do you have any ideas?"

I'd waved a careless hand in the direction of the hallway. "Use Brendan's room. I don't think he'd care."

Emily and Peter had disappeared, only to reappear a few moments later, looking disgusted. "Somebody beat us to it. What about the other bedroom?" she asked.

"It's locked," I told her.

Peter grinned. "It doesn't have to be."

If I hadn't been so wasted, I probably would have told them not to try and open that door. But, at that point, I just couldn't bring myself to care.

"Go for it," I told them. I knew that Emily had been talking about going all the way with Peter.

As they'd turned to head in the direction of the bedroom, I'd followed, deciding that it would be a good time to take a bathroom break. Emily and Peter had paused at the locked bedroom door, discussing what method they would use to pick the lock.

When I'd emerged from the bathroom, Peter had let out a victory howl and opened the bedroom door.

The smell had nearly knocked us down. Simultaneously, we'd put hands over our mouths. Emily had spoken between her fingers.

"It smells like somebody died in there," she mumbled.

"No kidding," Peter agreed.

Trying not to gag, I'd pushed between them and opened the door wider so that we could see inside the darkened room. My hand had fumbled along the wall for a light switch. I remembered thinking that I'd never smelled anything so awful in my life, and I didn't think that it could have anything to do with a malfunctioning sewer.

I'd found the light and flicked the switch.

Then, we'd all frozen, unable to breath—unable to speak.

Mr. and Mrs. Walker were lying on the unmade, king-sized bed. As if in a dream, I'd slowly moved into the room. I was vaguely aware of the fact that Emily and Peter were right behind me. Emily was pushed up against my back, and Peter was pressed against her.

If I hadn't had my hand over my mouth, I probably would have screamed.

The Walkers' throats had been sliced open. Dried blood stained the pillows, the bed, and the carpet. It was as if every drop of blood had seeped out of them. Their eyes were wide and staring, as if the horror of their death had been captured and recorded for all to see.

Emily's voice was a hoarse whisper. "Oh, no! Oh, no! Oh, no!"

She'd just kept repeating the words over and over.

"They're dead," I murmured in complete disbelief. "He killed them. Brendan killed them." I'd known, without a doubt, that he'd done it. I'd remembered the smell, and the conviction in his voice when he'd told me that they wouldn't return. I'd thought of the smile on his face, when I'd mentioned that he'd gotten his car back. All of those horrifying clues had come to mind as I'd stood in the middle of the bedroom with Emily and Peter.

"I feel sick," Peter said, his voice sounding young and afraid. I'd known exactly how he'd felt.

If I hadn't looked at Emily in that moment, we might have joined the Walkers on the bed. But God was watching over us—of that, I was convinced. I'd seen the look on her face, and I'd known that she was about to scream.

I didn't think that she'd stop screaming once she'd gotten started, because I wanted to do the same thing—just put my hands to my face and scream until it had all gone away.

But God was watching us. My hand shot out and clamped over Emily's mouth. When I finally spoke, my voice was strong and commanding.

"Don't scream, Emily. Don't you dare scream, do you hear me?" I ordered. I'd waited until she'd nodded. Her eyes were enormous with shock, and I'd suspected that mine were, too. Peter was as pale as any vampire that I'd ever seen on television.

It was instinct and God, I supposed, that directed my next move—and the moves that had followed. It was a gut instinct that had nearly paralyzed me, because I'd known, without a doubt, that we could possibly have died.

"Peter, walk very slowly to the front door and go outside," I told him. "Start the car. If anyone asks you where you're going, tell them that you and Emily are going to get some wine coolers."

"Wine coolers?" Peter sounded as if he were in shock. I'd shaken him hard. I was scared to death that Brendan would find us in the bedroom.

"Wine coolers," I repeated. "And stop looking so horrified."

"What about you and Emily?" he asked.

"We're going to follow you. If anyone asks me, I'll say that I'm walking Emily to the car. Got it?"

"Got it," Emily stuttered. She was shaking, and I was deathly afraid. I knew that if Brendan had seen her face, he would realize that we'd stumbled upon his horrible secret.

I'd given Peter a hard push that had sent him to the open door. "Get going," I told him. Then, I'd taken Emily's hand and hurried out of the room, closing the door very quietly. I hadn't breathed again until I'd realized that we hadn't been seen.

Emily grabbed my arms, her nails biting painfully into my skin. "Did he kill them?" she asked fearfully.

I didn't want to add to her shock, but I hadn't known what else to say. "Yes, Emily, I think he did," I answered honestly. "We've got to get to a phone and call the police." But the only phone in the house was in the living room, and I wasn't about to risk getting caught.

"Okay." Her teeth had begun to chatter. I shook her, just as I had done to Peter.

"Emily! You've got to chill out! Do you understand?"

"Yes," she whispered.

Clearly, she did, but it was obvious that she could do nothing about the shaking. I'd sent a fierce, silent prayer to God that Brendan was still engrossed in his guests, and that he was too wasted to notice how pale and shocked we'd looked. After the horror we'd seen, how could we have been anything else?

The path from the hallway to the front door was the longest walk of my life. Amazingly, I was able to force myself to talk to Emily about everything—and nothing. I was doing my best to look and act naturally.

We were almost to the door when Brendan had slipped his arms around my waist and pulled me against him.

"Whoa, there. Where're you two headed?" he asked.

"Wine coolers," Emily blurted out. She was staring at me with those huge, shocked eyes, and I knew that if she'd looked at Brendan she would have cracked.

"I was just walking her to the car," I added. I tried not to stiffen as Brendan nuzzled my neck.

"Coming back?" he asked.

Emily nodded vigorously, then shot out the door. I'd calmly slipped out of Brendan's grasp and followed her.

"I'll be right back," I promised, scared to death that he would follow me. If he had, I'd known that I would have to go back inside with him, and trust Emily and Peter to go to the police.

I'd also realized that the longer I spent in his company, the more likely it would have been that he would realize that something was wrong.

"Don't be long," he called after me, then laughed.

I knew that I would hear that laughter in my dreams forever. It was the laugh of the devil—of a monster, who was capable of the most gruesome crimes imaginable.

Emily was ahead of me. She'd made it to the car and had turned to look behind me. She was slumped against the car, holding a hand to her chest. She was so pale that I'd thought she was going to faint.

"He went back inside," she said. "Jessica, I can't believe this is happening!"

71

Peter had started the car. "Let's go!" he called.

I'd felt badly about leaving everyone else behind with that lunatic, but I didn't think that I'd had any other choice. Peter drove like a madman. I didn't blame him. I didn't think that I would have been capable of driving. He'd driven over curbs, run stop signs, and nearly hit another car before we'd reached the all-night convenience store that was located a few blocks from Brendan's house.

I was out of the car before he'd come to a complete stop. Emily was screaming. She was sobbing and hanging on to me so tightly that I'd had to shake her off me. I was close to breaking down myself. It was only my instinctive feeling that Peter wasn't in any better shape than Emily that had kept me going.

At the pay phone outside the store, I'd dropped the coins more than once before I'd finally hit the change slot.

When the 911 operator had answered, I'd frozen, unable to speak. Behind me, Peter was attempting to calm Emily. It was a lost cause, though. She was trapped in her own nightmare.

Finally, I'd managed to unlock my throat muscles. "My boyfriend—" I'd paused and swallowed hard, wishing that I hadn't said that he was my boyfriend. I didn't want to admit that I could even have known someone who was capable of killing his parents—or anyone else.

"I think my boyfriend may have killed his parents," I finally got out in a rush of words that I prayed made sense.

"Can you repeat that, please?" the operator asked.

I'd swallowed again before realizing that the lump in my throat appeared to be permanent. "His name is Brendan Walker." Then, I'd given his address. "He lives there with his parents, only, they're dead. The house smells awful. We found them in the bedroom." I'd broken down then, crying and sobbing the story out over and over again.

"Can you please calm down?" the operator asked. "We've got the police on their way. Can you tell me where you are?"

I was beyond speech by that time. Surprisingly, it was Peter who'd taken the phone from me and told them where we were. He'd hung up a moment later.

"They're sending a car for us," he said. Then he'd gathered Emily and me against him and held us tightly. I'd never forget him for his kindness at that moment.

The squad car had come for us and taken us to Brendan's house. Emily had grown hysterical again, screaming that she didn't want to go. Peter and I'd managed to calm her down. In my mind, I'd believed that we'd both wanted to see that we hadn't dreamed up the entire nightmare—or, that Brendan hadn't been playing some sick joke on us.

Once we'd arrived at Brendan's house, the officer had parked behind another police car. Behind us, I'd seen several more police cars turning onto Brendan's street. They had lights blazing, but their sirens were ominously silent. I remembered feeling relieved about that. I didn't want Brendan to know about the police before they'd managed to subdue him. I had mental pictures of Brendan screeching through the crowd, slicing and dicing his way to the door—and freedom. He was insane, so I hadn't felt foolish for the awful thought.

Emily, on the other hand, had watched more horror movies than I had. She was convinced that Brendan would kill the police officers, and then, he'd come after us while we sat helplessly in the police car. Her hysteria was contagious, and I'd found myself watching the door until my eyes had burned.

What could we do if he'd come after us? We could run. He couldn't chase after all three of us, but I knew that I would be the first one that he'd want to punish. He would feel betrayed. I'd been his girlfriend. I wasn't supposed to tell his horrible secret.

I was the girlfriend of an animal who had killed his parents, then partied while they lay dead in their bed.

I'd chewed my nails to the quick, making them bleed. Emily's hysterical screams had died down to horrible moans. Peter had rocked her like a baby, and I'd wondered how much therapy we'd all have to endure before we'd get over that nightmare.

It was a long time before the police had finally led Brendan out of the house. Everyone else had filed out behind him. Those who had been stumbling drunk were suddenly amazingly sober as they'd gathered on the lawn and talked in low, shocked voices.

I'd stared through the window at Brendan, unable to take my eyes from him. He hadn't looked scared, or guilty. He'd looked calm and unconcerned. A shudder had ripped through me. I had been dating an insane person, I'd realized. A killer. A young man who was capable of killing his parents, then going on his merry way while their bodies had been decomposing in the next room.

Over the next few days, the police and the investigators had grilled me relentlessly, trying to find out if I'd known what Brendan had planned to do. They were trying to implicate me in the horrible crime. It had taken some doing, but I'd finally convinced them that I'd had nothing to do with it.

I'd told them everything that I knew. I'd told them about the clues that I hadn't picked up on. I'd told them how much Brendan had hated his parents.

Mom and Dad were my anchors, standing beside me all the way. I knew that they couldn't help thinking the same thing that I had thought—that I might have been Brendan's next victim, if we hadn't stumbled upon the bodies of his parents when we had.

During the trial, I'd had to testify against Brendan. It was the hardest thing that I'd ever had to do, because he was there, staring at me with those beautiful eyes. I hadn't felt guilty for testifying against him—just scared. Scared that he could somehow break free of his handcuffs and chains, and get to me before someone could stop him.

I still have nightmares, and I don't see them fading any time soon. My therapist tells me that they will, and I hope and pray that she's right. I also pray that one day, I'll find someone else—someone I can bring myself to trust. It won't be easy.

THE END

RESCUE ME
I'm losing my battle with booze

I fell apart after my husband died. Clive was killed just after New Year's when his tractor trailer jackknifed on a mountain pass covered with black ice. It may have been the suddenness of the accident, his young age, or the fact that I was left alone with an eight-year-old child, but I just couldn't "move on" with my life like everyone wanted me to.

I've lost the love of my life, I would think. How can I possibly go on without him?

A thin layer of frost covered the nearby fields on the day we laid Clive to rest. In the churchyard I watched my daughter, Suzie, pull up the collar of her coat to keep her ears warm. I reached out and pulled her close. My body sheltered her from the wind, but inside I felt as icy as a marble statue.

Will my blood ever flow freely again? I wondered.

After the funeral guests had gone home and Suzie was sleeping fitfully upstairs, I stood in the middle of my empty living room. Panic gripped me like a vise; I felt a physical pain at my core. What am I going to do? I wondered. I can't cope by myself! I wanted to turn back the clock. I wanted nothing more than to discover that it was all a dream.

That's it! I thought. A dream! If I deny that anything happened, I can carry on with my normal life. I'll make believe Clive's away on business and everything will be fine.

"This is our secret, Suzie," I told my daughter the next day when I explained my plan. "No one else needs to know."

"But who's buried in the churchyard?" she asked.

"Nobody. It was an empty coffin, okay?"

"Okay, Mommy," she said with a small frown.

After I started living the lie, I felt less alone. Sometimes when the kitchen door opened, I could even convince myself that if I looked up I'd see Clive's grinning face.

My husband's life insurance money paid off the house and there was enough leftover to see my daughter through college. The day I signed the papers, I told myself that I'd won the lottery.

At home, Suzie and I pretended that Clive was away on business. When I ventured out, people seemed to respect my grief and didn't press me to talk about my loss. That made it easy to keep up the fantasy that my husband was still alive.

75

I returned to my job at the hair salon a few weeks later. The staff members are not only my work colleagues, but they're also my friends. Nina, the owner, and Jeanette and Michelle are really great, but I couldn't reveal my despair to them because they wouldn't understand. Clive's elderly parents were retired and living in Florida. I rarely saw them.

The salon staff always treated me like family and it was especially nice when I had none of my own. I'm an only child and my parents were killed during my first year at college when a fifteen-year-old lost control of his father's SUV and crossed the median into their car. Perhaps things would've been different if I still had them to talk to.

One special chair in the salon was set aside and curtained off for male customers. It was clever of Nina to make the men feel welcome. There have been unisex salons in the big cities for years, but it was something new for tiny Hamilton Creek.

Robot-like, I got through the days cutting and styling my regular clients' hair. Sleep, however, eluded me. My coworkers began to notice the deep shadows beneath my eyes.

"Gosh, Paige," Nina said one day. "Are you still not sleeping well? Why don't you go to the doctor and get something? You need rest, honey."

"I'm fine, Nina. And you know I hate taking pills," I said as I rinsed conditioner out of Mrs. Kennedy's hair.

"Paige, honey," Nina replied, giving me her I'm-the-boss-but-I'm-also-your-friend look. "You have to do something. Why don't you go see Doc Carroll? You can't carry on like this. Don't forget that you have Suzie to take care of."

"Everything's fine," I insisted, draping a towel over my client's head.

I couldn't tell Nina that I didn't go to see Doc Carroll anymore because I felt guilty. He'd been the only doctor in our small town since before I was born. In fact, he delivered me right at home in the living room. He never let me forget it, either, and he was understandably upset when I chose to have my baby in Rock Bluff's brand-new hospital ten miles away.

Doc Carroll and I bumped into each other in the grocery store when Suzie was about six weeks old. He gave me this sad look, like he thought I considered him too old to deliver my baby. He knelt down by the stroller and smiled at my daughter. "She's beautiful," he said.

But still I didn't take Suzie to his office for her shots or after she hurt herself playing in the yard. I always drove into Rock Bluff for that. And I avoided meeting Doc Carroll whenever I could, so how could I turn to him now? He'd probably written me off as someone who thought she was too good for the local practitioner.

Anyway, I didn't want a prescription. The sleepless nights were just a passing phase. I reminded myself that I didn't sleep well when Clive was out of town. As soon as he came home, I'd be fine.

Everything in the house was just as it had been before the accident. Clive's clothes were hanging in the closet and his toolbox was sitting on the workbench in the garage. It was ready for him to pick up and use at any time. I couldn't imagine things any other way. But I really do need a good night's sleep, I eventually admitted to myself.

Instead of taking Nina's advice, I listened to old Frank. He's the shoeshine guy who plies his trade around the town and he comes into the salon once a week. He polishes the shoes of the bank manager, the mayor, and other locals who feel that the barbershop across town is too geared toward young guys who want only buzz cuts. Frank's advice was to add a drop of whisky to some hot milk before going to bed. "Helps me sleep like a baby," he said, nodding his grey head.

Well, if it works for Frank, then maybe it'll work for me, I thought.

Clive and I had never been big drinkers. He'd have a beer after cutting the grass on the weekends and I'd sometimes have one, too. Occasionally I'd have a vodka and tonic—a drink that's very refreshing. But I don't like the taste of whiskey.

That evening, after Suzie was in bed, I poured myself a glass of vodka. Then I had another before going up to my room. I drank it quickly, telling myself that it was better than taking a sleeping pill.

Frank was right. That first week I slept like a log. Then the effects wore off, so I added a splash of vodka to my soda at dinner, being careful that Suzie didn't see me. The alcohol helped me feel pretty mellow and I got through even more nights without waking at the slightest sound.

I got into a routine of settling down on the sofa with a pillow, a blanket, and a bottle of vodka on the coffee table. After a couple of drinks, I believed that I was waiting for Clive to come walking through the door.

Sleeping better gave me more energy to do my work at the salon and take care of Suzie. Having two or three shots of liquor each night became a habit. Several weeks later, I began to add vodka to my morning juice and even took a flask to the salon so I could top off my sodas throughout the day.

It's helping me like an anesthetic dulls pain, I told myself. And it was better than tossing and turning at night only to end up with puffy eyes and a persistent throbbing in the back of my head the next morning.

I was styling Mrs. Kennedy's hair one afternoon and humming loudly to a song on the radio when Nina came over. "You okay, Paige?" she asked.

"Sure!" I gave her a wide grin. "Why wouldn't I be?"

"Well, I don't think I've seen you this happy since. . . ."

"Since before the accident? Oh, that's history," I said, telling her exactly what she wanted to hear and knowing all the while that I was talking about someone else.

Nina tilted her blond head and gave me a puzzled look. "I see."

I pushed out my tongue at her retreating figure. I knew what she really thought of Clive—that he'd held me back from achieving my full potential. I'd returned to Hamilton Creek without finishing my college degree because Clive had asked me to and after that I was content to be a wife and mother. Nina didn't understand the bond between us. She always wanted me to go back to school and I resented her motherly interference. I wanted to yell, "It's my life and I'll live it the way I see fit!"

"Ouch!" Mrs. Kennedy's wrinkled hand flew to the back of her head. "Are you trying to scalp me, Paige?"

I looked down and saw my fingers entwined in her hair. "I'm so sorry," I said, releasing my grip. She pursed her crimson lips and I tried to concentrate on the layered cut she liked. Thoughts of taking my scissors to her and giving her a spiked, punk style sustained me until she left the salon.

That night I mulled over Nina's views on my husband. There were some grains of truth to them, I had to acknowledge. Things between Clive and me hadn't always been perfect. I'd often toyed with the idea of going back to school or taking a course online, but I knew that it would make Clive feel bad and maybe even cause an argument. He had no aspirations to be anything other than a truck driver, so I never let him know how much time I spent in the library when he was out of town. I read all of the latest magazines and books on social studies and history—my two favorite subjects.

What am I thinking? I wondered. I'm too set in my ways to change. I switched off the TV, swallowed my glass of vodka, and set the alarm for six-thirty.

The next day, Naomi from Ruby's Diner came in for the lunch orders. She wrote down each person's request and then turned to me, expectantly.

"I'm not hungry, Naomi," I said.

Nina's voice rose above the hum of the hairdryers. "Paige, are you on a diet or something? That's the third time this week you haven't ordered lunch. And you're getting to be skin and bones, girl. You need to eat something."

The thought of food made me feel queasy. "No, thanks," I insisted. "I'm fine. I'm just not hungry."

"But—"

78

"Are you deaf? Leave me alone, will you? I've had enough of your advice."

Everyone's eyes—the staff's and customers' alike—swung toward me. I'd never spoken to Nina or anyone else like that.

"Sorry," I mumbled. My client's eyes were wide with fear, as if her stylist had suddenly been revealed as a mad woman. "Excuse me one minute, I. . . ."

I hurried to the small kitchenette where we take our breaks. A supply of sodas, iced tea, and lemonade were in the fridge. I leaned my forehead against the cold, metal door and took several deep breaths.

What's wrong with me? I wondered. I have to get myself under control.

I took out a soda, poured it into a glass, and then reached into my pocket for a small, silver flask. I unscrewed the top and tipped the vodka into the soda.

"So that's what you're doing," Nina's voice made me jump and some vodka splashed onto the floor.

"Shoot, Nina! Look what you made me do! This is only a pick-me-up—"

"Get that innocent look off of your face, girl," Nina said, closing the door. There was anger and disappointment in her voice. "I can guess what that is and it's not going to help you."

She pulled out a chair for me and then grabbed a cloth and wiped up the spill. Reluctantly, I sat at the table and sipped my drink. "It's helping, Nina. It's helping a great deal. I don't need any pills and I can quit this any time."

"Sure you can." Nina sat next to me and held my hand. I was trembling like an aspen leaf. I felt like my whole body was wired up with an electrical current running through it.

"You don't know what's it's been like," I said, my words tumbling out like beans from a can. The truth was finally exposed. "I can't sleep without Clive. I can't do anything without Clive. He's always been there. We were high school sweethearts!"

"Yes, I know."

"And those two years he was in the Army, he wrote to me every day. I still have the letters. I can show you. . . ."

I felt like an old, worn, rag doll coming apart at the seams. The tight grip I'd held over my emotions shattered like glass and tears came streaming down my face. Crying was something I'd never done over the past seven months because I had to keep up the pretense in front of Suzie. If Clive were really away on business, why would I cry?

My shoulders heaved as I sucked in huge gulps of air. Nina's arms slid around me and she held me until the spasm passed. Afterward, she silently offered a wad of folded tissues from her pocket.

I wiped my hot, swollen face. "I'm sorry."

"Honey, that was probably just what you needed to do—let out some of that tension that you've been holding inside."

"But—" I suddenly remembered my client. "Anita Howard's waiting!"

"Don't worry; I told Jeanette to finish her up."

I sighed. "Oh, Nina, what must you think of me?"

"I know it's been hard, Paige," Nina said. "But you'll get through this. You're not completely helpless, you know. You managed fine whenever Clive was absent and he was out of town a lot, remember? Now you have to think about the future, not the past. Promise me that you'll try and cut back on this . . . what is this stuff?" She picked up the flask and sniffed.

"Vodka," I said.

"Ah, vodka. Something you can't smell on a person's breath." She poured the remaining liquid down the sink. "I'll hang onto this for now," Nina held out the flask. "You can have it back when you're ready. And I'm here to help, Paige, whenever you need me. You won't forget, will you?"

I smiled my thanks. "I won't forget. And I'll do my best to stop."

After rinsing my tear-streaked face in the bathroom, I returned to the salon and thanked Jeanette. She handed me Anita's five-dollar tip, but I told her to keep it.

Her face lit up like it was Christmas. "Thanks, Paige!" she said.

At least I've made someone happy today, I thought.

I managed not to take a drink for a couple of weeks after that and I felt surprisingly good. I was quite proud of myself; I wasn't dependent on alcohol, after all. But telling Suzie that her mother had done a foolish thing was even harder to do, so I kept putting it off.

Then the sleepless nights returned. At the same time, I also had this strange feeling under my ribs. It wasn't an itchy or burning sensation—it was something I'd never felt before and it drove me absolutely crazy.

One night I tossed and turned, scratching at the strange pain as the wind whipped the tree branches outside my window into a frenzy. A late-summer storm was brewing and my thoughts turned to Clive. Is he safe in a motel for the night or did he park the rig somewhere and he's fast asleep in the cramped, little berth?

Then reality kicked me in the stomach like a bad-tempered mule. My husband wasn't away on a delivery—he was dead. He'd never come home again no matter how many times I tried to tell myself otherwise.

I pushed back the damp, crumpled bed sheet and padded into the kitchen. My mouth was dry, the back of my neck was sticky with sweat, and that spot under my ribs was hurting like hell. There was a full bottle of vodka in the back of the highest pantry shelf where Suzie wouldn't find it and I was tempted to take a slug. Instead, though, I warmed some milk and added chocolate powder to it. It reminded me of when I was young and Mom would make it for me after I'd been ice-skating on the big pond in winter.

Suzie doesn't like hot chocolate. Neither had Clive, I remembered, and the raw wound of my loss opened again. Maybe it would never heal. I felt lost, like I was wandering in the mountains and couldn't find my way home. I wanted to scream, "Clive! Clive! Find me! I'm here!"

I pushed down the simmering panic and told myself to go back to pretending that he'd come through the door any moment now. But I needed some help to do that, so I went to the pantry and grabbed the bottle of vodka.

As I started to unscrew the cap, Nina's concerned face appeared inside of my head. I'd promised her that I wouldn't drink anymore, but surely one wouldn't hurt. She'd never know, would she? The strange, burning pain nagged at my ribcage again. After this pain's gone, then I'll stop, I told myself and tipped the bottle to my lips. A few minutes later, I staggered back up the stairs.

As if through a fog, I heard yelling. "Daddy, Daddy!" It was Suzie.

I forced open my eyes and glanced at the clock. It said ten after three. Shoot! I couldn't have been asleep more than an hour. I thought.

The wind was stronger now, howling down the chimney and around the eaves of our old house. A loose fence panel clicked rhythmically outside. Dragging myself to my daughter's room, I lay down beside her. "Mommy's here," I whispered as I rubbed her back. "Don't worry; it's only a storm. Daddy will be home soon."

My voice soothed her, and after a while she drifted back to sleep. I should've told Suzie then that her father was never coming home, but it was the middle of the night and I didn't have the energy.

Tomorrow. I'll do it tomorrow, I told myself.

Light flooded the room and little fingers persistently tapped my face as I awoke. "Mommy, are you okay?" Suzie asked, a worried note in her voice. "I thought you weren't going to wake up."

I twisted my head away. "Stop that, Suzie. I'm fine. What time is it?"

"It's almost seven-thirty and I'm all ready for school." There was pride in her voice.

My body felt weak and I didn't want to move. The burning sensation had spread around one whole half of my body. I rubbed my hands over it. What the hell is this? I wondered. "Have you eaten breakfast?"

81

"I ate a banana," Suzie said. "The milk carton was on the table, but it smelled kind of funny."

Darn! I thought. I'd forgotten to put the milk back in the fridge. I'd have to buy some more later on. "What day is it?" I asked.

"Friday. TGIF, as Daddy used to say." Her face brightened for a second, but then her eyes grew fearful. "Sorry, Mom, I didn't mean to say that. I didn't mean to talk about him." Clamping her hand over her mouth as though she'd said something bad, she backed away.

I struggled to sit on the edge of the bed. "It's okay, honey. We need to—"

"What time will you be home tonight?" Suzie interrupted.

"I'm not sure." My brain wasn't functioning properly. After some thought, I said, "I think my last appointment's at four. Nina's closing early tonight."

"Okay. See you later. The school bus will be here soon."

I curled a finger, indicating she should come closer. When she did, I put my hands on her shoulders and kissed her freckled face. "Have a good day."

Suzie ran out of the room. My grown-up eight-year-old, I mused. She'd gotten herself up, dressed, and even fixed breakfast without my help. Suddenly I was frightened. If my daughter doesn't need me anymore, what good am I doing being alive? Then I told myself it was just tiredness that was making me feel that way.

I went over my actions the previous night. I'd weakened again when I needed to be strong for Suzie. Dragging myself to the bathroom, I checked my torso in the mirror for signs of a rash, but there was nothing. The weird sensation had me scratching at my skin, but that gave me no relief. I prayed that it wasn't anything serious and that it would go away.

TGIF—Thank Goodness It's Friday—was on my mind all day. The customers seemed to be in strange moods, too. It was like the barometric pressure was building up not only outdoors, but also inside their heads until they were about to explode. Every single one of my clients found fault with their hairstyles.

"Did you use the right shampoo?" asked Karen Lewis.

"My bangs aren't straight," Mrs. Hillard complained.

My feelings of frustration grew throughout the day and I wondered if I was cut out for the job, after all. Maybe I should go back to school and do something else, I thought.

Finally, Nina took me aside and told me to take a break and get something to eat. "And you might want to comb your hair before you come back," she added.

"What do you mean?"

"I mean you've stopped taking care of yourself," Nina replied.

"You never wear makeup any more. Your hair needs washing and when was the last time you had it styled?"

"What's the point?" I asked.

She put her hands on her hips. "The point is that you can't just let yourself go. You work in a hair salon, in case you've forgotten. You need to look smart and attractive for the clients. They won't want their hair cut by someone who looks like a bum."

"You're calling me a bum?" I was ready to erupt.

"Take a look at yourself." Nina took hold of my shoulders and turned me to face the mirrored wall.

I stared. My normally bouncy hair was flat and lackluster and the roots needed to be touched up. My face was the color of squash and my eye sockets were the color of eggplant. It wasn't pretty.

Though I hated to admit it, Nina was right. The closest I came to glamour was running a brush through my hair and putting on lip salve. Horrified, I twisted out of her grip and left the salon. There was a sandwich in a cooler in the trunk of my car. I got it out, sat in the driver's seat, and tried to open the plastic bag, but my fingers were clammy. I couldn't pull the edges apart.

I yelled with frustration and tossed the bag onto the passenger seat. It was just too hot and I was too upset to eat, anyway. My body ached and burned with a growing intensity.

My hand slipped down into the door pocket for a small bottle of vodka. A feeling of relief washed over me as I twisted off the cap. I swallowed half of the contents and then returned to the salon, tossing my sandwich in the trashcan outside. I stashed the bottle in my purse.

I got through the rest of the afternoon with only a slight fuzziness in my head. I watched the hands of the clock crawl around to four forty-five. I'd hoped the vodka would ease the pain and itching, but instead it only increased in intensity until my whole body felt like it was covered with fire ants. It scared me.

Something's very wrong! I thought.

My last client had gone home and I was pulling off my smock when Nina came over. "Paige," she said. "You know it's Hal's bowling league tonight. That's why we're closing early."

I stared at her, blankly.

She sighed. "Remember I told you that they're handing out trophies for the local competition and my darling husband's team won first place?"

"Oh, yes. That's right," I said, but in truth I'd completely forgotten.

"I have to get over to Rock Bluff before six for the presentation. Can you stay and cut that gentleman's hair for me?" She nodded to the curtained area. "He's a walk-in, but I hate to turn him away."

"Why me?" I asked, and then realized that we were the only two staff members there. "No, I really need to get home. And I have to go by the grocery store."

"Please?" Nina cajoled. "Tomorrow's your Saturday off. You can sleep late."

Each stylist gets one day off each week and every fourth week we get a Saturday, giving us a long weekend. I'd forgotten mine was the next day.

"Okay, okay," I snapped. I wasn't happy, but I owed Nina the favor.

As my boss hurried to her car, I called Suzie and told her to watch TV until I got home. I also reminded her that Mrs. Simpson, our neighbor, was home if Suzie needed her. Then I took a huge slug of vodka to get me through the next half hour.

The man in the chair looked familiar. I'd seen him around town and in the supermarket recently. He had thick, brown, curly hair, a round face, and metal-rimmed glasses.

He's long overdue for a haircut, I thought. He looks like a poodle.

As he sat there wrapped in the black-satin cape—he looked like Zorro without the mask—I bit my tongue to keep from laughing.

"Hi," the man said.

I mumbled something in return and got to work, resenting the delay he was causing me. My face felt flushed and my stomach was bunched in knots. I desperately needed food and regretted not eating that sandwich.

As soon as I was finished, I planned to hurry to the grocery store. I could munch on an apple as I drove home. Maybe the pharmacist would even give me some cream for my itch. My torso felt like it was on fire.

What on earth can it be? I wondered. Is it life threatening? Will my daughter be left an orphan? Panic rose inside of me like molten lava and sweat trickled down my sides.

The man was talking, but I hardly heard a word he said. I tried to concentrate on cutting his hair, but my trembling fingers kept losing their grip on the scissors. When I bent down for the third time to pick them up off the floor, I fell over.

And I didn't have the strength to get up.

The man jumped out of the chair and knelt down next to me. His face was out of focus. "Are you all right?" he asked.

"TGIF," I said, my eyes burning with unshed tears. "I have some terrible disease. Suzie will be all alone in the world."

The man moved closer to me. "Do you have a health problem? Do you need medication or something?" He spoke gently and calmly. "Perhaps I should—"

"I'm dying!"

The man's lips twitched like I was a child exaggerating a

stomachache to get out of a test. "I see," he said. He didn't contradict me or tell me not to be so stupid. Instead, he helped me sit up with my back against the reception desk. Grasping my wrist in his fingers, he looked at his watch.

"What are you doing?"

"Taking your pulse."

"Are you a doctor?"

"No," he said. "I'm an EMT. That's an—"

"An Emershency Medishal Technishian," I drawled. "I know."

He let go of my wrist. "Your pulse is fine, but perhaps I'd better get you to the emergency room—"

"No. No hoshpital. I'll be okay." I insisted that he help me up because my knees felt like rubber. I wrapped my arms around my body and the urge to scratch my skin until it was raw almost overwhelmed me.

"Should I call your husband?"

I shook my head and concentrated on the fact that Suzie was waiting for me. I had to get home to her.

As if reading my thoughts, the man said, "Then maybe I should take you home."

"Yesh. Must get home." I have to tell Suzie that I love her before it's too late, I thought.

"Come along." He placed an arm around my waist and I winced at his touch.

"Do you need to lock up?"

I picked up my purse, showed him how to set the lock, and together we walked out. The light pressure of his fingers felt like a white-hot branding iron against my flesh. He led me toward his car. I shook my head. "My car'sh over there." I pointed.

"You can't drive," he replied.

"Nonshense. I'm okay. I just need to get home and be with my daughter." The slurred words proved me very wrong.

The man ignored me and with a grim face helped me into the passenger seat of his car. I felt a burning sensation as the seatbelt slid across my ribs and I gritted my teeth to keep from screaming. When he got behind the wheel, I turned toward him. "I shouldn't be getting in a shtranger's car." My words held no conviction.

"I promise I won't harm you," he said, switching on the ignition. "Where do you live?"

Deciding to put my trust in the man, I gave him the address. What other choice did I have? I was too exhausted to defy him. My head felt heavy—like my neck couldn't hold it up properly—and sweat beaded my brow.

After a while, the air conditioning vents started blowing out icy blasts of air and it dried the moisture on my face. "Ooh, that'sh lovely," I murmured, closing my eyes. I felt tired, so very tired.

As we drove my rescuer told me that his name was Tim Murray and that he was currently based at the hospital in Rock Bluff. He preferred country life, though, and had just bought a house in Hamilton Creek where he could indulge his passion for fishing.

Then it was my turn. Somehow, it was easy to talk to the stranger. I found myself telling him about Clive's death and how I couldn't sleep. I also told him that I was worried about the weird pain I'd been having.

I didn't know whether he could make any sense of my words, but he asked about my neighbors and friends. I told him that Nina was at the bowling club and that my next-door neighbor, Jane Simpson, occasionally watched Suzie for me if I was late coming home.

Meanwhile, my skin burned and I scratched at my torso. I felt Tim's eyes on me. "Do you have any other symptoms, like a rash or blisters?" he asked.

"No, just this awful itching. It's been driving me crazy for days."

"Hmm." He nodded his head like he knew about my terrible disease. I bit my lip and stared out the window until we pulled up in front of my home.

Suzie gave Tim a suspicious glance as we entered the house, but he was brisk and cheerful and enlisted Suzie's help to get me upstairs. There he made me promise to go to bed.

"I'll be back in a few minutes," he said.

He returned about ten minutes later with a bowl of soup and some crackers on a tray. I was sitting up in bed. I'd freshened up in the bathroom and my hair was still damp from splashing cold water on my face. Suzie drew the curtains and the room dimmed. She fetched me a glass of water and some magazines and then sat next to me—just like I did whenever she was sick.

Tim placed the tray on my knees and my mouth watered at the smell of tomatoes and basil. "Your neighbor's going to let Suzie spend the night with her," he said. "So you won't be disturbed."

Suzie glanced at me. "Can I, Mom?"

I looked at Tim. "Are you sure it's okay with Jane?" I was relieved to be speaking coherently again.

"Yeah," he said. "She'd love to have Suzie." He glanced at my daughter. "Mrs. Simpson said something about the kittens growing up fast."

Suzie hopped off the bed. "That's right!" she told Tim. "Her cat, Freckles, has six kittens. They're really cute."

"Suzie," I said. She turned to face me. "Be a good girl."

"Sure, Mom!" She kissed me. "See you in the morning." I watched as she practically skipped out of the room to collect her pajamas and toothbrush.

Tim came toward me. I braced myself for a lecture, but maybe he decided it wasn't the right time. All he said was, "She's a great kid." I nodded in agreement. "Now, Paige," he continued. "I want you to finish that soup and then relax. How's the pain?"

"It comes and goes. Right now, it's more of a dull ache. What do you think it is?"

"I have a feeling it could be shingles," Tim said. "Some people have pain without a rash, but why don't you make an appointment with your physician on Monday and get it checked out?"

"Don't shingles happen to old people?"

"Mostly, yes, but it can also be brought on by stress. And it sounds like you've been under a lot of stress since your husband died. I'll come by and see you tomorrow," he said, turning for the door. "Try and sleep."

Sleep? Fat chance, I thought. How can I sleep without worrying?

Perhaps the knowledge that someone else knew about my symptoms and that maybe they weren't as serious as I believed helped. I finished the soup, savoring every mouthful as if I'd never tasted anything so good before. Then I flipped through a magazine, brushed my teeth, and was asleep before I knew it.

When I woke up the next day, the clock showed ten after eight. That meant that I'd slept for almost twelve straight hours. I couldn't believe it!

I showered and washed my hair, then chose a skirt and a top to wear instead of an old T-shirt and shorts. Suzie came in as I was finishing getting dressed and she talked about the kittens while I put on makeup. Cover-up helped to disguise the circles under my eyes and a dusting of blush on my cheekbones made me look almost human again.

As she rambled on, I realized that it was time I rejoined the real world and stopped telling myself—and Suzie—lies. I'd had a wake-up call. My daughter needed me and it was time to be honest with her.

Suzie deserved a mother who could take care of herself. I prayed that the pain in my body wasn't an indication of a serious medical problem and that I hadn't done too much damage with the alcohol. The implications of my actions finally sank in: If I didn't stop drinking, I risked losing Suzie.

That was just not acceptable.

Drinking hadn't solved my problems, anyway—it only blotted them out for a short time. It was time for me to get help.

I tuned back into Suzie's conversation and heard her mention Tim Murray.

"He was very kind to bring me home yesterday," I said. "Mommy wasn't feeling too well and couldn't drive."

87

Suzie shrugged and I was grateful that she was too young to understand the full meaning of my words. "Yeah, but he ought to go to your salon, Mom. His hair's funny-looking. It's shorter on one side, like he's slept on it, and the other side's all springy."

Oh, my God! I never finished his haircut! I thought. Before I could say anything, the doorbell rang and Suzie ran to answer it. I followed her into the hall.

It was Tim. He greeted Suzie and then turned to me. "How are you feeling?"

"I'm fine, thank you. Please come in."

As he stepped into the hall, I studied him. He's not much taller than I am, but he's sturdily built. He wore neatly pressed chinos and a button-down shirt, which revealed more curly hairs below his Adam's apple.

"Well, you look much better than you did yesterday." Tim looked at me and I was aware that behind the glasses his eyes were a deep blue. They searched my face as if looking for signs of drunkenness. When he saw how clear and bright my eyes were, he seemed to relax. "Are you still in pain?"

"Yes, but it's more like a prickly heat rash than a stabbing pain."

He nodded. "Well, if you're up to it, I thought you might like a ride to pick up your car."

"My car. Oh, yes."

"And perhaps later you'd like to meet me at Ruby's Diner? I could buy you both lunch," Tim said.

"Please, Mommy, can we go?" Suzie pleaded.

It had been a long time since we'd been out to eat. I'd been unwilling to risk having my self-deception revealed. It's time Suzie and I start living again, I told myself.

She pulled at my blouse. "Mom?"

"You want to treat us to lunch?" I asked Tim. "Why?"

"Why not?" he replied. "I'm new in town and it's not every day that I meet two attractive women." He looked at Suzie as he said it and her cheeks turned pink. "Plus, it beats eating alone."

I felt my own face flush with warmth. Since Clive's death, no man had called me attractive. I told myself that it was only for Suzie's sake that I agreed to have lunch with Tim. "All right, Mr. Murray, but first I really must finish your haircut. I don't know how I could've left it like that."

I worried that he'd refuse. Surely he wouldn't want me anywhere near him with a pair of scissors after yesterday's fiasco. Instead, though, an amused smile crossed his lips. "Sure. Folks have been giving me some odd looks. And please, call me Tim."

I fixed Tim's hair out on the porch where I used to cut Clive's. It felt a little strange and the feeling of my fingers in his hair sent chills down my spine. Suzie sat against the wall next to us. As I cut Tim's hair, she peppered him with questions. "Do you have kids?"

"No. I'm single."

"What does your house look like?"

Tim told her and then he talked to her about fishing. She seemed fascinated.

"Will you take me?" she asked.

"Suzie!" I removed the small towel I'd draped over Tim's shoulders and he stood up.

"Aw, Mom. I want to catch a fish. A big one!"

Brushing hair off of the nape of his neck, Tim winked at me. "Of course I'll take you fishing, Suzie. You don't get seasick, do you?"

Suzie's face turned solemn. "I don't know. I've never been on a boat before."

After I finished the haircut, Suzie and I ran a few errands in town and then we met Tim at the agreed upon time. Over lunch, I felt like I was emerging from hibernation to discover that the sun was still shining, the grass was still green, and life was continuing all around me. I felt eager to join in again.

Tim followed us home afterward at Suzie's insistence and she dragged him to Jane Simpson's house to see the kittens.

I stayed behind, replaying earlier conversations with Tim in my head. Had I come across as tongue-tied and awkward? He certainly hadn't made me feel that way and his desire to reach his goal of becoming a paramedic really impressed me.

Thoughts of returning to school began to creep into my mind. I pulled out the pamphlets on educational programs that Nina had given me months before and I'd stashed in a drawer. She'd circled one in particular—it was about becoming a paralegal. I read it through. The course would take three months full-time or six months if I went part-time.

I smiled. Nina knew me better than I knew myself, it seemed, and the program sounded perfect for me. But the thought of leaving the salon altogether was scary and I decided that maybe I'd enroll in the part-time course.

Baby steps, I told myself. I need to take baby steps. I can't change things overnight. But it would be great to have new skills that might lead to a successful and exciting career, I thought as I made a cup of tea. Thinking about the future was intimidating and exhilarating at the same time.

Later, I fetched all of the bottles of alcohol and was standing at the kitchen sink when Tim knocked on the door and let himself in. He grinned as I turned and my spirits lifted. I was glad to see him. I felt like I'd known him for years instead of only having met him a day earlier. I offered him some tea.

"Maybe later," he said. His eyes were drawn to the three empty vodka bottles. With trembling fingers, I placed them in the recycling box under the sink. My secret was out. If he hadn't known before, Tim now knew that I drank. But I was determined not to keep my problem hidden any longer. I'd been in denial about Clive's death and I wouldn't continue to deny that I had a problem with alcohol.

"I left Suzie next door so we could talk privately," he said.

"Okay." I wasn't sure what to expect. Will he turn me in to the authorities? I wondered. I hoped that he'd give me a chance to explain first. I'd never intentionally put Suzie's life at risk and I wanted him to know that.

Sitting at the table next to Tim, I lifted my eyes to his face and it seemed full of kindness and compassion. I took a deep breath and waited for him to speak.

"I, um. . . ." He was hesitant. "I had the feeling you'd been drinking yesterday at the salon."

My head dipped.

"I happen to be a recovering alcoholic," Tim said, "so I recognize the symptoms." Before I could register my surprise, he drew his chair closer. "I started drinking after work with the guys. I wouldn't admit that I had a problem for a long time, but when I finally did, I was lucky. My brother, Eric, and his wife, Anne, helped a great deal. They took care of me and persuaded me to go to Alcoholics Anonymous meetings."

"Did it take you a long time to get sober?"

"Not too long. It's still sometimes a struggle, but it does get better with time. Believe me." He cleared his throat. "Have you been drinking long?"

"Not really," I whispered, shame burning my cheeks. "Only a few weeks."

"That's good! Then you're probably not a full-blown alcoholic. But can I advise you to seek help, anyway? It's important to arm yourself with information. That way, you're more likely to make the right choices."

Tim's encouraging words helped me reveal my deepest fears. "I know I have to do something," I replied. "I've been living a lie and I don't know if I have the strength to change things by myself. But I want to try."

"Paige, it takes a strong person to admit that you have a problem," Tim said. "And it seems to me that yesterday was a turning point for you. I hit bottom when I drove my car off the road and into a tree. I realized later how fortunate I was not to have hit another vehicle.

The paramedics who rescued me impressed me so much with their dedication that I decided to become one. After my broken bones healed, I gave up my job as a mechanic and started the EMT training. AA really helped me get my life back. Maybe you'd like to give them a try?"

"What about my other problem? How do I deal with my loss?" I asked. "Can I get help for that, too? Can I learn to accept my husband's death?"

Tim sat back, looking pleased with me like I was a student asking all the right questions. "Of course. It sounds like you've been stuck in denial. Professional help will get you past that and through the other stages of grief. I also think the physical pains you're experiencing are shingles brought on by this form of stress."

"Really?" I absorbed his words and they were like a lifeline. There is a way I can get out of my black hole, I realized. Tim's done it, and I can do it, too. And once I got my act together I wouldn't ever risk losing Suzie again. She'd already had one tragedy in her short life and it would be too cruel for her to lose me, too.

Straightening my back, I said, "I'm going to ask Doc Carroll about counseling on Monday. I haven't been to him in a long time, but I'm sure he'll help me. I don't want to go through this alone."

Tim's eyes held mine and I got the feeling he'd taken a shine to me. "Dr. Carroll will have all of the information you need. He can also confirm whether or not you have shingles. And I'd like to help, too, if you'll let me."

"I'd like that." Resolved to make Tim proud of me, I added, "I can't thank you enough."

"You're welcome." He accepted my gratitude like it was all in a day's work, but I knew I'd be eternally grateful to him. His eyes twinkled behind his glasses. "Perhaps I could have that tea now?"

"Sure!" I jumped up from the table. There was a weightlessness that I hadn't felt in a long while. I put the teakettle on the stove. As I placed a teabag in a mug, Tim reached out and picked up one of the information sheets.

"Are you thinking of retraining?" he asked.

"Yes. Nina, the salon owner, thinks I'd make a good paralegal."

"I bet she's right."

Suzie burst into the kitchen just then like a mountain lion was chasing her. "Mom! Mom!" she shouted. "Can we have some kittens?"

My eyes widened. "Some?"

"Mrs. Simpson says she's only got people who want four of the kittens and if she can't find anyone to take the other two they'll have to be put to sleep."

"Honey, I'm not sure I could cope with even one kitten right now, never mind two," I said. "I'm sure she'll find homes for them both."

Her lower lip trembled. "But what if she can't? Doesn't it mean they'll never come back, like Daddy?"

I was embarrassed with Tim in the room. "Suzie, I can't talk about this now."

"You never talk about anything with me! You don't care about me!"

"Oh, Suzie." Had I been living so much in denial that my daughter thought I didn't care about her?

"We have to take the kittens!" Suzie yelled. "They'll die if we don't take them. Just like Daddy. I know he's dead. I know he's not coming back. Sally Evans said he's got to be in the churchyard and I'm stupid to pretend. . . ." She burst into tears.

Tim reached out and put an arm around Suzie's shoulders. She leaned into him and cried on his shoulder like she used to cry on Clive's when she fell off her bike or got her fingers caught in the closet door. Her little body shook with sobs.

I felt awful. My inability to acknowledge the truth and seek help had led to this. I knew I had to sit down with Suzie and explain everything, but later—not right then and not with Tim there.

Tim glanced at me and I was relieved to see sympathy, not hatred, in his eyes. He placed his fingers under Suzie's chin and gently lifted her face so that she could see him. "I have an idea!" he said. "I'm rather busy right now, but I'd like a cat to keep me company when I'm settled in the house. If your mother says you can have one of the kittens, I'll ask Mrs. Simpson for the other one. But you have to help look after it."

Suzie's crying subsided. "That'd . . . be . . . cool!" She sniffed and turned her tear-streaked face to me, trying to guess my reaction to his suggestion.

"Of course, that means I'll have to come here and visit my cat's sibling occasionally," Tim continued.

"Is that okay, Mom?" Suzie pleaded.

I handed Suzie a tissue and smiled at Tim Murray. What a kind man, I thought. He's come into my life at a critical point.

Then I reflected on the help that my friends and neighbors like Nina and Jane had already provided. I had the feeling that with the guidance of counselors and Tim's friendship, I'd be back to my normal self pretty soon.

I drew my daughter into my arms and glanced shyly at Tim. "I've read that petting small animals helps reduce stress. Is that true?"

"Very true."

I looked from Tim to Suzie. "Then I think that arrangement would be perfect. What shall we name our kittens?"

That was nine months ago. I'm fit and well again and I still attend AA meetings on a regular basis.

The kittens are full-grown cats now. Suzie and I have Mango and her sister, Muffin, lives with Tim. I'm helping him put some finishing touches on the decorating in his house and in return he's teaching Suzie and me how to fish.

Tim is halfway through his clinical training to become a paramedic. I completed the paralegal course and have joined a law firm here in Hamilton Creek. I'm being trained by one of the junior partners.

Tomorrow's my birthday. I'll be thirty. Tim's taking me out to dinner and then we're going dancing. It will be our first real date and I can't tell you how excited I am!

THE END

RAPED AT 55!

I opened my eyes and the streaming rays of the warm morning sun made me blink then moan with agony! Why was I, fifty-five-year-old Sara Chalke, lying on the living room floor?

I rolled over and glanced at my naked body and the browning red bloodstains on the beige carpet—and the memory sliced me like a knife. Every gory detail and the ripping pain of rape tore at my emotions—and a flood of sobs jerked out of me.

"Oh, God!" I groaned. "Why am I so darn trusting? Why did I let that man into my house, even if he needed to wash his grimy hands? Why did I trust his innocent face, so like my son, Al's, caring one? Why did Joe die and leave me alone after Al went to college?"

Why? Why? Why? The questions echoed in my brain as if I was still a child calling into a rain barrel at Grandma's house.

Somehow I managed to shower and shampoo. Then I cleaned the carpet. But the stains were indelible reminders of my stupid, trusting nature! And suddenly I didn't want to trust anyone! I would never tell my son about the horror. Thank God that Joe would not learn that I had been raped. It was a tiny consolation that he had to die so young— to be spared from hearing what happened to me.

I didn't even trust the authorities now. Someone might tell another and the word would get out that sedate Sara Chalke who lives in the quaint white ranch house on Spruce Street, the Sunday school teacher and poet who reads gentle rhymes to the Women's Club, had been brutally raped by a polite, young man who could have passed for a minister. One look at him had made me unlock the door at once to show him the way to the mudroom sink where he could wash his hands.

As I kept rubbing at the stain on the rug, my conscience nudged me to call the police. Report the man and give his description so he can be hampered from harming others, my mind told me. I wanted to pick up the phone right away. Padding over the carpet, I grabbed the hard beige receiver and punched out the number and then hung up!

I didn't even trust the police. I no longer trusted anyone! I couldn't chance Al finding out. I didn't trust how he would take the bad news. He might look at me as tainted, and I didn't want my son to see his mother as tainted in any way. We had enjoyed a wholesome family life and I refused to let that rapist ruin those memories—or my future!

I hung up the phone with a sharp click and returned to spray rug shampoo on the blood spots and kept rubbing and rubbing as my mind fled back to yesterday.

94

I was outdoors enjoying the warming sunshine on the cool fall day as I trimmed the lilac bush on the edge of my yard when the pleasant-faced, cordial-sounding young man who said his name was Sam, came from behind me without warning. I jumped with surprise and he chuckled.

"Oh, ma'am! I didn't mean to startle you! I'm looking for work. You see, I lost my job when the factory cut out their night shift. My parents both died in a plane crash—on a trip they had saved for during a long, long time. It ripped out my heart, ma'am. But I've got to carry on! Could you give me that job and let me earn some pay? I'd really appreciate it!" He gazed at me and his eyes shimmered just like my son Al's did when he wanted something like an apple pie and hoped I'd bake it for him.

Sam seemed to be desperate to earn money and the little bit this job would pay would certainly not give him much. But a little was better than nothing. That's what Joe used to say when we could save a few dollars at a time to put down someday on this little home we eventually bought. We both cherished our little love nest when we moved in because it would help soothe our awful sadness over our baby girl who had died from pneumonia when she was ten months old. Our Al was only two years old then and missed his baby sister. He cried so hard when she was no longer in her small, white crib.

Our home was bought as a fresh start for us three—we had sold the crib before we had moved in. So our home was our haven for over a dozen years until Joe got sick with lung cancer in the middle of his teaching year at West Side High School. Then it became a hospital as I tended him. Al came home from college as often as possible to sit by his father and hold his hand.

So now you can understand why I melted so at Sam's plea for work, knowing that my Al was also looking for odd jobs to pay his own education bills now that his father was gone. My evening office job kept me going, along with my reporting of community and county events for our local newspaper.

I told Sam he could finish pruning the bush and also cut the grass before trimming the edges of the yard. I had saved to buy a new dress for the newspaper-sponsored dinner to be held in a month. I would write him a check and put off buying the dress. I could always wear my blue suit and just get a new blouse.

Sam was buzzing around the edge of the yard and I felt secure and safe. It felt as though Al were home again! Maybe I could give Sam a meal and we could chat for a while the way Al and I did.

The doorbell rang and I rushed to let Sam inside. His request to wash his hands was no surprise, really. He had done a lot of work without gloves.

It was when he was suddenly behind me again like he had been when I was outdoors that I felt his warm breath on my neck. I whirled and faced his smile, but it suddenly seemed like a smirk!

"Get out your purse. I'm ready to collect—and I did a good job so I earned every dollar I'm asking for." He sounded mean and my flesh got goose bumps. My throat tightened and I wanted to call for Joe or Al but they were not with me. I was alone with a smiling man who had changed into a cold-eyed stranger. And I admit I was scared!

I'll pay him and get rid of him!

"What's the charge?" I said lightheartedly, trying to break the icy tension.

"I need five hundred bucks—now!"

"Five hundred dollars? You've got to be kidding!" I forced a laugh to get him to admit right away that he was only teasing me.

His hard hands grabbed my arms and his fingers dug into my flesh, making me cry out with pain. "Hand over five hundred bucks now! I don't believe in pussy footing. I'm getting out of this town fast and I need cash to do it. I earned the money! I'm not stealing from you, lady! You hired me. People who hire someone pay the price!"

This man is not normal. He is sick and dangerous and I've got to get him out of here—fast, my mind told me.

"I'll get my money. Wait here." I hurried from the kitchen and returned with my checkbook. But he stood so close to me that I felt his breathing on my cheek, so I went into the living room and he followed me. There is no way I can pay him five hundred dollars. I don't have it!

I emptied my wallet in front of him and there were two twenty-dollar bills, a five, a ten, and four ones. He sneered, twisting his handsome face into a grotesque mask. "Only fifty-nine bucks! No way, lady! No way will you get away with this!"

"I never thought you'd charge more than that." I wouldn't get my checkbook. He might grab it and write checks when he was gone. "This is all the money I have."

"You've got a nice little house here. A neat little yard. And you're going to tell me you're poor?"

"My husband died! My son's away at college! I manage somehow, but I'm not well to do!"

I regretted telling him I was so alone in life as the words spilled from my mouth. Why had I been so trusting with the information? Why did I tell him so much? I'm too darn trusting! He could use the information against me now! Oh, Joe, I wish you were still with me! I thought.

The information put a smile back on his face. He grabbed me and jerked off my blouse with a quick rip, then pulled at my jeans snap and zipper and pulled it down before pushing me down to the floor. But I fought! I kicked and struggled, scratching at his face even as he pulled off my jeans and underclothes! His strength was an iron vise as he slapped me before painfully and brutally raping me as I screamed before he shoved a ball of sweaty-smelling cloth into my mouth.

He was so powerful and violent I must have blacked out in an effort to escape. I had long ago stopped being a virgin, yet his forceful rape had made me bleed. He must have hit me hard on my head because it was sore when I woke up afterward.

My thoughts about yesterday faded as I kept rubbing at the bloodstains that were also fading.

Sara, you've got to call the police. You've got to get that man caught! But who is he? Where is he now? Is Sam his real name?

But I didn't know enough to even explain to the police! Many men do yard work. And he looked so gentle, kind, and harmless, too. And he had said he was moving on, anyway. Who knows where he could be now?

So I didn't tell. I kept quiet and tried to go on with my life. But everywhere I went and saw men working in yards, I thought about Sam. I always stared hard to try to identify him if I could, and maybe by then I'd have the nerve to turn him in to the police.

I did my work at the newspaper and evening office job. I tried to resume my peaceful life but many nights I awakened screaming in terror, sweating and trembling as I relived the rape again in a nightmare.

When Al came home I always had his favorite food waiting for him. I pretended that life was good and normal. But when someone came to the door one day and rang the doorbell, Al headed to answer it.

"Stop! I don't answer the door unless I know who it is!" I began to cry and shake.

"Mom? What's wrong?" Al said, hugging me as the doorbell chimed again. "I've got my own apartment now and you'd like staying with me for a while to rest. Could you ask for time off from work?" He sounded so sweet, gentle, and protective that I knew I needed to get a break from home and the horror that happened there nearly a year earlier. A change of scene might exorcise the nightmares so I could return home renewed and healed from the rape trauma.

"Al, I think I do need a rest—a break from my hectic jobs. I've got time coming since I passed up breaks just to keep busy."

I had been at Al's cozy two-room apartment near the college campus for over a week of my planned three-week visit when I took a walk around the neighborhood. And as usual while walking I scanned faces of yard workers just in case I might spot Sam by some chance.

97

It felt good to sniff the fresh air and see people in their daily routine washing their windows or mowing their lawns or trimming shrubbery or watering their flowers. I almost longed to move from my home with so many happy memories and start over in that city. It would be far from the horrible memory of Sam, anyway.

I walked every afternoon for four days in succession. Then in my habitual scrutiny I spotted a young man that resembled Sam! He was trimming burgundy-leafed shrubbery in a lush green yard where a middle-aged woman stood talking to him.

"Oh, I'll do a good job for you, ma'am," he said. "Not easy being alone and all. Sure, I'll be in for that lemonade when I finish."

Maybe it's Sam. Maybe it's not! But I've got to talk to that woman just in case. If I'm inside her house I can look through the window and recognize him. He has that gentle face that I'd recognize, I'm sure. But I have to get past the young man without being seen.

When his back was to me I hurried up the walk, hoping upon hope that he'd not turn and see me—and somehow, however unlikely, recognize me.

I sighed with relief when I saw the narrow walk leading to a side door, out of his sight. I rang the doorbell and the woman appeared with a questioning expression on her face. "Yes?"

"You don't know me and you have no reason to trust me. But I had a bad experience almost a year ago with a young man who did yard work for me. Do you want to hear more? I won't come in if you'll listen to me while I'm right here. I'll whisper so he doesn't hear me."

I gave her my story and her eyes widened with shock. "Oh, my goodness! Want to look at him through the garage window here?"

"Sure!" She hadn't invited me into the house and I didn't blame her. She didn't know if she could trust me. She stood near her door and could run into the house quickly if she thought I might not be truthful with my story.

I peered through the window at Sam and sickness swirled in my stomach. I knew it was the same man. How could I have forgotten that face as it stared into mine from above me when I was pinned to my living room floor?

I groaned. "It's him! Sam! May I use your phone to call the police?"

"Of course. And I'll lock the doors so he can't come in now. He's still working, so he'll be busy if the police come right away."

As I phoned the police, I admit I had little trust that Sam could be arrested on my word alone. There was no evidence now that I had been raped nearly a year ago. But I had to report him as a menace on the way he preyed on me and charged five hundred dollars, then raped me. Something had to be done! I was willing now to take the chance of my name being spread around even in my city.

Soon the sleek black police car pulled into the driveway and Sam stopped clipping and stared at it. He dropped the clippers and ran. He was soon apprehended, and when he saw me standing beside the homeowner, he spat. "You squealed! I'll stick to my story, too! You asked for it! I didn't rape you."

It sounds too easy to be true, but in his panic, Sam, who really was Elliot Marshall with a rape record, had spilled the truth. And it was held against him as evidence.

He is now in jail and awaiting trial and sentencing. He will be found guilty. I don't care now who knows that I was raped. I'll be glad to see justice done.

I regret that I lost my total trust in smiling people. But the world isn't all friendly and cozy. There are people out there like Sam—I mean Elliot Marshall—whom are harmful to defenseless widows. And it is time they are exposed.

Al did not look at me as a tainted or tarnished woman. He gazes at me with admiration and love for my new ability to live on my own with wisdom and wariness.

"You'll always be my sweet mom," he said after I asked him if my experience changed his mind about me as the mother he thought I was.

I now keep my door locked if someone rings the doorbell and has something to say to me. I don't hire anyone even to mow the grass unless I know the person or have a recommendation of someone I trust. Any contractor needs to show me his credentials before I even think of hiring him. And I need a written estimate before one bit of work is started.

I still trust in God, goodness, laws, and all that stuff. But total trust in everyone is foolhardy. So I had to share my story to warn you—so won't be a victim, too.

THE END

WILDFIRE!
We were driven from our home

W hen my husband and I bought our dream home in Colorado, I felt as if we'd settled in paradise. From a wall of windows in our living room we could see snow-capped mountain peaks, while our bedroom at the rear of the house looked out on a ridge thick with pine, blue spruce, and aspen.

Not that such beauty came without a price. My husband, Darren, had a forty-five minute commute to his job, tough going at times in the winter. And in the summer there was always the danger of fire. Only two years before we moved into the house, a wildfire a few miles away charred thousands of acres of national forest land and destroyed fifty homes.

But when I sat in my living room looking out on the green, sloping land, such devastation seemed far away from me. I preferred to think of all the things I wanted to do with the house, such as decorating and landscaping. I intended to make my dream home into a real showcase.

I guess some people are just natural homebodies. While my friends put their energies into their careers or saved their money for exotic vacations, all I ever really wanted was to stay home with my kids and take care of my house.

Wherever we've lived, I've always tried to make my house into a real home. Our first apartment was admired by everyone who saw it, and when we sold our first house, the real estate agent commented that it looked professionally decorated.

My family didn't exactly share my passion for housekeeping and decorating. My husband could care less what the house looked like, as long as he had clean clothes in the closet and meals on the table. Not that he didn't appreciate my efforts, but to Darren, walls were walls, no matter what color paint was on them. He couldn't tell the difference between café curtains or Roman shades and had no interest in learning to tell them apart. As for my son and daughter, once they hit junior high school, they would've just as soon had the whole house decorated like a big rec room, with bright, colored furniture and a giant TV.

Which left me to paint the walls, make the drapes, and buy the furniture that would make our home look and feel good. And I loved every minute of it. I spent hours poring over decorating magazines, walking up and down the aisles of the local home improvement store, and watching decorating programs on TV. I refinished garage-sale finds, faux-finished walls, and sewed my own curtains and pillows. When I looked around my house, I saw all these beautiful things I'd made with my own hands and I felt a great sense of satisfaction.

The nice thing about decorating your own home is that things don't have to always stay the same. When I grew tired of a color scheme or a window treatment or even a particular piece of furniture, I could change it. I experimented with different styles and fashions, and prided myself on having a home that always looked up-to-date.

I ignored any complaints my family might have about any new decor. After all, I was the only one in the house with any taste. One day they'd thank me for introducing them to so many new things.

So it didn't phase me a bit when I announced plans to redo our family room and Darren and both the kids howled in protest. "What's wrong with the room the way it is now?" Darren asked, looking around at the blue gingham slipcovers and yellow curtains and pillows I'd made two years before.

"I'm tired of it." I picked up a yellow striped pillow I'd embroidered with a blue and red rooster. "What would you think of a lodge look— lots of stained wood, red and green plaid slipcovers, and maybe an antler chandelier?"

Darren sighed and sank back in his chair. "What does it matter what I think? You're going to do it anyway."

I set the pillow aside and frowned at him. "Don't be like that. Your opinion does matter to me. What don't you like about the lodge idea?"

He shook his head. "I'm sure it's fine, but I already like the stuff you have in here now. What's wrong with keeping things the same for a while?"

"Because it's time for a change of pace. Trust me, you'll love it."

The kids' reactions was just as predictable as Darren's. My daughter, Mollie, who was twelve, wrinkled up her nose. "If we're going to redecorate, why not do something more hip?"

"More hip?" I raised one eyebrow. "What did you have in mind?"

She shrugged. "I don't know. Maybe big pillows on the floor and beanbag chairs so it would be real comfortable to sit around with our friends."

"Yeah, and a home theater system." My eleven-year-old son, Justin, flopped down on the sofa. "And a mini fridge so we could keep sodas and snacks down here."

"But the family room is for the whole family," I said. "Not just you and your friends."

Justin nodded. "Sure. But nobody's going to want to hang out here if they have to stare at dead animals and stuff."

I laughed. "They won't be staring at dead animals. You'll see. It'll look nice."

They rolled their eyes but didn't say anything else. Meanwhile, I took measurements for new drapes, ordered fabric, and began scouting flea markets and tag sales for the perfect accessories.

One evening I showed off my latest find. "Look what I got today for the family room," I said.

Mollie made a face. "What is it?"

"It's an antler chandelier." I held it higher and turned it to admire it from all sides. "As soon as I clean and rewire it, it'll be good as new."

"I think it's hideous." That was one of Mollie's favorite words. Everything was hideous.

"Honey, what do you think?" I asked Darren.

"Um, you don't think it's a little barbaric?"

"It's only deer antlers." I admired it again. "I think it's very artistic."

"Don't leave it on the floor or Rover might eat it," Justin said.

Hearing his name, our dog thumped his tail on the floor. Come to think of it, he was eyeing the chandelier as if it were an oversized chew treat.

I propped the chandelier on the counter and smiled at my family. "Trust me," I said. "It will look great."

When summer vacation started, I enlisted Mollie and Justin to help me repaint the family room. I chose a nice reddish brown hue called Adobe Dust.

"It looks orange," Mollie said.

"I like orange," Justin said. "We could do the furniture blue and we'd have a whole room in the Denver Broncos' colors."

"It is not orange, and we're not doing the furniture blue," I said.

"What are you doing with the furniture?" Justin asked.

I smiled. "You just wait and see. It's going to be great."

We were almost finished with the first coat of paint on the walls when Darren came home from work. "What do you think?" I asked him.

"It looks fine." He scarcely glanced at the walls. "Did you know there's a fire up on the ridge?"

The ridge was a line of hills only a few miles from our house, on the edge of the forest. "I've been down here in the basement all day and haven't even been outside." I set aside my paint roller and stripped off my rubber gloves. "Is it very bad?"

Deep worry lines etched Darren's forehead. He glanced toward Mollie and Justin. "Come outside and see."

Of course the kids followed us out. As soon as we stepped out onto the back deck, smoke stung my eyes and nose. I gasped when I looked toward the ridge. Billowing clouds of black smoke towered into the sky, blocking the sun.

"Is someone's house burning?" Justin asked.

"No, son. It's a forest fire." Darren glanced at me. "It's really dry out there. This could be bad."

I started to answer, but my voice was drowned out by the sound of a helicopter passing overhead. A huge bucket dangled from it by a long cord.

"What are they doing with that?" Mollie asked.

"They're scooping up water to fight the fire." I glanced over her head, exchanging worried looks with Darren. If helicopters were already on the job, it wasn't a minor spot fire.

Only two summers before, forest fires had destroyed ten thousand acres near our subdivision, and fifty families had lost their homes. Five years before that, another fire had blackened twenty-four thousand acres and left thirty families homeless.

Though we'd always known that forest fires were one of the things you dealt with when you lived on the edge of vast woodlands, we'd never dreamed that our own home would ever be in danger.

I glanced back at the billowing smoke cloud. If the wind picked up, it could easily blow the fire right down on us. "Come on, kids, let's go inside and get ready for supper," I said, herding them toward the door.

"I'm going to stay out here a while." Darren pulled his phone from his pocket. "I'll make a few calls and see what I can find out."

I was making hamburger patties when Darren came back in, looking more worried than ever. "Where are the kids?" he asked.

"I sent them downstairs to watch TV." I washed and dried my hands and turned to face him. "What did you find out?"

"They think it started from a lightning strike. It's burned a couple hundred acres so far." He pulled me close. "I think we should pack a few things and be ready to leave if we have to."

I pulled away, shaken. "You don't really think we'll have to leave, do you? I mean, they've already got helicopters and firefighters on the scene. Surely they'll get things under control."

"The man I talked to at the fire department sounded like it would take a while, several days even, before this is anywhere near under control."

I looked around the kitchen, my gaze resting on random objects— the potholders I'd quilted, the spice rack I'd made, the children's artwork on the refrigerator. How could I begin to decide what to take and what to leave behind?

"Let's wait a while longer," I said. "Maybe we won't have to go."

Justin was the only one who ate much supper. He thought the fire was exciting, and asked a million questions about the firefighters. "Do you think they'll bring in hotshots and smoke jumpers?" he asked. "What about slurry bombers? Do you think we'll be able to see them?"

"I hope they bring in all those things," Darren said. "It will probably take everything they've got to keep this under control, as hot and dry as it's been lately."

"Danielle and her family had to leave their house and go stay at a shelter when they had that big fire two years ago," Mollie said. "Do you think we'll have to leave?"

"We might," Darren said.

"I hope it doesn't come to that," I said. The thought of leaving behind so many things that were dear to me made me sick to my stomach.

After supper, Darren turned on the news. Every station had coverage of the fire, calling it "the first major fire of the season" and "potentially one of the most dangerous fires of the decade."

My heart hammered in my chest and I could scarcely breathe as I watched footage of tall pine trees exploding into flame and fingers of fire creeping down the ridge. Huge tanker planes dumped loads of fire-retardant slurry. It looked like a rainstorm of just-mixed strawberry gelatin.

For the children's sake, we tried to make light of the news. "It looks like they're really going after this," Darren said. "At this rate, they might have it under control by morning." But neither of us believed it.

We shut off the TV and put the children to bed. For the first time in years, they insisted Darren read them a story.

While he read a short story to them, I wandered through the house straightening a picture here, fluffing a pillow there. Everywhere I looked, I saw items that triggered memories. The quilt made from scraps of Mollie and Justin's baby clothes, the pottery vase my mom had given me, the trash-picked vanity I'd lovingly refinished. Every picture on the wall and every piece of furniture meant something to me. How could I bear to lose any of it?

When the kids finally settled down for the night, Darren returned to the living room. We turned the TV on low and listened to one more report about the fire. This one said firefighters would spend the night digging firelines, taking advantage of cooler temperatures and higher humidity overnight. "Tomorrow will be a pivotal day in this fight," the reporter intoned.

Darren punched the off button on the remote. "Let's pray things are better in the morning," he said.

"And if they're not?"

He took my hand and squeezed it. "We'll deal with that when the time comes. Right now, let's try to get some sleep."

I went to bed but sleep eluded me. I tossed and turned, the smell of smoke still in my head. I made mental lists: things to do in the morning, people to notify, things to take with us if we were forced to evacuate.

The last list grew longer and longer. Of course I had to bring the insurance papers and the deeds to the house and cars. Justin and Mollie's baby albums and our wedding pictures. The baby clothes quilt. My mother's vase. Would the vanity fit in the car? What about my wedding dress? The plaster handprints the children had made me when they were in kindergarten? My grandmother's rolling pin? My new dress shoes. The pearls Darren gave me for our fifteenth wedding anniversary. And I didn't want to forget the letters Mollie wrote to us the summer she went to camp.

Some time before dawn, I drifted to sleep. I woke to the sound of the TV. I found Darren in the living room, listening to the news. "What's the latest?" I asked, sitting beside him.

"They were able to dig a fireline last night. If the weather holds, we're in good shape."

I looked out the window, at the American flag that hung from our deck. It hung limp. So far, so good on the weather. Cool and calm was exactly what we needed. Rain would've been best, but the only clouds in the sky were formed from the smoke that still hung thickly in the air.

Justin and Mollie joined us. "Who wants blueberry pancakes for breakfast?" I asked.

"Wow, and it's not even anyone's birthday," Mollie said. "Thanks, Mom."

I smiled. "I'm sure it's somebody's birthday, somewhere. I just felt like making this morning special." I also wanted something to do with my hands while we waited to hear more news about the fire.

After breakfast, Justin grabbed his skateboard and headed for the door. "Where are you going?" I asked.

"I told Greg I'd meet him at the park so we could practice." Though our neighborhood is rather rural, two blocks from the house is a beautiful county park.

"You need to stay home this morning," I said. "The smoke is too thick to be out in." Plus, I wanted him nearby in case we had to leave in a hurry.

I was reluctant to resume painting the family room just then, so instead I set up my sewing machine at the kitchen table and began working on new draperies. The steady hum of the sewing machine soothed me and I felt myself begin to relax. I was sewing a tan denim fabric into full drapes to go under a padded valence I planned to make. The room was going to look gorgeous, like a cabin at a fancy ski resort.

Darren spent the morning fooling around in the garage. He'd just come in for lunch when the phone rang and he answered it. "Hello?"

"Hi, Lucy," he said. Lucy Hilton was our neighbor across the street.

Darren frowned. "Oh, really? Who told you that? I see. I will. You, too. Thanks for calling."

I set aside the tuna fish I'd been mixing and looked at him. "What is it? Is something wrong?"

"Lucy has a friend who's a dispatcher for the fire department. He says the wind has picked up and is blowing the fire our way. We're going to have to evacuate."

He called the children into the kitchen and gave them the news. "I want each of you to pack one suitcase with things you want to take with you," he told them. "There's no need to panic but we should try to hurry, so we'll be ready when the time comes for us to leave."

I tried to appear calm on the outside, but my hands shook as I put the uneaten tuna in the refrigerator. "I'll get the insurance policies and other important papers," Darren said. "What else should we take?"

I tried to remember my list from the night before. "Pictures," I said. "My jewelry. Clothes. Quilts."

"We should take food for Rover and Whiskers." Whiskers was our yellow tabby.

"Of course. I'll get that. Mollie!" I shouted up the stairs. "Find Whiskers and put her in her carrier."

The next hour passed in a blur, though I felt like I was moving through molasses. I stuffed two bags of pet food into the backseat of my car, then ran back upstairs and started filling a suitcase with clothing from our dresser and closet. That was only half-packed when I decided I'd better check on Justin and Mollie.

Justin had a suitcase open on his bed filled with baseball cards, sports trophies, and books. "Justin, honey, you have to take clothes, too," I said. I took out a baseball trophy and a stack of books. "We don't have room for everything."

He added his baseball glove to the growing pile in the suitcase. "I don't care about clothes. I'll wear any old thing."

A lump rose in my throat. Without another word, I pulled a duffel bag from his closet and filled it with his clothes while he stuffed the suitcase. We'd find some way to make it all fit.

When I returned to the bedroom, Darren was finished packing the suitcase. I took my jewelry case from the dresser, then retrieved my makeup from the bathroom. Darren raised one eyebrow. "You're taking that?"

"If I'm going to be homeless, at least I'll look good." I tried to make a joke, but it didn't come out sounding very cheerful.

Darren put his arm around me. "It'll be all right," he said.

I wrapped my mother's vase in the baby clothes quilt, then went into the hall and began stripping pictures from the wall. The children's school photos. A picture we'd had taken on a family ski trip. My parent's fiftieth wedding anniversary portrait.

I was looking for a box for the pictures when I spotted the plaster handprint plaques and added them to my pile.

Darren passed me, a gallon jug of water in each hand. "Your car is full now," he said. "What do you want in mine?"

"Do we have room for my sewing machine?" It was an expensive model that would be difficult to replace. I followed him into the garage with my stack of pictures. The back end of our SUV was filled with suitcases, Mollie's ice skates, the pet food, Darren's briefcase, and the tower from our computer. Darren added the water jugs and shut the hatch. "You can take the pets and Mollie with you. Justin can ride with me."

I settled the pictures on the backseat of his car and went into the house for another load. Through the open garage door, I could see all our neighbors loading cars, hooking up boats, and rounding up animals.

Above all this I could hear the drone of airplanes flying above the thick smoke.

I was trying to stuff one more box of photos into Darren's car when a sheriff's department cruiser passed the house, loudspeaker blaring. "For your own safety, please leave the area immediately."

I ran upstairs. Darren and the children were wandering through the rooms, blank looks on their faces. "Did you hear that?" I asked. "We have to leave now."

"Mom, I can't find Whiskers!" Tears ran down Mollie's cheeks. "We can't leave her behind."

"You and Justin go downstairs and get Rover into the car," Darren said. "Your mom and I will look for Whiskers."

"You have to find her." Mollie wailed.

"We will. Now go on and take care of Rover. And don't forget her leash."

When the children left, I turned to Darren. "What if she got outside? We'll never find her."

"She's probably hiding somewhere, upset by all the commotion."

With a pounding heart, I made a hurried search of the rooms, looking under furniture, on top of cabinets, and in closets.

"I found her." Darren emerged from Mollie's bedroom, the cat clinging to him. A long scratch down Darren's arm testified that Whiskers hadn't surrendered easily.

I helped Darren stuff the cat into the carrier, then took a last look around the house. Would I ever see my dream home again?

"Come on, we'd better go." Darren returned from carrying the cat to his car and put his hand on my shoulder.

"I'm sure we've forgotten something important," I said.

"Nothing is as important as you and the kids. As long as we're all safe, that's all that matters."

In my heart I knew this was true, but I also knew letting go of the other things in my life would be hard.

Following instructions given on TV, we left the house unlocked and headed toward the Red Cross shelter that had been established at the high school in town. We joined a long train of cars, each piled high with luggage, pictures, heirlooms, even furniture. Some of the cars pulled horse trailers, boats, or RVs. It reminded me of pictures I'd seen in the news of refugees fleeing a war zone.

At the entrance to our subdivision, sheriff's deputies were busy setting up a roadblock. Once we were gone, we wouldn't be allowed to return until they'd determined it was safe.

At the shelter, volunteers directed us to parking lots behind the high school. Already the lot was nearly full of cars, trailers, and RVs. Men, women, and children wandered in and out of the gymnasium, while news crews set up cameras and conducted interviews in the hallways and adjacent classrooms. Since the shelter didn't allow pets inside, dogs had been tethered all along the fenced-in basketball court, while triple tiers of cat carriers were lined up next to the gym entrance. We rolled down the windows and left Rover and Whiskers in the car, which only added to my anxiety.

Inside the gym, we waited in line to register. When the woman in front of us reached the front of the line, she burst into tears. "I left work as soon as I heard about the fire," she explained between sobs. "But when I got home, they'd already shut off the road and they wouldn't let me back in." She accepted a tissue from the Red Cross worker. "I have two dogs at home. What will happen to them?"

"We have workers from Animal Control who are going house to house, picking up pets," the Red Cross worker explained. "If you'll step over here, we'll put you in touch with people at Animal Rescue. I'm sure your pets are safe."

The worker returned to the registration table. "Welcome," she said. "Will you folks be staying with us tonight?"

"I guess so," Darren said. "We don't have anyplace else to go."

"What company is your homeowner's insurance with?" the worker asked.

"Family Mutual."

"Then you're in luck. We have a representative from Family Mutual here who will give you a check to cover meal and hotel expenses while you're out of your home. We also have a list of hotels in the area offering special rates to evacuees."

Darren and I looked at each other, and I couldn't help smiling. "I can't believe everything's so organized." I began to feel calmer, knowing so many people were here to help us.

I felt a tugging on my arm and looked into Mollie's worried face.

108

"What about Rover and Whiskers? Can they stay at a hotel?"

I turned back to the Red Cross worker. "We have a cat and a dog. What can we do with them?"

"After you speak with the insurance agent, Mr. Turner, go down to Room 116. Volunteers there have a list of people who have volunteered to keep pets in their homes."

In a fog, we followed a volunteer to a desk in the corner of the room, where an efficient man in a gray suit cut us a check for $100. "If you need more tomorrow, just let me know," he said. "I plan to be here every day until this is over."

We thanked him and proceeded to Room 116, where volunteers were doing their best to cheer up some very worried pet owners. The crying woman was talking on a cell phone to someone who was caring for her two dogs, who'd been rescued from her home by an animal control officer.

We explained that we needed to speak with one of the volunteers. "We have a couple south of town who'd be happy to take your dog and cat," she said. "We'll call them and they'll come pick them up."

"Will Rover and Whiskers like staying with strangers?" Justin asked. "What if they miss us?"

The volunteer turned to Justin. "I'm sure Rover and Whiskers will miss you. But the Mercers will take extra-special care of them, and you'll know they'll be safe."

The call was made, and we walked back out to the car to check on the animals. Justin persuaded us to let Rover out so he could walk the dog around the parking lot.

The Mercers turned out to be a young couple who had two dogs and a cat of their own. "We'll take good care of Rover and Whiskers," Mrs. Mercer assured the children. "We'll give them lots of treats and petting."

Animals taken care of, we drove to a hotel and checked into a room. When the manager learned we were evacuees from the fire, he gave us free drink coupons for the hotel bar. "You let me know if you need anything else," he said.

We settled into our room and turned on the TV. Though the kindness of so many strangers had begun to make us feel better, the news reports sent us crashing back down into despair. The fire had grown at an alarming rate, fed by high winds and low humidity. "We've had reports that several homes have burned," a reporter announced. "We've been unable to confirm that information at present."

As the cameras panned over a horizon on fire, Mollie began to cry. "All those trees gone." She sobbed. "All the forest animals. What will they do?"

I put my arm around her and pulled her close. "I know, honey. It's

109

awful. We just have to pray everything is all right."

"I'm hungry," Justin said from his spot on the room's second double bed. "What are we going to eat?"

"You can have whatever you want." Darren sat down next to Justin. "How about that?"

"I don't want to eat," Mollie said.

I patted her back. "Come on. You'll feel better if you eat something."

"How about burgers?" Darren said.

"Pizza," Justin said. "And ice cream sundaes."

So we went to a pizza parlor, then stopped off at an ice cream shop. Despite the grim reason we were there, the evening had a holiday feel to it. When was the last time the four of us had spent so much time together? Usually we were all busy with our own concerns.

When we returned to the hotel, I automatically started to turn on the TV. Darren reached out and took my hand. "Why don't we take the children down to the pool," he said. "Try to forget about things for a while."

"You're right. Maybe we'll all sleep better if we go for a swim."

Amazingly, I'd packed our swimsuits in my haste. I suppose all those times I'd filled suitcases for vacations had kicked in. I was grateful for that, because for the next hour we all forgot about the fire and enjoyed splashing around in the hotel pool. "This is like being on vacation!" Justin said, and I couldn't help but grin. Thank goodness for children to keep us from getting down in the dumps.

The next morning, reality intruded again in the form of news reports that several houses had burned yesterday. We packed the car and hurried to the Red Cross shelter, where volunteers served up a pancake breakfast while representatives from the fire department gave a press conference.

Ominous red pins on a map marked the site of five houses that had been destroyed. I breathed a sigh of relief when I saw that none of them was ours, then I felt guilty and said a silent prayer for those families who'd been left homeless.

The Mercers called to let us know Rover and Whiskers had settled right in to their temporary home. We met several of our neighbors at the shelter and exchanged evacuation stories. The woman I'd met the day before who hadn't been allowed into her home showed up wearing clean clothes. "A woman I didn't even know heard my story and brought these for me," she explained, dabbing at her eyes. "Everyone has been so kind."

Indeed, I was overwhelmed by the help everyone offered. A group of women arrived with stuffed animals for the children, while others brought cookies, video games, and art supplies to help pass the time.

110

Everywhere I turned, people asked, "Do you need anything? Is there anything I can do for you?"

I was touched, but of course, the only thing I really needed was to know that my home was safe and I'd be able to return to it.

The day passed slowly. We watched news reports on the television in one corner of the gym and checked the maps every hour as fire department representatives marked the growth of the fire. No more homes burned and we all kept our fingers crossed that today was the day things would turn the corner.

The children clung to us the first hour or so, but after a while they ran off to play with new friends and old ones. I checked on them at lunchtime and found them involved in a board game with several of our neighbors. I breathed a prayer of thanks that children were so adaptable.

By afternoon, boredom had set in. I approached one of the Red Cross volunteers. "Is there anything I can do to help?" I asked. "I'm used to staying busy."

She consulted a clipboard at her side. "Some people are taking food to the firefighter's camp," she said. "Would you like to help with that?"

So the four of us ended up at the ballfields on the other end of town, where a miniature city had been set up. Firefighting teams from all over the country had converged to do battle with the blaze. Teams of yellow-shirted hotshots—elite crews trained to fight wildfires—worked alongside local volunteers. The ballfields were crowded with fire trucks, battalions of tents, news satellite trucks, portable showers, and latrines. Even here smoke filled the air and the sound of air tankers and helicopters traveling from the fire to the refueling stations was constant.

Darren, Justin, Mollie, and I took our place on the serving line as firefighters began to troop in for their evening meal. A lump rose in my throat when I saw their soot-blackened faces and red-rimmed eyes. They looked utterly exhausted.

"Thank you so much for what you're doing," I told one young woman who looked scarcely older than Mollie. "My home is one of the ones you're protecting."

Her weariness receded and she smiled, her teeth startling white against her gray face. "You're welcome. That's good to hear."

When everyone had been served, we sat down to eat also, at a table filled with firefighters from another state. They'd rode all night on a bus to join the efforts to battle the blaze.

"How do you fight a fire this big?" Justin asked them.

"Believe it or not, the best way to fight it is by hand," one of the men said. "We go out with chainsaws and hoes and axes and cut

111

firelines, put out little spot fires, set backfires, and try to make a cleared area the fire can't jump across. Eventually, you get the fire surrounded and it burns itself out."

"Meanwhile, the local fire departments have crews doing structure protection," said another man. "They dig fire lines around houses, cut down trees, and direct the air support where to dump retardant. They save a lot of houses that way."

I thought of the home I'd grown to love. If only the firefighters could save it as well.

Back at the hotel, Darren and I relaxed by the pool while the children played. "What if our house burns?" I asked Darren.

He squeezed my hand. "Then we'll collect the insurance money and start over."

I thought of when we'd first married. In those days, we hadn't owned much, and what we did have was mostly hand-me-downs from family. We even used to talk of taking off and backpacking around Europe for a year, leaving everything behind.

Then I thought of all the things in my house that I'd spent so much time, effort, and love into fixing up. But I saw them now with a strange sense of detachment.

"I guess it wouldn't be so awful, having to start over," I said. I looked at Mollie and Justin playing in the pool, and thought of Rover and Whiskers, safe with the Mercers. "Everything that's really important to me is safe, and that's all that matters."

"We'll be all right, whatever happens," Darren said.

A sense of peace settled over me then, because I knew he was right.

As it turned out, that night the wind shifted, driving the fire back on itself. Firefighters acted quickly to cut more firelines. By morning, they announced they were well on their way to containing the blaze.

At noon, the sheriff's announcement that we could return to our homes was greeted with cheers.

We collected an ecstatic Rover and a pouting Whiskers from the Mercers and joined the caravan of families returning to our neighborhood. Though a smoky smell still hung in the air, the area around our house had been spared any damage. Our home was just as we'd left it, right down to the tuna fish can on the counter and the discarded clothes on the bed.

But now I looked at them all with a different eye. Though the memories I associated with every picture and item of furniture were still precious, the things themselves were not as important. These past few days I'd seen how much more valuable family and friendship were than any mere object.

I joined Darren on the back deck. Fingers of black stretched down the ridge behind the house.

"We came awfully close to losing everything," he said.

I took his hand. "Not the things that really count."

The children joined us on the deck. "What are you doing out here?" Justin asked.

"Just thinking." I put my arms around him and his sister.

"About what?" Mollie asked.

"What would you think about helping me redo the family room? But this time, we'll make it into a room everyone can enjoy."

"Can we have beanbag chairs?" Justin asked.

"And bright colors?" Mollie added.

I smiled. "Sure. After all, a family room should be for the whole family. These past few days have shown me just how important family really is."

Mollie glanced up at the ridge. "Do you think there'll be more fires?"

"There might be," Darren said. "But we'll be all right. We know what to do now."

"The important thing is to stick together," Justin said. "Right, Mom?"

I hugged him close. "That's right. As long as we're together, we'll be fine."

THE END

HOOKED ON
PRESCRIPTION DRUGS

Five years ago, if anyone had asked, I wouldn't have hesitated to say that I was an honest person. The only lies I ever told were white ones. And if anyone had ever suggested I would steal, I would've been so insulted I'd have probably stopped speaking to them.

But these days, I'm not so smug. I know that even an honest person can lie and cheat and steal when they're overtaken by addiction. I know, because it's happened to me.

It all started about four and a half years ago. I bent over to pick up one of my daughter's toys from the floor and I felt something pop in my back. One moment I was fine and the next I was in a heap on the floor, in agony as pain shot through me. Only the thought of my daughter, Lexie, finding me that way when she came home from school kept me from lying there all afternoon. Somehow, I managed to drag myself into the bedroom and up onto the bed, where I lay curled in a fetal position, trying not to cry.

When Lexie came in, I managed a smile and told her I'd hurt my back, but I'd be fine. At twelve, she was perfectly capable of looking after herself for an afternoon, and in a minute, I heard the stereo and Lexie's voice on the phone to her friend, Anna.

When my husband, Sam, came home from work a little later, I wasn't so cheerful. "I'm in agony," I told him. "I don't know what happened."

Sam was concerned enough to call our doctor, who agreed to see me right away. Sam helped me out to the car, where I lay in the backseat, gritting my teeth against new waves of pain every time we hit a bump in the road.

"Looks like you've ruptured a disk," the doctor said, once he'd had a chance to look at my X-rays.

That sounded bad to me. "Will I need surgery?"

He shook his head. "I don't think so. Most of the times these things resolve themselves. I'll give you some medication for the pain and some strengthening exercises to do just as soon as you're able. That, and time, are the best remedies."

I swallowed, not very happy with the diagnosis. Even one more day of this pain was going to be too much for me. As for exercise—I could hardly move. How was I going to exercise?

On the way home from the doctor's office, we stopped at the pharmacy to fill the prescription the doctor had given me. I took one pill there in the car, chasing it down with a soft drink Sam brought me.

I was amazed at how quickly the drug worked. By the time we pulled into the driveway, I was able to sit up and walk into the house without too much discomfort. I even managed to eat a little of the dinner Sam and Lexie fixed.

A few hours later, the pain woke me from a sound sleep, but I took one of the pain pills and I soon felt better. I drifted to sleep, thinking that whoever had invented Vicodin ought to be awarded a Nobel Prize.

I took it easy the next day. My back still bothered me, especially when the medication wore off, but I soon figured out that if I took the pills before I started hurting—say, every four hours—I felt better.

In fact, in addition to taking away my pain, the pills made me feel great. Sort of euphoric. Nothing much bothered me that first week. I drifted through my days a little light-headed, with a smile on my face.

By the end of the week, the bottle of pills was empty. I stared at it, frowning. Without the pills, my back didn't feel much better. How was I supposed to take care of my family if I was in pain?

I called the pharmacy and asked them in to call the doctor about a refill. To my delight, when I checked back later, my prescription was ready.

That second bottle of pills disappeared as quickly as the first. But the next time I called for a refill, the doctor's office called me.

"The doctor is concerned that you need a refill so soon," the nurse said. "These pills are designed to be taken only for a short while."

"My back still hurts," I said. "If I don't take the pills, I'm miserable."

"Have you been doing the exercises the doctor gave you?" the nurse asked.

"I hurt too much to exercise." Honestly, I was getting really annoyed.

"I'll have to check with the doctor and call you back," she said.

When I still hadn't heard from the doctor after four hours, I called the office again. "This is Carrie Anson," I said. "Has the doctor okayed my prescription refill yet?"

"Just a moment, Mrs. Anson. I'll check."

The nurse came on the line in a few moments. "Mrs. Anson, the doctor wants you to have some physical therapy," she said. "That should help with the pain you've been having."

"What about my prescription?"

"The doctor has authorized fifteen pills. But you're to take them only when you absolutely have to."

I chewed my lower lip. Fifteen pills would only last me a couple of days if I spaced them out. If I complained, the doctor was liable to refuse even that many. "Please call them to my pharmacy," I said meekly.

"I will. Now here's the information about the physical therapist."

I made myself wait an hour to drive to the pharmacy and pick up my prescription. In the parking lot, I ripped open the bag and struggled with the childproof cap. I swallowed one of the pills and sat back in my seat, relief flooding through me. Soon, I knew, the pain would dull and the good feelings would return.

I had my first appointment with the physical therapist the following Thursday. I didn't really want to go. I didn't have time for the twice-weekly appointments and besides, as long as I took the Vicodin, I could handle the pain.

I explained all this to the physical therapist, who seemed sympathetic. "I understand it's terrible to be in constant pain," she said. "But pain medication only masks the pain. It doesn't do anything to alleviate the cause. That's what we're going to work on together."

I'd been worried that all that stretching and reaching and pulling would only make the pain in my back worse, but the truth was, I did feel better physically by the time that first therapy session ended. Still, I took another pill on the way home, just in case.

When I emptied the pill bottle a few days later, I knew better than to ask my regular doctor for another refill. Instead, I flipped through the phone book and found the name of another doctor in town. Then I called and pretended I'd just injured my back.

"Have we seen you before, Mrs. Anson?" the receptionist asked.

"No," I answered brightly. "No, I'm a new patient."

After all, if my regular doctor was going to be so unsympathetic, it was high time I found a new one.

I left the doctor's office that afternoon with a brand-new prescription for Percocet. "That should knock the pain right out," the doctor reassured me.

The Percocet knocked the pain right out, all right. At first, it knocked me out, too. Soon I developed a tolerance for the drug and was able to go about my everyday activities, happy and pain-free. Like the Vicodin, the Percocet made me feel euphoric, as if I could do anything.

But if I ran out of medication, I began to feel anxious and irritable. By now I knew how to handle things, though. I'd simply pull out the phone book and call another doctor in one of the towns near mine. I'd repeat my story about having injured my back and being in pain. I learned to have the prescriptions called into different local pharmacies, even made up local addresses for my patient information, and then paid my bill in cash.

I didn't know it then, but I'd become what's known as a "doctor shopper"—a person who frequently changes doctors in order to obtain prescription medication. But if any of the doctors suspected me, they never said anything about it, and invariably, they wrote prescriptions— for drugs like Lortab, Vicodin, Percocet, and my personal favorite, OxyContin. Soon I was spending hundreds of dollars a month on doctor's visits and prescriptions, since I didn't dare file any claims for my painkillers with our insurance.

I didn't dare tell Sam what I was doing, either. I hid the pill bottles and the bills from him. Fortunately, I had my own charge card and I handled paying all our bills, so he didn't know what was going on.

I was sure no one else knew, either. After all, except for the doctor's visits and the prescriptions, I lived a perfectly normal life. I cooked dinner, helped Lexie with her homework, and went shopping with friends.

One Saturday, I took a historic homes tour with my friend, Jenny. The local historical society does this every year, arranging with the owners of restored historic homes in our area to open their houses for public tours.

Jenny and I had a lot of fun that day, strolling through gorgeous Victorian mansions, oohing and ahhing at the gorgeous furnishings and fixtures. We toured six houses that afternoon, and at the fourth, I had to go to the bathroom. I slipped away from the tour group, into a downstairs powder room. While I was drying my hands on an embroidered towel, I idly opened the medicine cabinet door. An excited flutter rose in my chest as I spotted an almost-full prescription bottle of Vicodin.

I glanced toward the closed bathroom door. Had anyone noticed me missing? With shaking hands, I reached for the bottle. This was a downstairs powder room, not a master bath, so that meant this prescription probably wasn't used much. I checked the date on the bottle—over three months ago. So nobody was likely to miss a few pills if I took them.

Feeling half-sick with fear and guilt, I opened the bottle and shook all but four pills into my hand, then dropped the pills into my purse, replaced the bottle in the cabinet, and hurried to catch up with my group.

Later, when I emptied my purse onto the bed and transferred each pill into one of my own prescription bottles, I knew I'd crossed a line that day. Though I told myself taking something someone wasn't even using—something I really needed—wasn't really wrong, I knew what I'd done was stealing.

And part of me knew that I did it because I couldn't get by any longer without the painkillers. I was an addict, though the label seemed absurd. Addicts were young thugs who stole cars and held up convenience stores to get money to buy crack and heroin. I was a suburban wife and mother. I had a bad back. I needed my medication.

117

And after all, I was taking medication prescribed by a doctor. Surely that made it all right.

Once I discovered how easy it was to get pills for free in other people's houses, I started a regular routine of visiting real estate open houses every weekend. I told my husband I went to get ideas for decorating, but at the first opportunity, I'd pop into the master bathroom and search the medicine cabinet. Over half the time I'd find some kind of pain pill. It was really amazing how common those drugs were.

I'd developed a tolerance to the most common strengths of medication. I had to take twice as many pills to feel the euphoria I craved. Even the medication I stole from open houses wasn't enough.

About this time, my friends and family noticed something was wrong. Whenever I ran out of medication, I'd become edgy, impatient, and snapping at everyone. One night when Lexie started bugging me about a new pair of boots she wanted, I lost it.

"I told you no and I meant it," I shouted, grabbing her by the shoulders and shaking her.

Lexie stared up at me, eyes wide and terrified. "Mom! You're hurting me!"

I choked off a cry and pushed her away from me, then ran down the hall and into my bedroom. I sat on the bed and hugged my arms tightly around me, trying to stop the shaking. What was happening to me?

Sam appeared in the doorway, his face full of concern. "Carrie, what's going on?" he asked.

I shook my head, unable to look at him. "I just—it's this pain in my back. It's hard to be pleasant when I'm hurting so much."

He sat beside me and rubbed my shoulder. "It's still hurting you after all this time? What does the doctor say?"

I shook my head. "There's nothing they can do."

"Maybe you should try another course of physical therapy."

"No. It didn't help me the first time." Actually, I'd only gone to two of the prescribed eight visits. I figured I didn't need therapy as long as I had the pills.

"Why don't you lie down?" Sam kissed my cheek. "I'll finish fixing dinner."

I nodded. "Tell Lexie I didn't mean to yell at her."

"I will. Now you get some rest."

But without my pills, I felt as if I'd never rest again. I got up and began searching through drawers, hoping to find a single pill. Anything to ease this horrible feeling.

All I found were a couple of empty pill bottles. One for Vicodin and one for OxyContin. They were from two different doctors, filled at two different pharmacies. I read the labels, noticing the doctors' license numbers on each. Just last month, I'd waited at a doctor's office while the receptionist called in my prescription. She'd read off the doctor's license number and the directions on the prescription and that was that.

I felt the same nervous excitement I'd experienced on the historic homes tour the day I found that bottle of pills in the powder room. My heart pounding, I crossed the room to the phone and carefully lifted the receiver. Sam and Lexie would be in the kitchen, preparing dinner, so they wouldn't hear me.

I dialed the number to the first pharmacy. When the pharmacist answered, I spoke in my best "professional" voice. "This is Marlo from Dr. Rieber's office. I have a prescription refill for Carrie Anson. OxyContin. Thirty tablets with one refill." I read the directions. Then the pharmacist asked for the doctor's DEA number. I read off the numbers on the bottle.

"Will there be anything else?" the pharmacist asked.

"No, thank you."

"We'll get this right out, then. Thanks."

"Thank you." I hung up the phone and stared at it, a giddy happiness swirling through me. I'd done it. With any luck, I wouldn't have to worry about getting new prescriptions again.

While I was still feeling so confident, I called the second pharmacy and refilled the Vicodin. I couldn't believe it was so easy!

The next morning, I picked up both new prescriptions, and then visited a couple of real estate open houses. I had a close call at the second house, when the agent walked in just as I was closing the medicine cabinet door.

"What are you doing?" he asked, his voice sharp.

I forced a pleasant smile onto my face. "I think it's important for a medicine cabinet to have adjustable shelves, don't you?" I said.

Before he could answer, I walked past him, still smiling. I made myself stay in the house half an hour longer, asking all kinds of questions about closet space and energy efficiency. I felt the agent watching me, but I ignored him. I acted as if I was a perfectly innocent housewife interested in finding a new family home.

I progressed from calling in my own refills to half a dozen pharmacies to calling in new prescriptions to pharmacies further away. If anyone questioned me, I made up a story about a vacationing patient who needed the pills.

By that time, I'd reached the maximum limit on my credit card. I couldn't afford to pay more than the minimum balance each month, and interest charges added up, but I told myself I'd eventually get everything paid off. Meanwhile, new credit card offers continued to arrive in the mail, so I opened a second charge account and began a new round of visiting doctors and emergency rooms.

One Sunday evening I told Sam I was going to a meeting at church and I headed for an emergency room in the city. Though I knew I'd have to wait several hours to be seen, I knew from experience that my tale of a terrible migraine would get me a new prescription for pain pills, and maybe even some free samples.

I was sitting in the waiting room trying to look miserable when a young man sat down next to me.

"You look like you don't feel so well," he said.

I nodded. "I have a terrible migraine."

He nodded. "My sister gets those sometimes. She says her doctor gives her something called Oxy something or other and it really helps."

"OxyContin. Yes, it works very well."

He leaned forward, elbows on his knees, and lowered his voice. "If you don't want to wait around here, I know where you can get OxyContin. No prescription."

I stared at him. He was a good-looking, clean-cut young man in jeans and a T-shirt. Not my idea of a drug dealer. "Um, suppose I was interested," I said. "How much?"

"Eight dollars."

"For how much?"

"One pill."

I gasped. "That's outrageous!"

He straightened, still not looking at me. "You want to wait around here, risk getting caught, that's okay with me."

I glanced around the room. The hospital was really busy that night. I could be there hours. Then what if the doctor refused to give me anything? Or wanted to give me a shot and send me home without a prescription? I mentally added up my cash. I only had about a hundred dollars on me.

"Can I have a dozen?" I asked.

The young man grinned. "Sure." He stood. "I'll go out first. You follow in a little bit and go to your car. I'll follow you there."

So that was how I began buying drugs on the street. I still used my other sources, but about once a week or so I met the young man, Bobby, and bought a dozen pills or so.

My life revolved around the pills now: how many I had left, when I could safely take another one, where I could get more. I stopped seeing most of my friends, lost interest in my hobbies, and felt cut off from everyone and everything. I existed in a fog, craving the high the drugs gave me, feeling listless and flat the rest of the time.

Lexie was fifteen, a difficult age for a girl, especially if she feels like her mother isn't there for her. She no longer came to me for help with her homework. I told myself it was because she'd reached a point where Mom wasn't much help. After all, I didn't know much about chemistry or advanced algebra. But the truth was, I'd become a stranger to my daughter. I no longer knew her friends or what was going on in her life because I was too involved with drugs to care to ask.

As for Sam, he and I had drifted apart as well. The drugs dulled my sex drive until I seldom felt like making love. When we did have sex, I was numb, going through the motions. I pleaded the pain in my back as an excuse, but Sam had heard this for so long, he was no longer sympathetic.

"If your back still bothers you, you should see another doctor," he said. "There must be something they can do."

But by then, even I knew there was nothing anyone could do to help me. I was an addict. Without my pills, I could no longer function.

I occasionally roused myself out of a stupor enough to make an effort with my family. When Sam asked me to accompany him to a dinner party his company was hosting for an important client, I eagerly agreed. I bought a new dress, had my hair done, and did everything I could do to make the evening a success.

Before we left for the restaurant where the dinner was being held, I took a Vicodin and an OxyContin. In the car on the way there, I felt the familiar warm rush from the drugs and smiled.

Sam glanced at me. "You must be feeling better tonight," he said.

I leaned over and kissed his cheek. "I feel great," I said.

He smiled. "I'm glad."

I was at my most charming that evening, mingling with Sam's coworkers and their spouses, smiling, and chatting. The drugs rushed through me, so I felt invincible. I loved everyone and I was sure they loved me.

I had a glass of wine before dinner, and more wine with the meal. Everything tasted delicious, and I scarcely noticed the waiters refilling my glass. At one point, I leaned toward Sam and whispered, "I think I'm getting a little tipsy."

He grinned. "I'm just trying to get you drunk and take advantage of you."

I giggled and drained the last of my glass. "I have to go to the little girls' room," I whispered. "I'll be right back."

The room spun when I stood and I had to steady myself on the back of my chair, but I somehow managed to walk, slowly and carefully, across the room.

The ladies' room was empty. I stared at my reflection in the mirror, trying to focus, then sank into a chair. The room was spinning again, and I felt sick to my stomach.

I really shouldn't have had all that wine, I thought, and tried to stand. I needed to make it to the toilet before I was sick all over myself.

I struggled to my feet and then pitched forward, onto the floor, falling into blackness.

I don't remember any of what happened next, but Sam tells me the company president's wife walked into the bathroom and found me sprawled on the tile, unconscious. When she couldn't rouse me, she called Sam, and he had the restaurant call an ambulance. Everyone was appropriately horrified and sympathetic, though I heard later that more than one thought I'd passed out "dead drunk."

At the hospital, the doctors diagnosed a drug overdose. When they broke the news to Sam, he denied it. "That's impossible," he said. "My wife isn't an addict."

But of course, I was. I was as hooked as any street junkie addicted to heroin. The drugs I craved were supposedly legal, most of them obtained by prescription. But I'd reached the point where they controlled every aspect of my life. They almost destroyed my family and me in the process.

When I was admitted to the hospital that night, I was close to death. How close I wouldn't know until later, but when I woke, it was with an angry doctor hovering over me.

"Are you going to let drugs kill you next time?" he asked. "Or are you going to do something about it?"

I don't think the doctor would've made much of an impression on me if it hadn't been for Sam and Lexie standing behind him. One look at their grief-stricken faces and I realized how much I'd almost lost.

I broke down into tears and they both came and put their arms around me. "I'm sorry." I sobbed. "I'm so ashamed."

"It's okay," Sam hugged me close. "We're going to help you get over this."

"The doctor says there's a program you can go into," Lexie said. "A treatment center."

I looked at her. Her eyes were red and swollen. It hurt so much to know she'd been crying for me.

"I'll do it," I said. "I won't let you down." I looked at Sam. "I won't let either of you down again."

That afternoon, I checked into the drug treatment facility that would be my home for the next eight weeks. There I met others like me: a nurse who worked in a doctor's office, where access to drug samples made it easy for her to feed her addiction; a grandmother who'd started taking pain pills following a hysterectomy and hadn't been able to stop; a rodeo cowboy who bought drugs from a dealer to mask the pain of his many injuries. Every one of us had become addicted to drugs we initially thought of as safe, because a doctor prescribed them.

I learned a lot in the treatment center, about addiction, and about myself. I learned that though the pain from the back injury had put me on the path to addiction, my own insecurities had kept me there. I had been at a vulnerable point in my life, with a daughter who was growing up and didn't need me as much, and a restlessness about what I was going to do with the rest of my life.

"Some people are more prone to addiction than others, for whatever reason," the counselor told me. "But you can beat this."

Sam and Lexie visited every weekend. They brought me flowers and candy and tried hard to be cheerful and encouraging. But I knew seeing me in this place was hard for them. Especially Lexie.

"I am going to get better," I told her on one of her visits. "I'll be home soon."

When I came home after eight weeks, I was five pounds thinner and a lot more fragile feeling. Stepping back into my old life was like wearing shoes that were a size too big. It wasn't comfortable, but I was determined to make it work.

The counselors at the treatment center had cautioned against sitting around the house all day, so I signed up for classes at the local community college four days a week. When I wasn't in class, I was studying or taking care of the house.

On Fridays, I went for physical therapy for my back. This time, I was determined to listen to the therapist and do whatever it took to get better.

And I did get better. As I worked to strengthen the muscles in my back, and to learn to handle the stress that made the pain worse, I began to feel better.

Which isn't to say that I didn't struggle. I did. There were times when I would actually have the phone in my hand, ready to call in another prescription. But then I'd think about Sam and Lexie, and I'd lay down the receiver and go for a walk. I walked miles in those first weeks, trying to get away from the craving that hounded me.

One morning I was looking through the paper when I came across a picture of Bobby. He'd just been arrested for dealing prescription drugs, along with a man who'd been at his apartment making a buy when the police busted in. A cold chill washed over me as I stared at the photo. That could've been me going to jail with Bobby.

Later, I cut out the article and photo and tucked them in the bottom of my dresser drawer. Whenever I felt my resolve weakening, I'd take them out and look at them to remind myself of how close to the edge I'd come.

It's been almost two years now since I passed out on that ladies' room floor. Two years of struggle and celebration. Lexie is seventeen now, a senior in high school. This spring, she'll graduate with honors and I'm thankful every day that I'm alive to be there.

Sam and I will celebrate our twentieth wedding anniversary next month. We're planning a trip to the coast to celebrate. Knowing that he stood by me when it would've been easier to walk away, I love him all the more.

I'm still taking classes, working toward my psychology degree. I hope to get work as a counselor after graduation, helping other men and women like myself. My struggle against addiction is easier these days. I have so many positive things in my life now I don't feel the need for that artificial high as often. I've learned to meditate and practice yoga to help me cope with the stresses of life and the normal aches and pains of growing older.

Looking back on the past five years, I can't believe some of the things I've done. The lies I told. The thefts. The laws I broke. And the hurt I caused the ones I loved. I'm so grateful I got a second chance.

THE END

MY BROTHER'S BATTLE
WITH BREAST CANCER
It's not just a woman's disease

"Sit down, Joanne," Jordan said. "I have something to tell you." We were in the kitchen of my apartment, and I was about to pour myself a cup of much-needed coffee. I knew from looking at my brother's face that it was bad news.

Of course, I'd already figured out something was wrong, since it was unusual for Jordan to visit me so early in the morning. It was Sunday, and I hadn't even dressed yet. He'd literally gotten me out of bed when he rang the doorbell.

I put the coffee pot aside and sat down at the small table across from him. "What is it?" I asked hesitantly.

Jordan didn't answer right away. Instead, he rubbed his hands over his face. "Do you remember me telling you that I had a physical?"

I nodded. But a physical exam wasn't unusual in Jordan's line of work. Since he was a construction worker, his company often required him to take physicals before he started a new project.

"Did they find something wrong?" I wanted to know.

"Yes." And that was all he said for several long moments.

I reached across the table and put my hand over his. "What is it?" But I was already starting to imagine the worst. My God, does he have some fatal disease? I just couldn't believe that. Jordan was the only family I had left since our parents had died three years earlier in a car accident. If anything happened to him, I didn't think I could handle it.

"It's cancer," he finally said.

I felt every muscle in my body go stiff. My heart slammed against my chest. "My God. Cancer. But you're so young." And he was. Jordan was only twenty-six, barely a year older than I was.

A million thoughts went through my head, but the foremost was denial. The test was wrong. Jordan looked healthy, and they must've mixed up his results with someone else's. My brother just couldn't have cancer.

"There's more," he continued. He kept his eyes focused on the table. "It's breast cancer."

I was certain that I had misunderstood him. Breast cancer? Men didn't get that, only women. I blew out a breath of relief. "Then the tests are wrong. You couldn't possibly have breast cancer."

My relief was short-lived. Jordan set me straight right away.

125

"That's exactly what it is. The doctor explained that men have mammary glands, and they can become cancerous just like they can in a woman." He paused. "I wish it were lung cancer or something else. Anything else. I don't want to have to explain to everyone that I have breast cancer. Can you imagine the jokes people will make about it?"

"No one will joke about you having cancer," I assured him.

But what if they did? After all, it wasn't a macho-sounding disease. And there wouldn't be a way to keep it a secret, either. In our small hometown of Jackson, Mississippi, news traveled fast. Especially bad news. People might be cruel and not remember just how dangerous this could be for Jordan. He hadn't said so, but I suspected this could kill him.

Because I didn't know what else to do, I got up and poured myself a cup of coffee. I offered Jordan one, but he declined. I took several long sips before I spoke again. "So, what can the doctors do about it?"

"I'll have to have surgery. A mastectomy of sorts. They'll cut out the lump and the surrounding tissue. Then I'll have to go through chemotherapy."

I had to sit down and try to absorb all the information. This just couldn't be happening. I couldn't get over the fact that my brother looked healthy. He still had his muscular build and tanned complexion. He always reminded me of the type of man who should be on one of those pin-up calendars. He definitely didn't look sick.

"When will they do the surgery?" I managed to ask.

"Tomorrow morning."

"My God," I whispered. "So soon." I put my coffee aside and pulled Jordan into my arms. I tried not to, but I started to cry.

"I knew this would upset you." He held me tight, and I realized he was actually comforting me. That shouldn't have been happening. Jordan was the one who had cancer, and I should have been consoling him. I knew I'd have to somehow find the strength to help him get through this.

A few minutes later, I wiped away my tears. I caught onto his shoulders so I could look him straight in the eye. "What can I do to help?"

"I have to tell Cassidy," he answered softly.

Cassidy was Jordan's girlfriend. They'd been dating nearly six months. I knew it was serious between them, and they'd even talked about getting married. I also knew that Jordan was very much in love with her.

"I don't know how she's going to feel about this," Jordan added.

Neither did I. Cassidy was only twenty-one and could get very emotional about things. Once she had cried for hours because she'd hit a bird while she was driving. I knew it wouldn't be easy for Jordan to tell her or for Cassidy to hear the news.

"Could you come with me when I tell her?" Jordan asked.

I didn't even have to think about it. "Of course. When do you want to do it?"

"I should get it over with. I'm supposed to check into the hospital tonight."

"Let me get dressed," I told him. "And we can go see Cassidy. I'll call my boss this afternoon and tell him that I need tomorrow off. I want to be there when you have the surgery."

Jordan only nodded, but I could tell from his expression that it was what he wanted me to say. He didn't want to go through this alone, and I'd make sure I was with him every step of the way.

"You'll get through this," I assured him. I guess I was also trying to reassure myself.

I realized, though, that I didn't see any such reassurance in his eyes. It sent an icy chill through me. He could be facing death. And I wasn't sure either of us had the strength to face it.

I watched Cassidy's usually vibrant face turn ashy pale. Fortunately, Jordan had insisted that we all sit down on the sofa at her father's house. If Cassidy hadn't been seated, she probably would've fainted.

"Breast cancer," she repeated. She drew in a hard breath and shook her head. "But how can that be? Men don't get breast cancer."

It was a question that I wished Cassidy hadn't asked. I wondered if Jordan would be faced with this same question from everyone he told. It made my heart ache for him.

Jordan explained to her what he'd already told me. Without saying a word, Cassidy listened. By the time he had finished, there were tears streaming down her cheeks. I waited for Cassidy to put her arms around him, but she didn't. She just sat there and stared at him.

"They'll do the surgery in the morning," I added to Jordan's explanation. "You can ride with me. I can pick you up on my way to the hospital."

Frantically, Cassidy shook her head. "I can't go. I have to work."

That wasn't what I'd expected her to say at all, and judging from Jordan's stunned expression, he hadn't expected it, either. "I'm sure your boss will understand that you need the day off," I quickly told Cassidy.

She bolted to her feet. "No, you don't understand! I can't go through this again. I just can't. My mother died from breast cancer when I was twelve. I won't go through that again."

I hadn't known about Cassidy's mother. Cassidy and her father had moved to Jackson just three years earlier. Of course, I knew her mother was not alive, but I didn't know she had died from breast cancer. I shivered. Women died from breast cancer every day. Would I lose my brother, too?

"I should go," I whispered to Jordan. "The two of you need some time alone so you can talk this out."

"I can't talk about this!" Cassidy snapped before I could leave. Both of her cheeks were wet from her tears. "Don't you see? I can't talk about this. Ever."

Since it didn't seem as if Jordan intended to say anything, I caught onto Cassidy's hand. I had to make her understand. I had to make her see that she needed to put her own pain aside and be there for Jordan.

"Cassidy, I did some reading last night about breast cancer. Jordan's chances are good that he'll make a full recovery. But he needs to stay positive. We all need to stay positive and strong. That's the best thing we can do for Jordan right now."

"I can't," Cassidy repeated. "I just can't." She ran out of the room, leaving Jordan and me there alone.

"She took her mother's death real hard," I heard Cassidy's father say. I didn't even know that he'd overheard our conversation, but he must've. He walked out of the hallway and into the room where we were. He placed his hand on Jordan's shoulder. "Just give her some time. She'll come around when she's thought all of this through."

Jordan nodded, but I wondered if he believed it. Was time all that Cassidy needed, or was she deserting my brother when he needed her most? It actually made me furious. My brother might die, and Cassidy couldn't get past her own hurt to support him.

That night, Jordan stopped by my apartment. We'd agreed that I'd drive him to the hospital since we didn't know how long he would have to stay. He'd even agreed to come back to my place when he was released. That way I would be able to take care of him. I'd still have to go to work, but at least he wouldn't be alone at night.

"Did you get a chance to talk to Cassidy again today?" I asked Jordan as I drove to the hospital.

He leaned his head against the window and stared outside. I couldn't remember ever seeing him so depressed. He was facing the biggest challenge of his life.

"Cassidy called me this afternoon," he answered. "She broke things off between us."

I clutched the steering wheel so tightly that my knuckles turned white. I wanted to scream at Cassidy for breaking up with him at a time like this. What kind of person could do something so cruel? I understood her pain over losing her mother, but I'd lost my mother, too. So had Jordan. It hadn't made us incapable of handling anyone else's suffering.

"Well, maybe Cassidy will change her mind," I said only to comfort Jordan.

But I realized I didn't want her to change her mind. She had let him down at the worst possible time. Maybe it was for the best that she was no longer in his life. Maybe in time Jordan would be able to get over her. Too bad he'd have to be battling cancer and chemo at the same time. It just wasn't fair.

"I'm scared," Jordan mumbled.

A lump swelled in my throat. I'd promised myself I wouldn't cry again in front of him. I wanted to be strong, but those two words had me fighting back tears. Jordan had always been the strong one. He was my big brother in every sense. Now he was scared, and there was nothing, absolutely nothing, that I could do about it.

"I know you are," I answered. "I'm scared, too."

He closed his eyes. "I'm not afraid of dying."

A ragged sob tore from my throat. "Jordan—"

"Just let me finish. I don't want to die, but that's not what scares me the most. I just don't want to waste away. I don't want to be stuck in some bed for months and months, so strung out on painkillers that I don't even know who I am. That's not living, and I don't think I could handle it."

I wanted to tell Jordan that wouldn't happen, but it would've been a hollow reassurance. Both of us knew that something like that could very well happen. Cancer patients didn't always recover, and they didn't always have an easy time of it if they did beat the disease.

We didn't say anything else on the drive to the hospital. There were no reassurances I could give Jordan. No words that would ease the pain that either of us felt. I could only promise myself that I'd be there for him, no matter what the outcome of the surgery.

Jordan checked into the hospital, and I stayed with him until visiting hours were over. It didn't seem right that I couldn't stay the night, but hospital policy prevented it.

"I'll be back first thing in the morning," I let Jordan know.

He nodded and gave my hand a squeeze. "Get some sleep," he told me.

It was an impossible request, but I gave Jordan a reassuring smile. "You do the same. I love you."

I started to go, but he called to me. "Joanne, you don't have to do this, you know."

Clutching my purse to my chest, I slowly turned back toward him. "What do you mean?"

"You don't have to pretend this isn't eating away at you," he said almost in a whisper.

Yes, I did. If I spilled out all of my fears to him, then Jordan would end up comforting me again. I didn't want that to happen. He needed his strength and emotions for his own battle, and I didn't want him to waste one bit of it on me.

I walked closer. "Remember when we were kids, and you beat up Craig Ellsford because he was teasing me?"

129

Jordan huffed out a frustrated breath. "Joanne, that happened nearly fifteen years ago."

"But you remember it," I insisted. "Well, so do I. I never did pay you back for that, so let's consider this partial payment." I forced myself to smile. "Besides, you're my brother as well as being an occasional pain in the butt. I'm allowed to let this eat away at me if I want to."

I barely made it to my car before I started crying. Despite Jordan's insistence that I didn't have to be strong, I knew that I did. I wanted him to be able to feed off my strength and love. But more than anything, I just wanted him to be all right.

I sat in the car and prayed.

Time crawled by while Jordan was in surgery. Every time a doctor or nurse walked by me, I jumped out of my chair, wondering if they were there to give me news. Fortunately, Jordan's friend, Tony, was there also, so I didn't have to wait alone.

I finally got up enough nerve to ask Tony something that I'd been wanting to ask since I first heard about Jordan's condition. Tony was Jordan's closest friend, and I thought he would tell me the truth. "Have any of the workers at the construction site said anything about Jordan's cancer?"

Tony shrugged. "There's been some talk."

I could only guess what kind of talk that had been. "I don't want them making fun of him," I said firmly. "And I don't want any of that kind of talk getting back to Jordan."

"Trust me, it won't."

I looked at Tony. Describing him as burly was an understatement. He was well over six feet tall and probably weighed over two hundred and fifty pounds. People didn't usually mess around with Tony, and I knew if he heard any unkind remarks that he'd put a stop to them.

"Thanks," I said to him. "It's just after Cassidy dumped him, I don't want Jordan to have to go through anything else like that."

"Believe me, I understand. But I think Cassidy will come around. She's crazy about Jordan."

I wasn't sure of that. After all, she wasn't at the hospital, and he was in surgery. How much could she care about him if she didn't even bother to show up?

Several hours later, the doctor came out and said the operation was over and that Jordan was doing as well as could be expected. The doctor explained that the lump was small, and they'd been able to remove it.

"Will he . . . " But I couldn't finish my question. I wanted him to tell me if Jordan was going to live.

The doctor must've understood because he answered me. "There are no guarantees with cancer, but we caught it early, and he's young and otherwise healthy. Your brother has the best possible chance of making it."

The best possible chance. That was even better than I'd hoped for. Of course it didn't mean that all was well, but it was the start that I had prayed for.

"Can I see him?" I asked the doctor.

"He's in recovery right now, but you should be able to go in soon."

Thankfully, Tony waited with me because those next few hours seemed to last forever. Finally, they let me see Jordan. He looked very weak, but I had to believe he'd get better now that the cancer was out of his body.

"I love you," I told him.

At first I wasn't sure he understood me, but I realized he had when he gave me a thin smile. I hoped there'd be many more smiles in the future, but I knew there'd be rough times ahead as well. Jordan would have to start chemotherapy. That would probably be harder on his body than the actual surgery.

Still, my brother was alive, and I had to be thankful for that. We'd deal with the rest one day at a time.

When Jordan was released from the hospital, he moved into my apartment. The chemo made his hair fall out, and he always seemed exhausted. Even with all his symptoms, however, he couldn't wait to get back to work. It was all he talked about.

"Don't push it," I warned him. "Just take your time and get better."

But I knew that was easier said than done. It wasn't long before Jordan became irritable and bored. That didn't surprise me. He'd always led an active life, and it was hard for him to stay around my apartment doing nothing.

I figured he was also irritable about the way Cassidy had reacted to his cancer. During his entire hospital stay, she hadn't come to visit him even once. She hadn't even called. I hated that she was able to hurt him that way. It made me try even harder to make his life easier.

One day, I came home from work and found Cassidy standing outside my door. I started to tell her she wasn't welcome, but the haunted look in her eyes made me hold my tongue. She looked as if she'd had as rough a time as Jordan.

"Why are you here, Cassidy?" I asked when she didn't say anything.

"I want to see Jordan."

That alarmed me a little, not because she wanted to see him, but because he should've answered the door. I prayed nothing was wrong with him. "He should be inside. Didn't he answer the doorbell?"

She shook her head. "I didn't ring it. I've been standing out here trying to figure out what to say to him."

131

I breathed a little easier, but not for long. I couldn't let her go in there and hurt him again. Jordan already had enough to deal with. "Listen, Cassidy, Jordan has been through a lot—"

"I know," she interrupted. "And it's all my fault." She started to cry. I noticed they weren't her first tears of the day. Her eyes were already red, and she had a wadded-up tissue in her hand.

"Well, it's not all your fault." But Cassidy sure hadn't made things easier for him. I tried to be polite, but just the sight of her made me angry. "Jordan's been through a lot with the surgery and chemo. He's tired, and he needs a lot of rest."

Cassidy started to bite her bottom lip. "I didn't plan to stay long," she quickly assured me. "I just didn't want him to think I didn't love him."

I nearly laughed. "Cassidy, how can you say you love him when you weren't even around when he needed you?"

That only made her cry harder. "I know, I know. What I did was awful. It's just that all of this is too hard for me to deal with."

It definitely wasn't the right thing to say to me. "And you don't think this was hard for Jordan?" I practically yelled. "You don't have a clue what he's been through because you weren't even around. My God, you broke up with him just hours before he had surgery!"

"But I love him." Cassidy sobbed.

"You don't even know what love is. It sure isn't running away just because things aren't perfect." I put my hands on each side of my head and groaned. "Just leave. There's no way I'm letting you get to Jordan again."

I went inside and slammed the door behind me so hard that the pictures shook on the wall. Jordan was in the living room, just a few feet away, and I could tell from his expression that he'd heard everything I'd said to Cassidy.

"I lost my temper." I tossed my purse onto the coffee table. "She just made me so mad."

He made it to me in one step and pulled me into his arms. "You can't let her get to you this way."

"I know."

I was already starting to feel guilty for yelling at Cassidy, not because I'd hurt her feelings, but because I'd no doubt upset Jordan. I should've just gone inside without saying a word and left her standing on the steps.

"She said she loves you," I mumbled.

If Jordan had a reaction to that, he didn't show it. He just continued to hold me.

"And she wanted to talk to you," I added in case he hadn't heard that part.

132

"You don't have to fight my battles for me, you know."

I pulled back and looked him straight in the eye. "I'm not doing that. Exactly."

The corner of his mouth lifted slightly. "That's exactly what you're doing. Now, don't get me wrong, you've been great through all of this, and I'll never be able to thank you—"

"I don't need your thanks. I'm your sister. I love you, and I just want you to get well."

"I am getting well," he reminded me quickly. "You're partly responsible for that. And whether you need to hear the words or not, I do want to say thank you for standing by me the way you have."

Jordan rubbed his thumb over my cheek, and it was only then that I realized he was wiping away a tear. I hadn't even known I was crying.

"Why do I get the feeling there's a 'but' at the end of your sentence?" I asked.

"Because there is." He paused. "Remember when I told you I wasn't afraid of dying?"

I nodded. He'd said that the day I drove him to the hospital.

"Well, I was," he admitted. "I was scared out of my mind. But then I made it through the surgery and the chemo, and I had to stop worrying about dying and concentrate on living again. Easier said than done."

"Things will get back to normal soon," I assured him.

"That's just it. I don't want to settle for plain old normal again. I want things to be better than they were. We're off to a good start. We're closer than ever. And all of this has made me realize what a special bond we have." He chuckled softly. "And don't you dare tell anyone I said that. It'll make me sound like a genuine wuss."

I laughed despite the fact I was still crying.

"You have to let me take chances," Jordan continued. "You have to let me fight my own battles."

The laughter stopped as quickly as it'd come. "Do those battles include Cassidy?"

"Especially her. There are a lot of things between Cassidy and me that are unsettled."

It made me ache to hear him say that. I still wanted to protect him from her, but that obviously wasn't what Jordan wanted.

"So, what do you want me to do?" I asked.

"How you deal with Cassidy is up to you."

I swallowed hard, afraid to hear his answer to my next question. "And how will you deal with her?"

Jordan shrugged. "I'm not sure yet. But I didn't fight this disease so I could go through life with blinders on. Or so I could put off living, and that includes the good with the bad."

133

He brushed a kiss on my cheek and smiled. "So, no more fighting my battles, okay?"

I nodded. But I wondered if I could truly do what Jordan had asked. It would mean getting past the fear of losing him, and I wasn't sure I was capable of doing that.

The following morning, the doorbell rang. Somehow, I knew it was Cassidy before I even answered it. I was right. She was standing on the doorstep.

"Don't tell me to go," she started.

I wanted to. I wanted to shut the door right in her face. But I didn't. I stood there and stared at her.

"Jordan's still in bed," I let her know, hoping that she'd get the hint and leave.

"I need to talk to him. And you."

I wasn't sure I could hear what she had to say, but then I remembered the conversation I'd had with Jordan the night before. He was right about one thing—we both had some unresolved issues with Cassidy. Maybe it was time to try to resolve them.

"I came to say I'm sorry," Cassidy said softly. She shook her head and pushed her hand through her hair. "I just couldn't stand the thought of watching Jordan die the way my mother did."

Cassidy had said almost the same words before, the day that Jordan told her that he had cancer. Her words had made me angry then, but I didn't want that anger to take over this time.

"I'm not strong like you are," Cassidy continued.

"I'm not strong," I assured her. "I just did what I had to do."

She nodded. "And I didn't. For the rest of my life, I'll have to live with the fact that I let Jordan down."

Her bottom lip trembled, and her tears were a steady stream. I knew this was no act. Cassidy was in as much pain as I was.

I put my arm around her. "Jordan isn't going to die. The doctors say his chances are excellent for beating this. He's already had a great checkup."

She looked at me. "You're not just saying that?"

"No." I paused. "But there could still be tough times ahead. His chemo isn't over, and it'll be years before we know for sure that the cancer won't return."

"That's what I figured."

"Did you also figure you'd walk out on him again if things don't go exactly the way you plan?" I hadn't intended to say that so bluntly, but I was glad I did. I didn't want Cassidy to go inside and see Jordan unless she was sure she could face what was going on in his life— everything in his life, especially the cancer.

"I love him," she finally said. "And I want him to forgive me."

"You won't break his heart again?"

134

She didn't even hesitate. "No. I know how awful I've been. I swear it won't happen again. Over these last few weeks I've realized how miserable I am without Jordan. I know how much he means to me, and I want to be with him for the rest of our lives. We were meant to be together."

I couldn't disagree with that. Before this incident with Jordan's cancer, I had believed they were truly in love with each other.

"Go in and talk to him," I said, stepping aside. "But if he tells you to go, then that's what I want you to do."

She nodded and slowly walked inside. I didn't go in with her, but I listened in case Jordan needed me.

I heard them talk for a while. Once Jordan even raised his voice. But after they talked for nearly a half hour, they ended up in each other's arms. I glanced inside and could see how happy they were. Jordan was actually smiling in between the kisses he was showering on Cassidy. I found myself smiling, too. I didn't know if things would actually work out between them, but I knew this was a good start.

It's been nearly a year since Jordan's surgery, and the cancer hasn't returned. I know he and Cassidy are happy. They're planning their wedding.

And as for Jordan and me, we've never been closer. I suppose when I almost lost him, I realized just how important he was to me. I think he found out the same thing, and he knows he can count on me no matter what.

THE END

THE PAIN THAT
ONLY LOVE CAN HEAL

Sweat drenched my nightgown as I awakened, screaming. Breathing heavily, I gazed at my alarm clock. It was one in the morning and the familiar nightmare haunted me. Still shivering, I got out of bed and walked to the kitchen to fix some hot chocolate. As I placed the mug into the microwave, I thought about my past. It had been years, but I still couldn't shake the ugliness. I had tried to put it behind me, but it continued to creep into my life.

So right after I graduated from high school, I left home. I hadn't spoken to my mother or stepfather since.

The microwave beeped, and the phone rang at the same time. I answered the phone as I removed the cup from the microwave. "Hello?"

"Nancy?" The deep voice of Reese Bolton, a man I'd recently started dating, made my fear melt away.

"Reese? Why are you calling me in the middle of the night?"

"I just wanted to hear your voice." He paused. "I had a dream about you. You were wearing that pretty yellow dress and you were standing in a field, the sun shining on." He chuckled softly.

As Reese continued to tell me about his dream, I knew that I would not have the courage to tell him about the dream that I'd had earlier that night.

"Nancy? Are you even listening to me?"

"I'm sorry, Reese. I guess I'm just kind of tired." My hands shook as I continued to sip my cocoa. At least talking to Reese was helping me to feel better.

"Nancy, I still don't know you too well, but, sometimes, you act like you've got a lot on your mind."

I sighed, finishing my drink. "It's just your imagination. I'm fine. Things have just been stressful at work," I lied.

"Oh, okay. Well, I guess I'll see you tomorrow?"

I placed the cup in the sink and returned to my bedroom. "Yes, I'm looking forward to visiting that special bakery you told me about."

"Good night, Nancy. I'll see you at two o'clock tomorrow."

"Good night," I said as I hung up the phone. I thought about Reese's friendly smile. Being with him felt so nice. When we were together, I forgot all about my stepfather's abuse.

The next day, I wore my favorite dress. Reese appeared at my door, bearing a bouquet of yellow roses.

"Hi, Nancy."

He kissed my cheek, handing me the flowers. "Reese, these are nice!" I placed my nose in the roses and sniffed. "And they smell good, too." I placed the flowers in a vase and filled it with water.

A half hour later, we entered the bakery. "Reese, this is such a cozy place!" We ordered hot cinnamon rolls and two coffees. As we munched on our desserts, he took held my hand.

"Nancy, I was wondering about something."

"What?" I took a bite of the delicious roll.

"I wanted to invite you to come to my church with me tomorrow." My heart skipped a beat as I dropped my roll on the plate. I pulled my hand away.

"Reese, I don't think I can go to church with you tomorrow, I'm sorry."

"Why?"

I shook my head. "I don't go to church."

The thought of God, forsaking me, filled me with anger. If God existed, why did he allow those awful things to happen to me?

"Nancy?" I didn't realize I was crying until his fingers brushed my cheek, wiping away my tears. "Nancy, what's the matter?"

I gazed at Reese. His dark eyes were full of sympathy, and I knew he wanted to help.

"It's hard for me to talk about this."

He placed his hand over mine. "Nancy, I've sensed that you have something heavy on your mind. Please share it with me."

I sighed as I stared at our hands. He rubbed his fingers over my palm, and I got a delicious sensation in my arm from his gentle touch. Taking a deep breath, I started talking about my past. I started crying again, and Reese gave me a napkin.

"I just can't stand it, Reese." I sniffed loudly. "My stepfather raped me, made me feel like I was a useless nobody, and my mom didn't believe me when I told her what her new husband had done to me." My voice took on a cruel hard edge. "I hate them. I hate both of them."

"Oh, sweetheart." He took me into his arms. "Nancy, I want to help you with your pain. God wants to help you—"

I pushed him away. "Who cares about God or your dumb church? Where was God when my stepfather was on top of me?"

"Don't talk about it, anymore." He kissed me and stroked my arm. "Come on, let's go for a walk."

I nodded, eager to get out into the warm, sunny day. Reese paid our bill and led me outside.

As we spent the day together, my anger melted away. Reese was kind and patient. A few times, I caught him staring at me. I felt I could fall in love with him, however, I didn't think I could ever trust his God.

When Reese dropped me off at my house, he kissed me again. The crickets chirped, and the stars were bright in the dark sky. "Are you okay, Nancy?"

I nodded, wishing he could spend the rest of the evening with me, talking, and drinking hot chocolate. "I think I'll be okay."

"My invite for tomorrow still stands."

"Reese—"

He placed his fingers over my lips. "Just give it some thought. You don't have to go to church with me tomorrow, but maybe sometime in the future?"

Just to please him, I agreed to give the matter some thought.

During the following week, Reese called me every night, making sure I was okay. The following Saturday, we went to the amusement park. The weather was beautiful, and the wind whipped through my hair as we rode the roller coaster. He held my hand as we stopped at a small theater in the amusement park and watched a show by a well-known comedienne. I laughed so hard at her jokes that my throat ached after the performance.

Afterward, Reese treated me to a nice dinner of steak and baked potato at a nearby small restaurant. When our day ended, Reese drove me home. He pulled into my driveway and cut his ignition. He then held me and buried his nose into my hair.

"You smell so nice, Nancy." He gazed into my eyes, stroking my cheek. "I want you to know that this was one of the best dates I've had in my life."

His kind words brought me comfort and joy. I'd never had a man to say such nice things to me before. Since my stepfather's abuse, I'd sworn off men, that is, until Reese came into my life. I was just starting to realize that I couldn't blame all men for my stepfather's sexual abuse.

"Thanks, Reese." I swallowed as he released me. He took my hands and rubbed his fingers over mine.

"I was wondering if you've given much thought about what I asked you about last week," he asked.

I turned away, staring into the descending darkness outside of the car window. I knew I had to be honest with him, just as I knew he wasn't going to like what I had to say.

"As a matter of fact, I have given the matter some thought." I pulled my hands away from his. "Reese, I can't go to church with you. I just can't."

He frowned and gripped his steering wheel. I touched his hard muscular arm, but my caress failed to give him comfort.

"Nancy, you don't know how much I've been praying for you."

"Praying for me?" I'd never had anyone to pray for me before, that is, not that I knew of.

138

He nodded. "Yes. I want you to open up your heart and trust in the Lord. Just give Him a chance."

My eyes became moist as I recalled how the Lord had forsaken me. "Why should I give Him a chance when He never gave me one?"

He sighed, and his voice suddenly sounded sad and tired. "Have you ever given faith a chance?"

I shook my head.

"Well, the first step is to accept His grace." He released the steering wheel and touched my face. Tingles of pleasure and delight coursed through my skin. When he kissed me, it felt like fireworks were exploding in the sky. "Good-bye, Nancy."

As I exited the car and walked into my house, I sensed that Reese was saying good-bye to me forever. I lifted the curtain and watched his car drive away. I sniffed and wiped away my tears, wondering if I would ever hear from him again. Even though I had only known Reese for a few weeks, I felt in my heart that I was falling in love, but I wasn't sure if he could love me since I didn't share his beliefs.

As I got ready for bed that night, I recalled one of the conversations I'd had with Reese the previous week. He told me to release my bitterness, and then I'd be happier. Should I follow his advice and give God a chance? I didn't think I could open up my heart to the Lord since He had forsaken me.

The next day was Sunday, and my friend Sandie came over for lunch. After we'd eaten our tuna fish sandwiches, we sipped coffee and shared a chocolate cheesecake for dessert.

"Okay, Nancy, how are things between you and Reese?" she asked as she helped herself to another piece of cheesecake. Sandie was kind of chunky, and she loved to eat desserts. Her dark eyes sparkled as she feasted on the sweet treat, awaiting a response.

I toyed with my cheesecake, no longer hungry. I'd found since I'd fallen in love with Reese, my appetite had lessened considerably.

"Reese wants me to go church with him." I pushed my plate away and folded my arms in front of my chest.

She raised her arched eyebrows, still chewing on her dessert. She swallowed and took a sip of coffee before responding. "Are you going to go?"

"Sandie, you know me better than that! I never go to church."

She shrugged, still looking at me. "Well, maybe you should start. I've been inviting you to my church for over two years now, and you have yet to take me up on my offer."

I frowned, gripping my white napkin. I was surprised when Sandie placed her hand on my shoulder. "Hey, I know you have a grudge against God. I don't know what happened to you or why you're hurting, but all I know is that you have to lean on Him in order to make things right."

139

I didn't respond to her as she continued to sip her coffee. I had never told her about my stepfather's abuse. As a matter of fact, Reese was the only person I'd ever told. My stepfather's abuse was so shameful and private. I figured if I told others about my abuse, they would end up saying the whole thing was my fault.

Before Sandie left, she asked if she could take the rest of the cheesecake home with her, so I gave her the rest of the dessert as we said our good-byes.

I didn't hear from Reese all week, and I missed him like crazy! I missed the deep lull of his voice. I missed his twinkling eyes, but most of all, I missed his kisses. His absence from my life was driving me crazy, and I wondered if he had cut me out of his life completely because I did not share his faith in the Lord.

The following weekend, I called Reese on Saturday morning.

"Nancy!" He seemed utterly surprised to hear from me.

"Reese, I—" Suddenly, I couldn't think of what I should say. I decided I should tell him the truth. "Reese, I miss you."

He was quiet for so long, that I wondered if he had heard me. "I miss you, too."

"You do?" I was starting to wonder if I'd only imagined all of the fun we used to have together.

"Yes, I do. It's just that, well, I think I was starting to fall in love with you. But I didn't know if I should get emotionally involved with a woman who didn't share my religious beliefs."

I was shocked that he was so honest with his feelings. "Reese, you know how you invited me to church?"

"Yes."

"Well, I'm willing to come with you tomorrow, if the invite is still open."

"You're always invited to come with me."

"What time is the service?"

"Eleven o'clock. Why don't I pick you up around nine-thirty? I can treat you to breakfast at the pancake house before the service begins."

I agreed but I knew I would feel nervous before church, so I didn't think I would be able to eat a thing before the service.

Reese picked me up at nine-thirty, sharp. He was wearing a charcoal gray business suit and his cologne smelled heavenly. He touched the sleeve of my white dress. "You look pretty."

"Thanks." I smoothed my hands over my dress, pleased that he liked what I was wearing. Both of us were silent as he drove to the pancake house.

After we were seated and had ordered our food, he took my hand. "Nancy, you don't know how much this means to me. I've been praying hard about this all week, and that's why I haven't called you.

140

I didn't want to push you into going to church with me. I wanted you to reach that decision on your own."

The waitress approached and set a plate of steaming hot pancakes in front of Reese and a plate of Belgian waffles in front of me. I didn't respond to his comment as I poured warm syrup over my breakfast.

"Nancy, do you mind if I prayed before we ate?"

Going to church was a huge step for me, but I didn't think I could open up my heart and actually pray to God, too. I hesitated as I set the syrup bottle back onto the table.

He patted my hand. "Never mind. I won't push you to pray if you don't want to. I'm just grateful that you'll be worshipping with me this morning." He bowed his head and said a silent prayer before he sliced his fork through his hotcakes.

I sipped coffee and nibbled on my breakfast, still too nervous to eat.

He looked at my plate. "You're not hungry?"

I shook my head. "Not really."

"Well, you'd better at least try to eat. The service lasts for two hours, and I don't want you to get hungry during the service."

He put his fork aside and caressed my arm. "You look like you've lost weight. Are you all right?"

I quickly shook my head. I didn't want to tell him that his absence from my life had caused me to lose my appetite. As I forced myself to eat some of my waffles, I tried not to think about what would happen between Reese and me. Would I ever be able to accept his God? Would he ever learn to accept me into his life if I never accepted Christ into my life?

"Nancy, what's wrong?" He pushed his empty plate away and signaled the waitress to refill his coffee cup.

"Nothing." I quickly shook my head, not wanting him to know what I had been thinking about. My plate was only half empty, but I just couldn't eat another bite of food. "I'm just a little nervous about coming to church with you. I haven't set foot into a church since I was a little girl." He didn't seem surprised by that fact.

We left the pancake house, and he drove to the church. Voices, raised in harmony, wafted out of the open wooden church doors. A white cross sat on top of the building. As we entered the church, several people came forward giving hugs and kisses to Reese. He introduced me to his church friends, and they embraced me as if they'd known me for years. One of the church sisters even invited me to a midweek Bible study she held in her home. She gave me her phone number and encouraged me to call her if I decided to attend.

My heart pounded as we entered the sanctuary. The wooden pews were filled with parishioners and bright sunlight cascaded through

141

the stained glass windows. The choir sang "Amazing Grace," and I'd never heard the song sound so beautiful.

The preacher was a tall man with gray hair. His eyes seemed to soften as he preached about accepting God's grace and forgiving others for their sins. I didn't think I could bring myself to do the things he preached about in his sermon, but I did find that he gave me some things to think about.

After the service was over, Reese drove me home. He grabbed my hand before I could get out of the car. "Do you think you'd like to come back to church with me next week?" His eyes were full of hope as he looked at me.

I knew my saying yes would mean a lot to him. However, I still had many questions about God and salvation, and I was still angry about God's absence from my life. So I shrugged, not sure of how to answer his question.

"I'm not sure, Reese."

He sighed. "You were moved by the service today, I can tell. Just think about it awhile and call me this week if you do decide that you want to come back to my church with me."

I nodded, agreeing to think about his request.

During the following week, I didn't call Reese as I thought about the sermon the minister had preached the previous Sunday. I thought about Reese's church friends. They seemed happy and peaceful, worshipping in the house of God. I wanted the peace and serenity I had seen on those parishioners' faces.

I found myself thinking about a lot over the next few weeks. I didn't call Reese to accept his invitation to his church. I had so much on my mind that I needed to sort through.

My friend Sandie came over one night for dinner. She had baked a lemon pound cake for our dessert. I had fixed a small pan of lasagna for dinner, but I barely ate my food as Sandie took large bites of the tasty meal.

"Nancy, you'd better start eating! I know you're upset about Reese and everything, but you're starting to get so skinny!" She touched my arm, her voice filled with the sounds of concern.

I gazed down at my loose-fitting pants. I had been to the tailor's the previous week to have some of my clothes altered.

Sandie pushed my plate closer to me. "Here, eat!" She glared at me until I managed to eat half of the lasagna on my plate.

"Maybe you should go to see a doctor or counselor or something, Nancy. Your eyes are all red and puffy, and you're so thin. I can tell you're suffering, and I wish there were something I could do to help you."

"Oh, Sandie. There's just so much on my mind that I need to

work through and sort out. I have so many questions about God and salvation. I also wonder about my stepfather—"

Sandie's dark eyes snapped to attention. "Your stepfather? What's he got to do with anything?"

I knew I was getting delirious since I mentioned my stepfather to Sandie. I never told her about my stepfather's abuse. The lasagna toiled in my stomach, and I felt like I was going to puke. My hands shook as I drank a glass of water.

"Nancy?" Sandie seemed scared as she looked at me.

I sniffed and wiped my damp eyes. "Oh, Sandie. I know you're my friend, but there's so much about me that you don't know."

In a tired voice, I told her about my stepfather's abuse and about the nightmares I'd been having for the last ten years. I also told her how I'd been blaming God for what had happened to me. Sandie listened, her dark eyes full of kindness and concern.

I was shocked when Sandie revealed that a relative had also abused her. She said that the only way she released her anger and hurt was by developing her faith, and by meeting with a support group.

"I wish I had known what you've been going through, Nancy. All I want to do is help."

I nodded. "I know, but, Sandie, I guess it's just hard for me to trust people after what happened to me."

I took Sandie's advice, and I joined a support group of women who had been sexually abused. Just speaking to them helped to heal the ache that I had been carrying around with me over the last ten years.

After meeting with the support group for a month, my nightmares ended, but my life was still not totally on track. I was still holding a grudge against God, but that grudge was softening as the days passed.

I missed Reese, so I called him late one night. "Hi," I spoke hesitantly into the phone.

"Nancy?" He seemed surprised and pleased to hear from me.

"Reese, I've missed you so much."

"I've missed you, too, sweetheart. People at my church have been asking when I was going to bring you back again to visit." It warmed my heart that people at his church had missed me, even though I had only been there one time.

"Reese, there's so much I have to tell you."

"Really?"

"Yes, can you come by early tomorrow morning? I know church starts at eleven o'clock, and I'd like to go with you, but I'd like for you to come by early so we can talk."

"Okay, Nancy. What time would you like for me to come?"

Reese came by at eight o'clock the next morning. I'd fixed expensive gourmet coffee and had purchased his favorite cinnamon rolls from the bakery. I smiled as I opened the door.

"Nancy!" He kissed my cheek and took me into his strong arms. He caressed my face as he gazed into my eyes.

He then fanned his fingers over my small waist. "You're so slim! You've lost a lot of weight, Nancy. Have you been okay?" His deep voice was full of concern as he followed me into the kitchen. The scent of coffee and cinnamon filled the small space. For the first time in years, I actually felt happy.

"I'm better than I've been in a long time." I poured the hot coffee into my white china cups and served rolls onto the floral-patterned plates. "Did you want to pray?" I asked.

Reese seemed surprised by my request, but he took my hand as he bowed his head and closed his eyes. As I shut my eyes, I listened to his strong voice, lifting up to the Lord, thanking Him for this wonderful breakfast. After we said Amen, he touched my thin arm.

"You seem happier. Your eyes don't look as sad and haunted as they used to," Reese commented.

I nodded, taking a bite of the delicious cinnamon roll. "I am happier, Reese. I've been through a lot over the last month."

His dark eyes were full of concern as he watched me eat my breakfast. "Tell me about what you've been through, Nancy."

As we feasted on coffee and rolls, I told him about how my friend Sandie had been there for me and about how she had helped me to find a support group for sexually abused women.

"This group has meant a lot to me, Reese. After ten years, I feel like I'm finally starting to heal from my stepfather's abuse."

I continued to talk after we finished eating, and soon we walked into the living room and made ourselves comfortable on my couch. Reese wrapped his strong arms around me as I told him how my anger against God had practically disappeared.

He squeezed my waist, kissing my neck. "I'm glad to hear that, Nancy. You don't know how hard I've been praying for you over the last month," he whispered in my ear.

Being with Reese gave me an exciting thrill, and as he held me, I felt like I never wanted him to let me go. When we went to church later that morning, I officially allowed God into my life. I accepted Him, and I'm so glad that I did. God's love and my support group have helped me to forgive my stepfather and not allow the past to determine all of my future.

Reese and I were married in his church, now our church, one year later. We've been married for over five years now, and we have two beautiful children. I still thank God each day for bringing Reese into my life.

THE END

144

SUICIDE AND BETRAYAL
How could she do it to me and the kids?

I never thought there could be anything worse than losing someone you love. Nothing more horrifying than seeing your cherished one lying pale and motionless, her eyes closed forever. Nothing more heart-wrenching than knowing that someone close to you had chosen to end her own life.

But there is something worse. Imagine learning that the person you thought you knew better than anyone in the world had been leading a secret life for years, and you never had a clue.

Two years ago my wife, Edie, committed suicide. We'd been married for almost seventeen years. We have two beautiful children. Our son, Andy, who is sixteen, and our daughter, Lilly, who is eleven. I had hoped that we'd have more children, but among the many things I learned about my wife in the past two years is that she had her tubes tied years ago, and she never told me.

I discovered that particular fact when I started going through her appointment books from past years. She kept them in a shoebox in the closet in her office. When I started learning the truth about her—when my whole perception of our marriage began unraveling—I sat down and spent hours pouring over those records of her daily existence.

Six years back, in faded ink from the fountain pen she always used, I found an appointment at a hospital more than two hundred miles from the town where we lived. Why would she go so far, and for what?

It took many phone calls, but I finally reached the doctor who'd performed the procedure.

"Yes, Mr. Meadows, I remember you and your wife," he said briskly, when I explained who I was.

"I don't think so. My wife was Edie Meadows—she passed away last year."

"I'm so sorry to hear that," he said, and his brusque tone softened. "I do remember her, though, even though I hadn't seen her in a long time. If you'll forgive me for saying so, she was a remarkably beautiful woman."

"Yes." That undeniable fact no longer brought me any pleasure. "But you said you remembered me as well? I never met you."

"You came to the hospital with your wife," he prompted, as if trying to jog my memory. "We had her spend the night because of her reaction to the anesthesia?"

"Doctor, I never even knew about this operation," I told him. There was a long silence. "This man you thought was her husband—what did he look like?" I asked.

"I really can't say." His voice had become distant.

"Look, Doctor, it's not like I'm going to go tell her you told me. She's dead. I'm just looking for some answers."

"But I really can't tell you," he said. "I'm sorry, but it's her I remember, not the man. I see so many couples, and it was many years ago."

I knew I wasn't going to get any further with him. I thanked him for his time and hung up.

She'd kept so many secrets from me. The man who'd accompanied her to the hospital—was he the same man who had appeared briefly at her funeral and then left before I could ask who he was? Had there been many lovers over the years? Or had she betrayed me with just one?

The strange man at her funeral—that had been the first clue. But in the weeks that followed Edie's death, many other unexpected pieces of information began to surface with increasing frequency.

"Dad, some guy keeps calling and asking to speak with Mom," Lilly told me one night when I got home from work.

"What guy?" I asked. "Did he give his name?" I was standing in front of the open refrigerator, loosening my tie and trying to decide what to make for dinner.

"No. I asked, and he just said, 'I need to speak with your mother.' He sounded like he was angry or something."

"Did you tell him that Mom . . . that she . . ." It was still hard for me to say the words. Lilly slipped over and took my hand.

"Yeah, the last time he called I told him, but he acted like he didn't believe me. He said he'd call back later."

"You let me answer the phone tonight, okay, sweetheart?" Who was this creep, harassing a nine-year-old girl who'd just lost her mother? "I'll handle it."

He did call that night, at around eight o'clock. Lilly was doing her homework at the dining room table. Andy, who was then fourteen, was up in his room, supposedly studying, but the persistent bass pounding from his stereo made me doubt it.

I pounced on the phone when it rang. "Hello?"

"Is Edie Meadows at home?"

"Who is this?"

"My name is Alan Peterson. I'm calling from Whitman and Associates."

The name of his company meant nothing to me. "Listen," I demanded. "You called here this afternoon, right?"

"That is correct."

"And my daughter explained to you that her mother passed away? What do you mean, calling and bothering us like this? Don't you have any shame or common decency?"

"I'm sorry, sir," he said. "I'm sorry for your loss, and I apologize for forcing your daughter to speak of it to a stranger on the phone. But I have an important matter to discuss with your wife. I guess I'll have to take it up with you. I tried to contact your wife several times in the past few months, and she never returned my calls."

He went on speaking, and the words he said made me weak. I sank down onto a chair, holding the receiver to my ear with a hand that had suddenly gone numb. I felt I could barely breathe. When Alan Peterson finished speaking and waited for my reply, I couldn't speak; my mouth was completely dry. At last I managed to tell him that I would have to call him back.

I hung up and sat there, staring into space for several minutes. Lilly passed me on her way upstairs and stopped.

"Daddy? Are you okay?"

"Fine, honey," I said mechanically. "I'm fine."

I was anything but fine. Alan Peterson was a collections agent. He had just told me that Edie owed over eighteen thousand dollars on a credit card I never even knew she had.

I was almost sure that there must be some kind of mistake. I say almost, because although I thought it was totally out of character for Edie to keep such a secret from me, in the weeks following her death, I had been plagued by questions about why she would kill herself. What reason did she have for ending her own life? Although I thought it unlikely that she would run up eighteen thousand dollars worth of debt without my knowledge, it might be a clue to her motive for suicide.

I went upstairs to our bedroom and, for the first time since her death, opened her closet door. If she'd kept purchases secret from me, where were they?

The contents of her closet were not much help. Her clothes were there, the sight of which brought tears to my eyes, and her shoes and handbags. I rifled through the dresses hanging from the bar. Almost all of them looked familiar to me; images flashed through my head as I recalled places she'd worn them, things we'd done. There were perhaps two or three that I couldn't remember seeing before, but my memory for women's clothing had never been particularly sharp. I took one of the dresses down and went along the corridor to Lilly's room.

"Lil? Quick question. Did you ever see Mom wear this?"

"Huh?" She turned away from her desk, where she was putting books in her knapsack, and stared at the simple black dress in my

147

hands. She shrugged. "I don't know. She mostly wore pants and stuff."

"I know. I was just looking at some of her things and I don't remember seeing this before."

She came over and looked at it, felt the silky fabric. "I don't think I ever saw her in it. I think I'd remember."

I looked at the label. "Bergdorf Goodman? That mean anything to you?"

"That's a department store in New York City," she said. "A really expensive one. I think Aunt June took us there once when she was trying to get Mom to wear nicer clothes. Remember that, how she always said that Mom shouldn't dress like a soccer mom just because she lived in the suburbs?" She tried to smile, and it pained me to see her.

"Okay, honey, go back to whatever you were doing." I started to leave the room.

"Dad? Why were you asking? Why are you looking at her stuff?" With her usual sharp intuition, Lilly had sensed that something was wrong, that there was a reason for my sudden interest in Edie's clothes.

"Just looking, that's all," I said. "I just felt like it for some reason."

I could see that she didn't believe me. I left her room and went back to mine.

I laid the dress on our bed and looked at it. Where would Edie have worn such a dress? We often went out to dinner together, and there had been plenty of weddings and christenings that required formal attire. Now that I looked hard at the dress, I saw that its simplicity was deceptive. It was elegant but very sexy, too, in an understated way. I fingered the material and pictured how it must have clung to her slim body.

Feeling suddenly sick, I thrust the dress back into her closet and slammed the door.

That night, I couldn't sleep. I kept seeing Edie in my mind's eye. It occurred to me that in the months before her death, her eyes had acquired a hunted expression. Had she been wondering how long she could dodge Alan Peterson's calls? Was she trying to figure out how to keep the credit card company at bay?

I was soon to learn that she had not one, but many creditors. Three separate collections agents, in addition to Alan, contacted me and dropped additional thunderbolts into my lap. Edie had owed a total of eighty thousand dollars when she died. As copies of her old bills poured in, I went over them with a sense of disbelief. Restaurants and expensive hotels were among the most frequent charges. There was a single six-thousand dollar purchase at Bergdorf Goodman's. Had that plain black dress cost six thousand dollars? My mind reeled.

There were other mysterious purchases. Eighteen hundred dollars at a store in New York City. I called the shop and learned that it sold men's wristwatches.

"Do any of those watches cost seventeen hundred, eighty-four dollars, and seventy-six cents?" I demanded, consulting the credit card statement.

"I'm sure we have many watches in that range, sir," the haughty salesman replied icily. I slammed the phone down.

Then I called Edie's sister, June, who lived in New York. I'd never liked her. Her sharp features were not beautiful and there was no warmth in her demeanor.

"When was the last time you saw Edie?" I asked as soon as she picked up the phone.

"What? Before her death, you mean?" She hesitated, and I wondered if she was stalling. "A couple months ago, I think. Why?"

"I want to know exactly when you saw her last. I want to know how often she went down to New York to see you, and I want to know what you two did when she was there."

"David, really!" she exclaimed, sounding disgusted. "Why are you being such a brute? What's gotten into you?"

"Never mind. Just answer the question, all right?"

"I don't wish to have this conversation right now." She sniffed. "And anyway, I'm not about to discuss the details of my poor dead sister's personal life."

I pounced at that. "You mean her secret personal life? Is that what you meant, June? What secrets was she keeping from me? I think I have a right to know!"

"I don't know anything about her secrets, David! Try to behave with a little decorum, could you? I'm not going to let you bully me."

I tried to rein in my anger. It was getting me nowhere. "June, I'm asking because apparently there were many things Edie didn't tell me. I've had quite a shock in the past few days. I've learned that she owed a lot of money. I mean, a lot. And I don't know where she was spending it, or for what. I think she might've spent six thousand dollars on a dress. Is that even possible?"

"Yes, David, there are dresses that cost more than those you'd find at department stores in the suburbs," June intoned in her infuriating, upper-class drawl. Oh, how I hated her! She never let me forget that she and Edie had grown up in a world of wealth and privilege, and that she thought Edie had married far beneath her.

"Look, June." I made one last attempt. "Is there anything you can tell me about her? Anything at all?" I tried not to sound like I was pleading.

"Nothing I can say will make any difference to Edie now. Will it, David?" she replied and hung up.

She knew something, I was sure of it. If I wanted answers, however, I was going to have to look elsewhere.

Had Edie been so unsatisfied by the state of our finances, our way of life? If so, she'd never given any indication of it.

Since our second year of marriage we lived in an affluent suburb of a small, rather charming metropolis about two hours north of New York City. Our house, although nothing like the turn-of-the-century Connecticut mansion Edie grew up in, was a large and tasteful Tudor, with a beautifully landscaped yard. I worked as the director of human resources at a large investment firm in the city near which we live. We always took the kids on two vacations each year, and Edie and I slipped away for frequent romantic weekends.

In addition to our material comforts, I had also always thought of us as rich in other, more important ways. Our marriage seemed solid and happy. Our children were well-mannered and appreciative of all the opportunities we gave them. Edie loved her part-time work as an interior designer, and she spent hours each week doing volunteer work in our community. She complained about the frequent travel required by her work to design showcases, arrange furniture auctions and estate sales, saying she enjoyed the work but would much rather be at home with her family.

But now I was beginning to wonder about all those trips. When she was away, she called frequently to check in and see how the kids and I were doing, and I could always reach her on her cell phone. I had never, ever thought that she might be lying about her whereabouts. Now, however, it occurred to me that cell phones are the perfect accessory for liars. When she told me that she was in South Dakota for a furniture show, she could easily have been anywhere.

Andy and Lilly could tell that something was distressing and preoccupying me.

"Dad, what's going on?" Andy asked one night. "Is everything okay?"

He was almost old enough to discuss adult matters, but I didn't want to tell him anything that might change his perception of Edie. She'd always been a good mother to both our children, and if it turned out that she hadn't been such a good wife to me, well, that wasn't anything the kids needed to know about.

"Everything's all right, son. Work is stressful right now, that's all. I'll get through it."

Lilly had begun spending quite a bit of time at her friend Alison Cooper's house. Alison lived down the street; her mother, a divorced woman named Barbara, had been friends with Edie. Although I'd only met Barbara a handful of times, she struck me as warm and sensible, very down-to-earth. Perhaps I could talk to her. I felt like I was going out of my mind with all the secrets I was learning and keeping.

The next time Lilly was over at Alison's house, instead of calling and telling her to come home for dinner, I walked down the street and rang the Coopers' doorbell.

"Hi, David." Barbara answered the door, wiping her hands on a dishtowel and gesturing for me to come in. "The girls are upstairs. Want a cup of tea?"

"I'd love one." I followed her to her cheery blue and white kitchen. She put the kettle on the stove and began taking mugs and teabags out of the cupboard.

"I haven't seen you since—since the funeral," she said. "I'm so sorry—I've been meaning to stop by to see how you're doing. How are you holding up?"

"As well as can be expected."

That's certainly no lie, I thought.

"Lilly seems to be doing all right."

"Yes, I think both the kids are handling it pretty well. Lil talks about Edie a lot, which I think is healthy. Andy keeps his feelings inside a bit more; you know how boys are. I think he's angry at Edie, in addition to being grief-stricken. But that's natural, too, you know?"

"Sure it is. She abandoned them—she abandoned all of you. I don't mean to speak ill of her—obviously she must've been suffering enormously to do something like that. But the fact remains that she left all of you with the burden of her suicide. I imagine it would've been less painful if she had died in some sort of accident."

I was sitting on a stool at the counter. She pulled up another stool and set the steaming mugs in front of us.

"David, can I ask you a question?" She seemed hesitant, worried about causing me pain.

"Sure."

"Forgive me if this is none of my business, but did she leave a note or anything? Did she give you any explanation for why she did this?"

At last. Aside from the police, I'd never discussed the subject with anyone. Edie's parents and sister had gotten the details from the police; they had not seemed to want to discuss Edie's death with me. And everyone else had been too shocked, and too afraid of seeming to pry. They all thought they were being considerate, leaving me alone with my grief, when in fact I was dying to talk about it.

"There was no note," I said. "Nothing. Do you know how she did it?"

Barbara shook her head. "Not really. I heard something about pills, but I think that was just neighborhood gossip."

"No, that's right." I closed my eyes for a moment, reliving that terrible evening.

151

"David? We don't have to talk about this. I'm so sorry I asked—"

"No, I'm glad you did," I said quickly, opening my eyes. "It's such a relief to be able to talk about it."

Wordlessly she pushed the sugar bowl toward me and waited while I tried to figure out where to begin.

"She must've done it right after the kids left for school that morning. Took all the sleeping pills and . . . and never woke up. Can you imagine? She stood there in the kitchen that morning, making scrambled eggs, packing Lil's lunch, kissing us all good-bye like it was just an ordinary day. And all the time, she knew what she was going to do. I mean, she must have known. After we all left, she cleaned up the kitchen, vacuumed the living room, and then did it."

"My God," Barbara breathed, her expression horrified. "How could she have been so unemotional about it?"

"Maybe it was the only way she could go through with it. But she definitely had it planned. She'd been stockpiling the pills for weeks. And by the time I came home and found her, she'd been dead for over nine hours. There was no hope of reviving her."

"How fortunate that it was you and not the children who found her."

"She planned that, too. It was a Friday. Lil was going straight from school to a slumber party. Andy was going on some kind of pre-season retreat with the lacrosse team. She knew I'd be the one to find her. At least she spared them that."

"She didn't spare you, though," Barbara observed softly.

"No, she sure didn't," I said bitterly. "And she left me quite a mess to clean up."

"What do you mean?"

"I mean, she didn't just do away with herself. She was leading some kind of double life. She was keeping all kinds of secrets from me, from us."

"Are you sure? How do you know that?"

I found myself telling Barbara all of it, everything I'd discovered. The debts, the tubal ligation, the man at the funeral, the man who'd accompanied her to the hospital. Barbara listened with an expression of growing incredulousness.

"I don't believe you." She cried, and then quickly lowered her voice, with a quick look toward the stairway, which suddenly echoed with the girls' footsteps. "I mean, of course I'm sure you're telling me the truth, but I just can't believe Edie would do those things. I've known her for years. Hi, girls!"

Alison and Lilly bounced into the kitchen and looked surprised to see me.

"Daddy! What are you doing here?"

"Came by to get you, sweetheart. Alison's mom and I were just talking."

"Why don't you two stay and have dinner with us?" Barbara suggested.

"Oh, I don't want to impose—" I began, pushing my mug away and getting to my feet. "Besides, Andy will be home soon, and—"

"I'll run home and leave him a note to come over here!" Lil interrupted excitedly. "Please, Daddy, can we stay?"

Barbara smiled at me over the girls' heads. "Please stay," she said. "It's no trouble. I'll order us a pizza."

It would be good for Lilly, I realized, looking at her hopeful face. It was good for her to be around happy people, in a normal house where nobody had taken an overdose of sleeping pills, where there was no empty seat at the dining room table to constantly remind us survivors of our loss.

And it would be good for me, too. Barbara's home was cheerful and cozy, and her relaxed demeanor set me at ease. It was nice to have some social contact for the first time in weeks.

"All right," I agreed. "But pizza's on me."

"I'll make a salad," Barbara said.

The girls yelled and then went running out to leave Andy a note.

"So you didn't have any idea about Edie?" I asked Barbara after they'd gone. "She never said anything to you about her activities or relationships outside our family?"

"Never," she said firmly. "She never gave the impression that she was anything but very happy with her life, in all respects. But, now that I think about it. . . ."

"Yes?"

"There was always a slight distance between us. Not just between me and Edie, I mean, but between Edie and everybody. She had such nice manners, and she was very kind and considerate, but she never really let her guard down. She never talked very openly about herself, or about what she was thinking and feeling. So even though I knew her for many years, you could almost say that I didn't really know her at all."

"Well, apparently you weren't the only one," I said.

"David, this must be so hard for you. Anytime you feel like talking, you can call me. Okay?"

The girls came back and we ordered the pizza. Later Andy joined us, and we all sat around the table, talking for a long time after the meal was finished. It was the first time I'd heard my children laughing out loud since Edie's death.

Later that night, after the kids were asleep in their beds, I thought about what Barbara had said. Edie had never been really open with

153

anybody. I could easily see how Edie might seem that way to an outsider. As Barbara had said, she was always courteous and gracious, but she had an aloof quality that set her apart from others. When I first met her, at the Ivy League college we both attended, I had been attracted to that aloofness. She seemed distant and unattainable, with her cool beauty and quiet intelligence. Later, when we began dating, I learned that she could be funny, affectionate, even silly. I thought that I was one of the privileged few to know her as she really was.

How disorienting it was to realize that I knew only one side of her. How could she have kept so much hidden from us? What a master of deceit she was to behave every day as if she were a normal, loving wife and mother, while she was doing who knows what else in her spare time!

It began to gnaw at me, my curiosity about her "other life." I thought about it almost constantly. I pictured her in her six-thousand-dollar black dress, sitting in some of the fine restaurants whose names I'd seen on the credit card statements. Did she act differently—talk differently—from the way she did at home? Who accompanied her at those dinners? In my visions, there was always a man hovering near her, but his features were indistinct. Was there just one man, or were there many? Had she loved them?

One night I returned home from work quite late, past nine o'clock. Andy was out with friends, and Lilly was spending the night at Alison's house. It was a moonless night. As I pulled into our long driveway, my headlights illuminated our garage down at the end, beyond the house. Edie's home office had been in the small guest apartment above the garage. Right before I turned the lights off, I thought I detected something amiss about the garage. Something unfamiliar, something wrong. I froze, studying the small building from the front seat of my car.

The shades were closed. That was it. I knew the shades on her office windows had been open; I had opened them myself the day I retrieved her appointment books from the shelf in the closet. I'd raised the shades to let in the daylight while I sat on the floor and perused the contents of those books.

I turned off the headlights, got out, opened the trunk, and removed the tire iron I kept stored there. Holding it steady in one hand, I moved quickly toward the garage and opened the door as quietly as I could. I closed it behind me and slipped up the stairs, silently cursing the slight creaking of one tread, and straining my ears to catch any movement from above.

Her office was pitch black, and I wished I'd thought to bring the flashlight from the car. My heart was pounding. Standing in the doorway, I shouted in a voice as loud and deep as I could make it, "Who's there?"

154

Silence. I strode across the dark room and fumbled for the lamp on her desk. I knocked it over, but caught it before the bulb could shatter. I set it gently back down and turned the switch. Her office sprang into light and shadow, familiar and unmenacing.

There was no one there.

Yet someone had drawn the shades. Someone had been there. I put the tire iron down on the desk and began looking around. The top drawer of her filing cabinet was slightly open, I noticed. The closet door had swung ajar, as it does when not shut firmly.

Someone had been going through her things. What had he wanted? Some instinct told me that it was a man. Had he found what he was looking for? Had he taken something away with him?

Just then I heard something down below in the garage. My hearing seemed unnaturally sharp. Someone was easing the door open.

"Hey!" Snatching up the tire iron, I bolted down the stairs. The garage door was wide open, and a man was running away across our backyard.

I sprinted after him, and just as he reached the woods behind our house, I threw myself headlong and tackled him.

We hit the ground hard, and he seemed momentarily stunned. Before he could regain his senses, I grabbed one of his arms and twisted it behind his back.

"You're coming with me," I growled into his ear. "I think you have some explaining to do."

I stood up and roughly jerked him to his feet. His face was in shadow, and I couldn't see his features. I brandished the iron.

"If I let go of your arm, can you walk in front of me to the house?" Fearfully, he nodded.

"Well, move!" I shoved him and he started walking slightly ahead of me toward the house. I saw him glance from side to side, but he knew that I was armed, as well as a faster runner than he, and he made no attempt to escape.

My keys were in my pants pocket. I retrieved them, unlocked the patio door, and pushed the man into the house ahead of me. While his back was still toward me, I deactivated our alarm system and then reached out and took him by the back of his shirt. I propelled him through the living room, down the hall, and into the kitchen, where I pushed him toward a stool and flipped the light switch.

He was the man from the funeral. I had already been fairly sure of it, but in the bright overhead light, his features revealed something I had not noticed before. He was young. Considerably younger than I— possibly in his mid-twenties. He had a good build and was handsome in a rough-hewn sort of way. I studied him for a minute, then gestured at the stool behind him.

"Sit. And start talking."

155

Nervously, he backed into the stool and sat down. "What do you want to know?" he stammered.

"Who are you, for a start. Then, what were you doing in my wife's office. And after that, you can explain the nature of your relationship with my wife."

"I'm Rick Bryce. Say, could you put that thing down?" He gestured at the iron.

I laid it down on the counter, within my reach, too far for him to grab. Then I folded my arms and waited for him to go on. He seemed to relax a bit.

"I've known your . . . Edie, that is, for about a year. I met her when I worked on her car."

"You're a mechanic?"

"Yeah. And she . . . we . . . you know."

"Had an affair?"

"Yeah."

"You were at the funeral."

"Uh, yeah, I came by for a few minutes. I just wanted to see her one more time, but it was a closed casket, and I felt weird once I got there and saw all her relatives and everything."

"And her husband and children?" I prompted sarcastically. "Did we make you feel 'weird,' too?"

He looked at the floor, ashamed. "I just felt so bad, you know?"

"About her death?"

"Well, yeah, and because I thought maybe she did it because I broke up with her. I mean, I was trying to break up with her. I told her that what we were doing was wrong, that if she wasn't going to get a divorce and be with me, then I didn't want to go on seeing her."

"And this was right before she killed herself?"

"Well, a few weeks before. But I don't know. Maybe that wasn't the reason. She didn't seem too heartbroken about it, you know? I think I cared about her more than she cared about me."

I wanted to hate him with all my heart, and yet he seemed so dejected I almost felt sorry for him. I couldn't imagine that such a smitten young man could easily engage the deep affections of a sophisticated older woman, although I could imagine that she found him very physically attractive. I didn't want to think too much about that, but I made myself ask the question.

"So, was it just basically a sexual thing? Rather than a love affair?"

He shrugged. "I guess so. For her, anyway. I couldn't help falling . . . feeling more for her, though. When I told her I loved her she just laughed at me."

"So what were you doing in her office?"

"I was going to see if there was any kind of evidence of our affair. I

156

didn't want anyone finding out about it and thinking badly of her after her death, you know?"

"Kind of late for that," I said grimly. "If that was your reason, why did you wait so long to come here? Why didn't you do it much sooner? Don't you think I've been through her things myself already?"

He hesitated, looked confused, then looked me in the eye.

"Okay, that wasn't the real reason. I wanted to see if she'd kept anything from our relationship. Anything to remind her of me. . . ." His voice trailed off.

"You mean, you wanted to know if she'd really cared about you?"

"Yeah. I can't get her out of my head. Now that she's gone, I just keep thinking about her and wondering if maybe she did love me, after all."

Poor kid. Edie had had him wrapped around her finger, evidently. "Did she buy you any gifts?" I asked.

He looked startled, wary. "Uh, a few."

"A seventeen-hundred-dollar wristwatch, perhaps?" My tone was wry.

He stared at me, then shot back the cuff of his jacket and looked at his watch as if he'd never seen it before.

"Did it really cost that much? I had no idea. I mean, I knew it was a really nice watch, but I didn't know—"

"What else?" I asked crisply.

"I don't know. Some clothes. A new stereo system for my car."

That explained a few of her mysterious purchases.

"So you weren't the guy who went with her to get her tubes tied six years ago."

"No! I told you, I just met her a year ago."

"Did she ever tell you about other guys she'd been with?"

"No details. I knew I wasn't the first . . . the first guy she'd had an affair with, though. Look, Mr. Meadows." He shot another glance at the iron lying on the counter. "Are you going to call the cops on me?"

I thought about it for a moment. He didn't deserve it, I decided.

"No. But let me ask you one more question."

"Okay."

"What was she like with you?"

"Huh? What do you mean?"

"Edie. How did she act with you? What was she like?" How could I explain to this kid that I was trying to figure out who my wife was, that the mystery I was trying to unravel had more to do with her personality than with the specifics of her secret life?

"Uh, well, she was kind of cold, you know? Not that affectionate, never clingy like some girls I've dated. She'd show up in her car and announce that she was taking me someplace, and we'd go off to

157

some really nice hotel in, like, Boston or New York or something. I sometimes joked that she was just using me for sex, but I think maybe she really was. She'd buy me gifts and take me to great restaurants and everything, but it wasn't like she really cared. I don't know how to explain it."

I understood what he meant. Her cool beauty, so desirable and unattainable. I had always thought her aloofness, her polite but distant demeanor, was the face she showed to the world, while her true self was the warm and sweet woman she was at home. Now I wondered. Was the warmth an act, and was there really an iceberg at the center of my wife's heart?

"You can go," I said, suddenly tired.

He got up, stammering an apology, but I cut him off with a wave of my hand. "It's okay. Forget it."

After he'd gone, I dragged myself upstairs to my bedroom. I got ready for bed, then looked around in sudden anger. Everything in the room reminded me of Edie. I didn't want to sleep in the bed we had shared one more night. I went to the linen closet, took down sheets and pillows, and made myself a bed on the couch in the upstairs study.

I lay there in the darkness, trying to sleep. I felt exhausted emotionally, but my mind kept racing. I still didn't know who she really was. I didn't know what other men she had shared her bed with, her time, her feelings—if she actually had any genuine feelings, that is. And what about her debts? She must have known that she couldn't pay them, must have guessed that one day they would be discovered. I remembered how, in the months before her death, she had often answered the phone, listened, then hung up, telling me that it had been a telemarketer. I knew now that those calls had been from the collection bureaus. She had to have known that it was only a matter of time before I took one of those calls and learned all about her shameful secret.

Was that why she had killed herself? To avoid the shame of being discovered? Or had she run up all that debt because on some level she wished for her secrets to be known? I've heard that murderers always reveal their crimes to someone, either out of guilt or because they're so proud of their own cleverness at getting away with it. Was that what Edie had wished for, consciously or unconsciously? To rub her deceptions in my face, to gloat over what a colossal fool I had been?

My bitter thoughts kept me awake late into the night. I heard Andy come in and tiptoe up the stairs to his room, and then I lay staring into the darkness for hours longer, with my eyes burning but dry.

A few days later I talked to Barbara Cooper again. We'd begun having dinner about once a week, usually at Barbara's house, where Lilly and Alison could go upstairs to work on homework or watch TV while Barbara and I talked.

I told her about Rick Bryce and what he'd said to me.

"So, it sounds like you've gotten answers to some of your questions," Barbara said. She was stirring a pot of soup while we talked, and I'd opened a bottle of red wine I'd brought from home. I poured each of us a glass. By this time, I knew where to find just about anything in Barbara's orderly kitchen.

"Only some," I replied. "Sounds like she was just stringing this Bryce kid along for her own amusement. But what about the other guys? How many of them were there over the years? When did she start cheating on me? Was it right away? Or after the kids were born? I hate not knowing these things!"

"You need closure," Barbara said reasonably, adding some seasoning to the soup. "You know, you might never learn the answers to all your questions, David, and it would be a shame if you made it a lifelong obsession to find them all. But you need to get some more information, somehow, so you can at least get the gist of it. I think once you have an understanding of who Edie was, get the general idea of the extent to which she was deceiving you, you'll be able to put the matter to rest and move on."

"You're right," I said. "You know what I'm going to do? I'm going down to New York, and I'm going to make her sister, June, tell me everything she knows. Then maybe I'll be able to put this all behind me."

That night, when Lilly and I were leaving the Coopers' house, something unexpected happened.

Alison liked to walk part of the way home with us, and she and Lilly started down the Coopers' walkway ahead of me. They were giggling over a dirty joke Barbara had asked Alison not to repeat at the dinner table. Barbara was standing in the doorway, her silhouette framed by the warm golden light behind her. I leaned forward to give her the good night kiss on the cheek that was our habit, and then somehow I ended up kissing her on the lips.

After a startled intake of breath, she kissed me back. Her lips were warm and soft, her breath sweet. I suddenly realized how much my feelings for her had grown over the past few weeks.

I pulled back and looked at her. We were both speechless for a moment; then she gave an awkward little laugh, and at the same time I smiled and started to apologize.

"No, don't be sorry," she interrupted. Then her face grew serious. "Just don't toy with me, David. I don't want to get hurt."

"I would never hurt you," I promised, and I meant it.

"You've come to mean so much to me," she whispered, and then, as if she wished she hadn't said so much, she stepped back and let the screen door closed between us.

"Alison!" she called. "Time to come back in!"

"Okay, Mom." Alison's voice came out of the darkness. A moment later she came trotting up the walk.

"Dad? You coming?" Lilly called from down the sidewalk.

"Right here, honey!" Before I turned to go, I looked at Barbara one more time. Her pretty face in the glow of the lamplight stayed in my mind all the way home. All that night I couldn't stop thinking about her. It was the first time in years that I had been preoccupied with a woman other than Edie. How pleasurable it was to let my thoughts dwell on a woman without bitterness and pain!

That Saturday I left Lilly with the Coopers. Andy was still sleeping when I left, but he had told me that he would spend the day with his friends. It was about eight-thirty when I got in my car and drove down to New York City. I hadn't been to June's apartment in years, but it was easy to find it. I parked and walked to the building's entrance on Fifth Avenue. I hadn't called ahead to inform her that I was coming, because I didn't want to give her a chance to find a way to put me off. I hoped she would be home.

A uniformed doorman asked for my name and called up on the house phone to announce me. Evidently she was home, because someone answered the phone. He had to repeat my name twice. Then he listened for a moment.

"Go on up," he told after he had hung up. "Apartment 6A."

I crossed the elegant, marble-floored lobby and rode up in the glossy, mahogany-paneled elevator. When I reached her floor, there were only two apartment doors, one on each side of the elevator. I hesitated, and the door on my left opened before I had a chance to ring the bell.

"David. Come in." June was wearing a cream silk negligee and holding a coffee mug. She made no move to hug me, or give me her usual kiss on each cheek, which I'd always thought was pretentious. "I'm having breakfast. Come into the kitchen."

I followed her into her sunny, large kitchen, filled with every appliance imaginable and equipped with a restaurant-style range and vast expanses of granite countertops. I knew June had never cooked a meal in her life.

"Where's Ray?" I asked as I took the seat opposite hers at the breakfast table and shook my head at her offer of coffee. Her husband, who was independently wealthy, served as a director on many boards and was often away.

"In Switzerland." She did not trouble to explain further or to make small talk, which I appreciated. I had no desire for meaningless chitchat. "David, why are you here?"

"I want you to talk to me about Edie," I said bluntly. "I won't leave until you tell me what I want to know."

160

She sighed and looked at her watch. "I have someone coming to give me a massage in ten minutes."

"Cancel it."

She looked into my eyes and saw my determination. "I won't cancel it," she said, arching a well-groomed eyebrow. "But I'll talk to you while she's here."

So ten minutes later I found myself in a situation I couldn't possibly have imagined. June, naked except for a white towel draped over her hips, was lying face-down on a massage table in her living room overlooking Central Park while a young woman rubbed her limbs with fragrant oil. I sat nearby on a chair and fired questions at her. It was impossible not to notice that June had a lovely figure, slim and well-cared for, but looking at her, I felt nothing.

"Did Edie tell you about her affairs?" I asked.

"Yes. Some of them."

"So there were many?"

"Depends on what you call 'many.' One a year, perhaps. A few lasted longer."

"When did she start seeing other men? Right after we were married?"

"Before."

"Before!" I repeated, shocked. I thought we had been so happy then.

"Edie was fundamentally incapable of monogamy," June said. She squirmed luxuriously under the masseuse's hands. "Oh, yes, right there. That muscle's all knotted up."

The next question was hard for me to ask. "So, she never loved me?"

"Oh, sure, she loved you," June said carelessly. "As much as she could love any man. You were very good-looking, and she found you exciting because you were the exact opposite of everything we'd been brought up with, you know? I think she married you mainly as an act of rebellion against our father. Little did she know that you'd make good, that you'd pull yourself up by the bootstraps, as they say. It was a surprise to everyone when you became such a success."

"So, if I no longer served the purpose of angering Daddy, then why did she stay with me?" I asked bitterly.

"Well, you had Andy by then. David, whatever else she may or may not have been, she was a good mother. She loved those children."

"Not enough to stay alive for them."

"Well, no, that's true. But as much as she could. You have to admit that she was good with them."

This was true. "But it was just an act, right? The perfect mother routine?"

161

"Everything she did was an act. Sometimes she had sincere feelings about something or someone, for a brief time, but mainly she played at trying on different roles. She played the mother role, the wife role, the lover role. She would be the soccer mom one day, and the next she would be zipping down to the city in her little convertible and taking some young stud back to her hotel."

"So she got a kick out of fooling everyone."

"I think that was the primary thrill, yes."

"Did you know that she had her tubes tied?"

"No," she said, raising her head up to look at me for a second. "I'm not surprised, though. Having more children would've interfered with her lifestyle."

"A man went with her to the hospital, pretending to be her husband. Do you know who that might have been? It was six years ago."

"Hmm, six years? I can't be sure. She was seeing someone rather seriously for a couple years, back around that time. He was an attaché at the United Nations. Perhaps that was who you're talking about. But of course I can't be certain."

"What about all her debts?" I asked. "Why do you think she spent all that money when she must have known I'd find out about it sometime?"

June gave her contemptuous little laugh. "David, you might have been making very good money, but it's nothing like what she was used to. Edie had no sense of money and what it's worth. She did interior decorating for fun, and because it gave her an alibi for her other activities. She never worked a day in her life for money. Daddy had always paid her bills before she married you. She'd use a charge card without even thinking about where the money was going to come from. Perhaps she was thinking that eventually she'd get around to wheedling the money out of Daddy for those bills, or perhaps she didn't even think about it, aside from trying to hide the debts from you."

At a signal from the masseuse, June rolled over onto her back, carelessly arranging the towel over her body. I was amazed that, the entire time we were talking, the masseuse's hands had never once faltered. Perhaps she didn't speak enough English to follow our conversation.

The time had come to ask the most painful question of all. "June, why do you think she killed herself?"

There was a long silence. June's eyes were closed. "I don't think Edie was ever truly happy for one day in her life," she said at last. "She got her thrills, she played her little games. She bought things and gave them away. She bought people and threw them away. She never let anyone get really close enough to know her. She never found anything to bring her deep and lasting happiness."

162

I'd learned everything I could, I felt. The massage was over, and June slipped into a fluffy white robe and walked me to the door.

I pushed the button for the elevator and turned to face her. "Thank you." I still didn't like her, but I knew that she'd been as honest with me as she possibly could.

She brushed away my thanks. "David, what are you going to do about the money? Edie's debts?"

"Raid Lilly's college fund, I guess. I don't have much choice. And then work my butt off to replace it."

"Let me call my father," she said. "I'll tell him to pay it. Eighty thousand is nothing to him."

"That's not necessary," I said. I didn't want to take money from their father, who had never treated me with anything but contempt.

"It's only right," she insisted. "He was the one who raised Edie and me to be such spoiled brats."

The elevator door opened. I held it open with one hand, while I asked her one more thing.

"June, what have you found to bring you lasting happiness?"

For the first time since I'd known her, her face lost its studied composure. She looked a little sad surrounded by all her beautiful, expensive things.

"I'll let you know when I find it," she said.

I drove slowly on the way back home, thinking about everything June had told me. She had been unable to clear up every last detail, but she had shed some light on Edie's personality, the characteristics that drove her to deceive me and destroy the world that we'd built together. It was strange to think that I had married a woman who just wasn't capable of the kind of deep affection and steadfast loyalty that most people think of as love.

Instead she craved excitement, deception, and role-playing to the extent that she risked the well-being of her children. What if I had found out about her double life sooner and insisted on divorcing her? Or, even worse, what if one of the children had discovered her secrets? I imagined Lilly picking up the phone and hearing part of an illicit conversation, or Andy, out with his friends, seeing his mother in a car with a stranger.

Was that what ultimately led to her suicide? I thought June was right when she said Edie had never been happy, but was that what had driven her to swallow those pills? Her suicide had been so methodical, so premeditated. Perhaps she was doing what she thought was best, saving us all from any further pain she might have caused us.

I would never know the entire truth, but I felt that I now knew enough. I could start trying to put it behind me and move on. I wanted a wife, a partner, a true love—and I had married the wrong woman. If

I ever married again, I would choose much more carefully.

I drove straight to the Coopers' house to pick up Lilly. It's hard to describe the feeling that washed over me when I walked through their door. I had spent the past few hours talking about Edie, dwelling on her sordid secrets, saddened and angered by her abnormal behavior—and then I walked into a house filled with light and music. Classical music was playing on the stereo, the girls were baking chocolate chip cookies in the kitchen, and Barbara was welcoming me in with a smile. It felt like I was home.

Over a plate of freshly baked cookies I told Barbara what I had learned.

"That makes me so sad!" she exclaimed when I had finished. "Poor Edie! Of course that kind of life could never bring her happiness. She was chasing after all the wrong things."

I thought about what a good person Barbara was, how she was such a loyal friend to me, and yet she was still able to have compassion for my poor dead wife. Somehow, when Barbara expressed sympathy for Edie, it didn't make me feel that she was betraying me, and it made it easier for me to have some compassion for Edie myself.

Lilly begged to stay at the Coopers' until dinnertime. I agreed, and Barbara walked me to the door. Impulsively, I tried to kiss her again, but this time she pushed me away gently.

"Not now, David. You need time to heal. And I don't want to get hurt. If and when you choose to be with me, I want it to be for me, not because you're looking for an antidote to Edie."

What she said made sense. And it did take many months for me to heal. Sometimes I would think I was over Edie, that I no longer had strong feelings about her at all. Then, at other times, I would hate her for how she had deceived me, and especially for depriving her children of a mother.

A few weeks after my visit to June I received an envelope with a Connecticut return address. It was from Edie's father. It contained a check for eighty thousand dollars and a note that said, simply, "I'm sorry."

Grateful, I immediately paid off Edie's debts. A weight was lifted off my shoulders.

Gradually my anger at her disappeared and was replaced by sadness. By the end of the summer, I realized that when I did think of her, it was with more pity than anything else. Her brief life seemed like such a waste. I was ready to get on with my own life.

I went to Barbara and told her that I knew for sure that she was the woman I wanted to share my life with.

"I want so much to be with you," I said. "Not because you're not Edie, but for your own beautiful soul. But I'm afraid, too. It's so hard

164

for me to trust anyone after everything that's happened."

Tears came into her eyes, and she reached for my hand. "You're going to have to learn to trust again," she said. "Even if it seems almost impossible, you're going to have to take that leap of faith. Otherwise you will never be able to love again, because without trust there can't be love. What's it going to be, David? A life with love... or without it?"

I looked deep into her warm brown eyes.

A leap of faith, she had said. It was a little like stepping off a cliff. But I knew she was right. If I didn't allow myself to trust anyone, I would never know true joy and intimacy again.

"Teach me to trust you," I whispered, "and I will love you with all my heart and soul."

"You can always trust me," she said firmly. "I will never do anything to hurt you. I will love your children like they're my own, and I will love you—" She stopped and corrected herself. "I already love you more than I can say."

It turned out that trusting her was easy. Each day I find that I love her more.

One year ago we were married, in a small ceremony with two very enthusiastic young bridesmaids. Every day since has been full of love and laughter, erasing the old painful memories, creating joyful new ones.

THE END

I LOST MY LITTLE GIRL
I was so high, I couldn't
remember where I left her

I looked at my daughter as she cried in the backseat of the car. I couldn't take her incessant wailing anymore. She was driving me insane. I needed a hit to take the edge off. I needed one puff on the pipe; then I'd be able to deal with the sound of her crying.

Krista was generally a good baby, but times were tough and I was hurting for money. I was running low on my food stamps, and whatever cash I had I needed to support my habit. The pipe was the only way I was able to handle motherhood. No one told me it was going to be this hard. No one said that the crying, dirty diapers, and constant nurturing would never end. I loved Krista, but I wasn't prepared for what having her entailed.

Krista was generally a good baby, but times were tough and I was hurting for money. Food stamps were running low and whatever cash I had, I needed to support my habit. The pipe was the only way I was able to handle motherhood. No one had told me it was going to be so hard. No one had said that the crying, dirty diapers, and constant nurturing would never end. I loved Krista, but I wasn't prepared for what having her entailed.

I made my way to Ninth Street. There was always someone there, ready to sell me a bump. It would be enough to take off the edge. Only then would I be able to deal with Krista and her crying. I slowed my pace as I rounded the corner. I scanned the sidewalk and porches for someone familiar, someone with a quick fix. As my car inched down the road, I spotted someone I knew. I was sure he would hook me up. My fingers tapped nervously on the steering wheel as I waited for him to come off the porch and sell me some crack.

Finally, he recognized me and came off the porch. He looked around to make sure the coast was clear of any police. Once he was certain it was safe, he approached the car.

"What do ya need?" he asked, his eyes scanning the area.

"I need a bump."

He laughed nervously. "A bump? What's that gonna do for you?"

I shrugged. "It's all I can afford for right now."

"You should seriously consider coughing up more money. Save yourself all these trips here. It's not a nice neighborhood for children," he said, pointing to my crying daughter.

"Don't worry about her," I said, shrugging it off. Krista was my concern—not his. If I wanted to bring my daughter down there, well, too bad. Besides, I really didn't have a choice. I didn't have anyone that I could leave her with.

He shrugged. "Whatever. Let me see the money."

I handed him a ten-dollar bill. "Let me have the stuff." He gave me the packet.

"Go on and get out of here," he said. "Just think about what I said. This ain't the neighborhood to be bringing your baby to. Next time, come with more money."

"I'll take that into consideration," I lied. How did he think I was going to come up with more money? I was barely making ends meet. I didn't have a lot of money to be spending on drugs. I drove away, excited to get to my house and smoke the hit. I needed it more than I had thought. I grabbed Krista out of the backseat and brought her into the house. As soon as I walked in the door, I placed her in her walker. In the kitchen, I took out a few cookies and put them on her tray.

"Here you go, baby. That should keep you quiet for a few minutes while Mom relaxes herself."

Taking the pipe out of my pocketbook, I stuffed the hit inside and lit it. Inhaling a deep breath, I held onto it until I thought my lungs would explode. Unable to hold it any longer, I let out the big puff of smoke. It didn't faze me that my daughter sat in her walker, walking around the same living room where I was smoking my pipe. After the second hit, my world began to feel much better. My muscles were relaxing and things just didn't matter anymore. I was on cloud nine and nothing could bring me down.

Going to the kitchen, I took out a bottle and handed it to Krista. It was wonderful once she'd started holding her own bottle. It gave me a break from having her on my lap. At ten months old, she was doing well. She was crawling and pulling herself up on the furniture. I had to watch her every second or she would get into everything. I loved the walker, because it kept her from totally trashing my house.

The phone rang. "Hello?"

"Jane, how are you?"

"Fine, Aunt Barb. I'm just feeding the baby; can I call you back?"

"Uncle Brian and I were wondering if we could come over and see you and Krista. We've missed you. It's been a long time since we've seen the munchkin. She must be getting really big."

"She is." I couldn't deal with family just then. "She's a bit cranky, though; do you think we could make it for another night?" I didn't want them in my house, where I was safe from anyone interfering in my world and was able to smoke my pipe whenever I wanted.

"We won't stay long. We have some gifts for her—and you, too."

She was trying to buy her way into my house. If I hadn't been high, it might have worked.

"Aunt Barb, it's really not a good time. How about I stop over there tomorrow and you can visit with her? We can stay for a few hours if you want."

"Tomorrow's fine, Jane. I'll cook dinner for you both. It will be nice."

"Sounds great," I lied. It didn't sound like fun to me. It sounded boring, and personally, I knew I would want to be leaving five minutes after I got there. But if going to Aunt Barb's kept her from coming to my house, then that was what I had to do. I couldn't risk them noticing what went on in my house. I would lose Krista, for sure.

"Come over around four. We can visit with the baby and play."

"Okay," I said. I hung up the receiver before she had a chance to say anything else. I picked up the pipe and took another puff. I felt like I would have to be stoned to survive over at Aunt Barb's the next day, so I had to come up with some fast cash. Thoughts of just how I would manage to come up with more money circled in my mind.

I could sell the DVD player my parents had bought for me. They wouldn't know the difference; they never came to visit, anyway. They sent gifts for holidays and birthdays, but anything other than that, they couldn't be bothered with. They thought I was too young to have a child, and really didn't want to be involved in Krista's life. They hadn't been ready for a grandchild and they felt that if they got too close, they would end up raising her. Having raised their own children, they definitely didn't want the responsibility of Krista. I didn't blame them. She was my responsibility, not theirs, and I knew that. But once in a while, it would have been nice to have a break from motherhood, just for a few hours. Just enough time to smoke and relax on my own. That was not to be for me, though.

The question was, to whom could I sell the DVD player? I only wanted twenty-five, maybe thirty dollars. Enough to get me through the night and the next day. I had a week to go before I would get more money from public assistance. Something had to give soon. I wanted a big score with money. I wanted the big payoff. Maybe Aunt Barb would give me some money if I cried poverty long enough.

I made a few calls to some friends and was lucky enough to find someone who was interested. Sue said she would love to buy the DVD player.

"I've been considering buying one for a while now. I just haven't had the money, but if you're sure you want to sell it for thirty dollars, I'll be right over."

"Score!" I yelled, hanging up the phone.

Krista, startled, began crying. I rushed over to the baby and picked

168

her up out of the walker. "Hush, baby. It's okay. Mommy didn't mean to scare you. I'm just happy. Sue is coming and she is bringing Mommy some money. Then we are going to take a ride."

Sue came over with the thirty dollars. She looked concerned, but didn't say anything. I gave her the DVD player and sent her quickly on her way. I had to get a supply. I would not make it through dinner the next day if I was clean.

Krista quieted down in the car that time. In fact, she fell asleep, giving me some much-needed relief. I cruised down Ninth Street again, looking for the guy who had sold me the crack earlier. I didn't see him sitting on his porch, so I drove on. I made my way around the block and slowly cruised down the street one more time.

A group of guys on the corner started whistling and calling to me as I rounded the corner of Ninth Street for the second time. I stopped. A few guys surrounded the car. I rolled the window down an inch to talk to them, my heart pounding. Hadn't that guy told me not to come into this neighborhood alone, and with a baby? And there I was, driving alone again with Krista asleep in the backseat. A gang of drug dealers and users surrounded my car.

"Hey, honey, wanna have some fun with us?" The guy's gold teeth shone when he grinned.

"I'm just looking to score some stuff." I trembled.

"We're looking to score, too, so maybe we can help each other out," he suggested. He looked around at the guys surrounding the car. "Right, boys? We want to score, just like she does."

The guys started whistling and bouncing on my car. I wanted to call the police or dial 911 on my cell phone, but if I did that, I would never be able to show my face on the street again, and it was the only place where I knew that I could score.

"Hey!" a voice from behind the guy at my window shouted. "What's going on here?"

The gold-toothed guy turned around. "Hey, what's up? We just found ourselves someone looking to score. We thought we could score with her, too. You want in on the action?"

"Get out of the way, moron." I knew the voice before I saw the face. When he appeared at my window, his anger was evident on his face. "Stop bouncing on the car and get lost. Now!" he demanded. The crowd dispersed immediately.

He turned to my window. "I thought I told you how dangerous it was for you to be here!"

"You did, but I need more. Here, I have thirty dollars." I fumbled with the money, trying to shove it out the window.

He took the balled-up money and started counting. He pulled out some packets. "This is the last time I'm going to warn you. You're

169

lucky that I saw what was going on. They would have raped you and never thought twice about it. Take this—and I don't want to see you here again at night."

He threw the packets into my lap. He started digging in his pockets again and pulled out a piece of paper. Grabbing a pen from his back pocket, he wrote down something. "Here's my pager number. Page me when you're gonna be in the neighborhood and I'll meet you. Don't venture in here alone. Next time, you might not be so lucky. It could get ugly. They have the potential to kill."

Swallowing hard, I bit back the fear. "Okay, I'll call—and thank you again."

"Get going." He slapped the side of the car. "Now!" he ordered.

I put the car in gear and pressed the pedal to the floor. I drove until I was in a safe neighborhood, where I pulled over, pulled out my pipe, and filled it. I immediately took a hit, taking the edge off. I took another hit. It would be enough to stop the shaking and get me home.

Krista slept quietly in the backseat. She would need to eat and have a bath, and then I could put her down for the night. Once she was in bed, I could smoke as much as I wanted. The high taking control, I drove us home. I was invincible now. Nothing fazed me. I was carefree and ready to face the world.

The next day, I got ready to go to my aunt's house. I smoked a few hits and got Krista dressed. I didn't really want to go, but they'd insisted, and they had bought her some things. Money, money, money was the only thought running through my head. If I could get my hands on some of their money, I could get a bigger supply, and then I would be set for a while. It was a temporary solution, but it would buy me some time to come up with more loot.

Krista looked pretty in her little yellow dress. She was happy, and that made me happy. Life was good when I had my stash and Krista was in a good mood. We would eat dinner, get the gifts, and be on our way back home.

"Hi, Jane," Aunt Barb said. "Let me see that precious baby." She scooped Krista out of my hands. The two went bouncing into the living room, with me in tow. My eyes started scanning the house. Aunt Barb had really nice things. A plan was building in my mind.

"Where's Uncle Brian?" I asked.

"He went to the store. He should be back in a few minutes."

I excused myself, claiming to have to use the bathroom. Aunt Barb didn't really notice. She was so wrapped up in Krista that my existence didn't even matter right then, which was good. It would give me time to find out if she had anything that I might be interested in taking.

I quietly made my way into their bedroom. I found jewelry boxes on

170

both dressers. I went through them as fast as I could, checking to see if there was anything worth hocking. I found a few things that would probably net me a couple hundred dollars. It would help in supplying me until I got my money the following week. The only problem was, I couldn't just steal the jewelry right then. I would be the number-one suspect when they noticed it was missing. I had to formulate a plan to get the jewels without them knowing that I'd done it.

The wheels spun in my mind. How could I get into the house and steal the jewelry? How? I wasn't sure just yet, but before the night was through, I would have a plan. I would get my hands on the jewelry and have extra cash in my pocket by tomorrow night. That was a guarantee.

Satisfied, I went back into the living room with Aunt Barb and Krista. Just as I walked into the room, I heard Uncle Brian call out from the back door: "Is that Janie and Krista?"

"Yes, Uncle Brian, we're here." I wasn't sure if he detected the boredom in my voice. If he did, he chose to ignore it.

Uncle Brian came into the living room and gave me a big bear hug. "How are you, sweetie?"

"I'm okay."

"Let me look at you." Holding my shoulders, he stepped back and looked me over. Shaking his head, he said: "I don't know, Barb. The girl is looking mighty skinny. I don't think she's eating right."

"Well, we'll make sure she has a good dinner tonight. Haven't you been eating properly, Janie?"

"I eat, when I have the money. I make sure Krista has everything she needs before I worry about myself."

"What does that mean? You go without eating sometimes?" Uncle Brian asked, concerned.

"Not all the time. Just sometimes toward the end of the month when my public assistance runs out. I can only concern myself with my little girl. It's more important that she gets enough to eat." Tears formed in my eyes. I wasn't lying when I said that. Krista was just a baby; she couldn't go without food. I really didn't eat much, anyway. I was usually too high to eat.

Uncle Brian fished in his pocket and pulled out some money. "Here," he said. "Take this for now." He handed me a twenty-dollar bill. "Aunt Barb and I will go get you some groceries. We can't have you starving to death. What does your mother do to help you two out?"

I shrugged. "She doesn't talk to me very often. Honestly, I don't think that she can be bothered with us." Sadly, that was also the truth. I knew that my mother didn't want anything to do with Krista or me. I didn't like it, but I got on with my life.

"I don't know about that sister of mine," Aunt Barb said, standing. She had been playing ball on the floor with Krista, who kept squealing with delight. "I have to check on dinner."

"Let me take over. I haven't gotten to play with Krista yet." Uncle Brian sat on the floor and picked up where my aunt had left off. Krista was so happy. I hadn't seen her that happy in a long time. Maybe it was time for me to go buy her bigger toys. She really seemed to enjoy the ball. Maybe I would take some of the twenty dollars and buy her a new toy.

The thought vanished as quickly as it came, replaced by the thought of calling the dealer and getting a little more crack. Maybe once I had a bigger stash, I could entertain my daughter better.

Shortly after dinner, I made excuses for us to leave. I had to go give Krista a bath and get her ready for bed. I couldn't stand the thought of having to hang out with my aunt and uncle any longer. They handed me a bag full of toys as we were leaving.

"Here, I know she'll enjoy these," my aunt said.

"We'll stop by tomorrow with some food for both of you. Don't worry about anything," Uncle Brian said.

I thanked them for everything. When I got in the car, I drove around the block, pulled over, and took a quick hit. That was how I spelled relief. All my tension slipped away.

As soon as the hit started to take effect, I put the car in gear and drove the rest of the way home. Thoughts began forming in my mind. I had to devise a perfect plan to get my aunt and uncle out of the house so I could get inside without them knowing. I couldn't take the blame for stealing their jewelry.

After putting Krista down for the night, I continued smoking. My mind gave up on worrying about how to get them out of the house. At that point, I didn't care. Nothing mattered when I was high.

The next morning, Krista was up at the break of dawn. I hadn't had much sleep, having stayed up smoking all night long. I was miserable and running low on crack. I still had the twenty dollars that my uncle had given me, but now I knew I had to have more. It was getting harder and harder every day to deal with my life in a straight state of mind. More and more, I was becoming dependent upon the drugs. And I didn't care anymore.

That afternoon my friend Lisa called, asking me if I wanted to hang out. She wanted to go to the beach and get some sun. She said she had an umbrella to put Krista under, but I refused. I couldn't sit on the beach and make small talk when I wanted to be hitting the pipe. Knowing Lisa wouldn't understand, I told her that Krista wasn't feeling well.

"I'm sorry, Lisa. Krista hasn't been feeling well lately and I don't want her sitting out in the sun all day long."

"If she starts getting cranky we can bring her home. Fresh air will do her good. You're always cooped up in that apartment with her. She needs to get out and get some sunshine. They say it's very healthy for kids."

"I appreciate the offer, but I can't." I didn't really appreciate being spoken to like that. Who did Lisa think she was, telling me what was good for my baby? I knew how to raise my child. It was none of her business if we stayed in the house all the time. I didn't like being out in the daytime if I could help it.

"Suit yourself, Jane. I just think that you really need to get out of that house once in a while. It can't be healthy for your daughter."

"I don't think that's any of your business, Lisa. What do you know about raising children?"

"Nothing, Jane, but I do know you can't keep them inside all the time. It's not fair to do that to your daughter, just so you can try to hide your habit."

"What the hell is that supposed to mean?" Fear rose in my voice. How did Lisa know what was going on in my life?

"Jane, you think I'm stupid, but I'm not. I know that you're doing drugs, and I know that your child is suffering. She deserves to have a life, even if her mother doesn't want one. You might not care about your own life, Jane, but you have a child to think about. Maybe it's time to wake up and get some help, before you lose your daughter."

"Lisa, you are not a friend of mine, and you certainly don't know what you are talking about. Mind your own business and stay out of my life!" With that, I hung up the phone.

"Who does she think she is?" I yelled. "She doesn't know what she's talking about."

Krista looked up from playing with the ball. She looked like she could care less about what I was saying. She was happy in her little world. What did Lisa know? Absolutely nothing. She didn't have a clue. Krista was a very happy child.

Later that afternoon, I paged the dealer and asked if I could meet him. I explained that I only had twenty dollars, but that I was about to come into some money and that I would be back for more.

"Okay, I'll meet you in front of my house. I'll sit on the porch and wait for you. If for some reason I'm not there, I'm only a few minutes away. Just park there and don't look or speak to anyone at all. If someone approaches the car, keep looking forward with the windows up and the doors locked. I should be there, though. But no matter what, do not speak to anyone."

"Okay," I said nervously. What was I getting myself into? Why did things have to be so complicated? I just wanted to go there and buy what I needed. Why must there be hassles involved?

I drove there and he was waiting on the porch as promised. I was thankful.

"This is not the type of neighborhood you would want to break down in," David, as I'd learned his name was, said as we made the exchange.

"No, it's not." I had started driving away when the thought had hit me like a ton of bricks. I knew what I was going to do to get my aunt and uncle out of the house.

I had to go home and get high for a bit before putting my plan into action. At home, I smoked until all twenty dollars worth was gone. I knew what I had to do, and I knew when it was over I would have enough money to get as much crack as I needed.

Around three that afternoon, I drove to the grocery store a block from my aunt and uncle's house. I went to the pay phone and dialed their number.

"Hello?" Aunt Barb said.

"Aunt Barb, it's me, Janie." I pretended to be crying.

"Janie, what's the matter?"

"My car broke down and I'm in a really bad neighborhood."

"What happened?"

"I must have taken a wrong turn and I ended up on Eighth Street. My car won't start and I'm scared. There are drug dealers hanging out all over the street and I'm afraid they might try to rape me or hurt Krista. Can you and Uncle Brian come and get me, please?" I begged.

"Oh, sweetie. Get back in your car and lock the doors. We'll be there shortly."

"Okay. Thank-you, Aunt Barb."

"Just stay safe, you and Krista."

"We will." I hung up the phone and smiled to myself. It had worked. I had her leaving on a wild goose chase. Now I just had to make my way to the house and get the jewels. I looked at Krista in the car. She was sleeping quietly. I would hurry down the road and be back within minutes. I knew she would sleep the whole time, so I locked the doors and quickly walked toward my aunt's house. By the time I got there, they were gone. I went in the back door and found it unlocked. I snuck into the house and went straight for the bedroom.

I pocketed many different pieces of jewelry. I left very little. Hurrying, I ran out the door and down the road. I ran as fast as my legs would allow. I had to get back to my car and get home before Aunt Barb and Uncle Brian found me near their house. I would call them from home and tell them that my car had mysteriously started, and that I'd driven off before anyone tried to hurt us. They would understand.

I ran blindly until I got to the store. When I got there, I couldn't find my car. Frantic, I looked up and down the parking lot over and over. Nothing. Where were my car and my baby? What had happened? I hadn't been gone that long. Fear seized my heart. Krista was gone!

174

Someone had stolen my car with her in it. But how? How could anyone have taken my car?

I ran to the pay phone and called 911. That time, the tears were real.

I frantically told the operator that I'd gone into the store and when I'd come out, the car, along with Krista, was gone. She told me to stay put and they would send the police over. I waited for what seemed like hours, when in reality, it was merely minutes.

The police showed up and I explained to them the same story I had told the 911 operator. They went into the store and questioned the workers while an officer questioned me. I couldn't help but wonder why they weren't out looking for my baby.

"Is anyone looking for my baby?" I demanded. I couldn't handle any more of their questions. I just needed to know that my daughter was okay.

"We have police officers looking as we speak," the cop said.

"Well, shouldn't we be doing something? I can't just stand here."

"You have to wait here while we do our job. If we don't find the car soon, we'll have to take you down to the station for further questioning. You can wait there for answers."

I shook my head; this wasn't happening to me. Where were my car and my daughter?

A few minutes later, another officer came over and whispered something to the cop that was questioning me. Before I knew what was happening, the cop was back, telling me that I was under arrest. The events that took place afterward are still a little blurry. I remember crying and begging to see my baby, but they kept denying me, telling me I wasn't in any shape to see her.

It turns out I ran in the wrong direction when I left my aunt's house. I ran in the opposite direction to another grocery store, and that's why I couldn't find my car or daughter. They were both safe at the other end, right where I had left them. I was just so high, I couldn't remember where I had left my car.

I was charged with abandonment and being under the influence of a controlled substance. I lost my child that day. The crack left me childless.

Krista went into foster care until my aunt and uncle were able to get custody of her. I'm in treatment now, but it will be a long time before I'll be able to see my daughter again. I'm not sure if I will ever get custody of her. Only time will tell.

THE END

175

USAA

Made in the USA
Middletown, DE
09 April 2024

52813715R00106